The Tale
of the
Bathtub Sailor

The Tale of the Bathtub Sailor

A dangerous encounter with the darkest side of the Caribbean

JAMES HADFIELD-HYDE

THE CHOIR PRESS

First published in the United Kingdom in 2018 by the Choir Press in association with Bernini Publishing

ISBN 978-1-78963-002-2 paperback
ISBN 978-1-78963-003-9 hardback

Dedication

This book is dedicated to all of those immensely courageous lone sailors and rowers who have single-handedly battled against the oceans of the world. Some have attained glory; some have paid with their lives.

To name but a few, I include Dr Alain Bombard, Sir Robin Knox-Johnston, Tom McNally, Hugo Vihlen, Sir Francis Chichester, Peter Bird, Dame Ellen MacArthur and the flawed, but nonetheless brave, Donald Crowhurst. I hope that a little of each of their experiences is contained within this novel. However, its content is entirely fictional and any similarity to any individual is purely coincidental. My apologies to those not mentioned.

Acknowledgements

Yet again, I must thank my friend Mike Healing for his unstinting dedication to completing his homework in the construction of this book. I thank my dear brother Paul, for his enthusiasm and invaluable contribution to the storyline. Not least, I include my mother, my sister Andrea, my brother-in-law David and my son Sebastian, for all of their encouragement.

CHAPTER ONE

When your name is 'Bill Smith' the odds seem to be stacked against you attaining any kind of noteworthiness right from the start. *His Imperial Highness, Bill Smith. His Grace, the Archbishop of Gigglesworth, Bill Smith.* Nope! Somehow it just doesn't seem to cut the mustard. After all, in his childhood, his father had always told him that he'd never amount to much, and who among us can shake the tree of destiny?

Bill sat at the kitchen table of their council-owned house, whilst Janice, his wife, prepared dinner. An all-too-familiar plate was placed in front of him.

'Egg and chips, love, your favourite. Sorry, I forgot to get the tomato sauce when I was passing the Co-op this afternoon. I'd forget my head if it wasn't screwed on. I keep saying to myself that I'm going to start writing lists one of these days. Never mind, I think there's a bit of brown sauce still left in the bottle in the cupboard. You don't mind brown, do you? You like brown!'

Bill's mind was elsewhere. The tedium and drudgery of working in the Goods Inwards department of a brake lining factory, and living in a council house which stood in the shadow of a football stadium, was stretching his sinews of tolerance to near breaking point. He could see his future as hopelessly bleak. After all, Bill was in the very prime of his life, he was thirty seven years old, and in a marriage that was as stale as last month's bread. His only solace was to retreat to the sanctuary of his large garden shed. Bolted and padlocked from prying eyes, it held the secret of his dreams!

Bill arose from the empty plate. 'I'm going to the shed,' he declared.

'You're always in that bloody shed, knocking and banging and sawing,' Janet retorted impatiently. 'What the hell are you up to in there?'

'None of your business,' came the reply.

Janice decided to let him have it with both barrels. 'Mum always said there was something not quite right about you. I should have listened to her. It was my father that pushed me into marrying you the minute I got pregnant with our Jack. "He'll be a good provider," he said. "You think on it, girl, he's got a steady job for life at Rawley's. The world will always want brake linings, you know." Fat bloody chance.' She drew in a breath. 'And another thing: what have you ever done for Jack? Nothing! Don Wilson does everything with his lad. They're always going off to football matches together, and last week I heard that he's managed to get him an apprenticeship at his works. That lad of ours has always looked up to you, Bill. God only knows why! You know how introverted and sensitive he is, but you just bloody well ignore him. You hardly give him the time of day. He's your only son, for God's sake. You'll live to regret it one day, you mark my words, Bill Smith.'

Bill made his way to the back door, turned, and said again, 'I'm going to the shed!'

'So you keep saying,' replied Janice. Before he had time to close the door she tried to make one last plea. 'Bill, why don't you let Jack help you with whatever crackpot thing you are making in that damned shed of yours? I'm sure he could help you hold things or whatever. It would make him feel wanted!'

The now-teenage Jack's arrival in the marriage had been a complete mystery to them both. During many previous arguments, Janice had made reference to the fact that if she didn't know better, she'd think Jack must have been the result of an immaculate conception.

As so often before, Bill left quietly without answering her.

Bill's own father had been a drunkard and a gambler, and so it was his father's older brother, Arthur, who had been his childhood hero. Arthur was a Merchant Navy man from Liverpool. He'd travelled the world! He'd done something with his life! Whenever he returned from far-off lands, he would tell tales of adventure and bring back all sorts of weird and wonderful presents. Uncle Arthur was a truly great storyteller, and he fired Bill's imagination with tales of great men like Shackleton, Scott, Lawrence, Hillary and Livingstone. Once, he gave Bill a genuine shrunken head that he'd got in Ecuador in the 1950s. Bill treasured it for years, until next door's dog found it and chewed it to bits. It got thrown in the bin. Sometime later, Bill read that one had sold at Sotheby's for more than two hundred thousand pounds. That was the story of Bill's life: an endless chronology of disappointment.

Domestic violence played a big part in the deprived area in which Bill was brought up. His father's behaviour was more normal than abnormal. The weekly ritual of going straight from work to the pub, rolling home blind drunk and beating your wife before going to bed was standard.

Life in those back-to-back terraced houses in northern England was wretched right up until the mid-1970s. Some still only had gas lighting, and many had outside communal toilets. Row after row of blackened houses on linear cobbled streets belched out smoke from each coal-fired chimney. Central heating was almost unheard of and Bill distinctly remembered having piles of coats on his bed before the days when continental quilts became accessible. As a child he had assumed that bed covers always came with sleeves.

His real hatred of his father had begun shortly after his tenth birthday. His mother had baked him a cake, and friends and neighbours gathered round to share in the celebration. His father walked in with a huge present wrapped in brown paper.

It was a bicycle, the best present ever! Bill was unaware that without a crossbar, it was a woman's bike, but that didn't matter. Mother spent time teaching him to ride it, and Bill was the envy of every kid in the neighbourhood. Only adults had a bicycle of their very own in that area. A few weeks later Bill came home from school. The bike was missing. His father had sold it to pay off a gambling debt.

But what was the mystery of Bill Smith's shed? Many more people than Janice had tried to find out, but so fortified was the security that the place had developed its own legend. Bill had even installed a camera which would record any approach past a certain point on the driveway. On occasion, rumours would fly that scaffolding poles and rolls of some sort of fabric had been seen going in after dark, but nobody could confirm with any certainty. There were only two members of Bill's inner circle, and they had sworn the oath of blood brotherhood never to tell.

Tommy Duckinfield had attended primary school with Bill, and the two of them had remained privy to all of each other's secrets to this very day. Les Cohen owned the local second-hand furniture and junk shop, just off the high street; he'd known Bill from infancy. Bill's father would pawn the odd bit of stuff at Les's shop in order to top up his drinking money.

As usual, Janice was fast asleep by the time Bill returned to the house and locked up. His pyjamas were always neatly folded and left in the bathroom so he could change without disturbing her.

Their relationship had never really burned with the fires of passion, even at the very start. They'd met when they were fifteen at St Bernadette's youth club, which had been run by the Sisters of Mercy, so it wasn't exactly sex, drugs and rock 'n' roll. It took Bill six months to feel Janice's breasts, and that was only because Tommy Duckinfield told him what to do. At the time, Janice had wondered what the hell he was doing it for, and for weeks after that they had had endless discussions as to whether they should admit it to Father McGuire in the confessional box.

As soon as Bill was in his teens he no longer accompanied his parents to Holy Mass, and would do anything to get out of going. It was only when he and Janice got married that he was sufficiently independent to abandon his faith altogether. He had always resented the fact that even though his family were very poor, the priests seemed to be on an endless quest for money.

In those days, a pre-planned visit to his parents' house by the local priest was akin to a royal visit. It meant that the entire house had to get a thorough cleaning and the best china would make its annual appearance. After a hearty meal, the whole family would have to kneel on the stone parlour floor in order to receive the priest's blessing, after which, they would be reminded to think of all the poor starving people in Africa by making as large a donation to the church as they could afford.

Bill couldn't quite get his head around the fact that the poorest people in England had to look after the poorest people in Africa. What were all the rich people doing, in both places?

Bill's parents were devoutly Catholic, and above the old blackened kitchen range was one of those miraculous pictures where if you looked at it from the left, it would appear as Jesus, and if you were to the right of it, it would appear as Mary, the mother of Christ. Bill's mother would bless herself with the sign of the cross in front of it each night before retiring to bed. Below it, there was always a stew bubbling away on the range, which would be topped up with potatoes or carrots or whatever was at hand. More meat was added when they could afford it.

On the afternoon following a visit from the priest, Bill was busy at the kitchen table, attempting to show willing with his school homework, when his mother shouted down to him from upstairs. 'Bill, stir the stew!'

To get up and get a spoon was more effort than was required, and Bill leant over to stir it with his Biro pen. The stew instantly turned blue! Bill's panic and fear subsided when his startled mother was convinced that the sudden appearance of blue stew was most definitely a sign from the Blessed Virgin herself. His father took a little more convincing when, later on, he reported from the bathroom that his lips, teeth and tongue had also turned blue!

As a youth, the first serious act of rebellion that Bill ever committed was one time when the fairground came to town. Bill and Tommy dared each other to get a tattoo each. They scraped up enough money between them, and Tommy got a dagger piercing a heart. Bill got an anchor on his forearm just like Uncle Arthur's. His father knocked seven bells of hell out of him when he noticed it several weeks later.

Bill's obsession with the sea and all things maritime had stayed with him since his infancy. One of his failings at school had been his inability to concentrate, and he would frequently be chastised by the teacher for staring out of the window in a dream. His mind was forever drifting into a land of pirates, palm tree islands, and fighting the elements alone against all the odds in stormy seas. His father resented his own brother, Arthur, for his wild and carefree attitude to life, and for filling Bill's head with such nonsense.

So great was the dominance of Bill's father, and the obsequiousness of his mother, that Bill's request to join the Sea Cadets was refused, point blank. His father gave the excuse that because Bill couldn't swim, he wasn't eligible to join. 'But the Cadets only train on the local canal,' pleaded Bill.

What hurt him more than anything happened two weeks later, when Tommy Duckinfield turned up wearing a new Sea Cadet's uniform. Just to add salt to the wound, Tommy started to show Bill how to tie a mooring hitch and a bowline knot with a piece of rope that he carried around with him.

The humiliating pain of it was almost too much to bear, but it drove Bill to be even more determined, and he made a point of becoming a master of the art of tying knots. He got a book on the subject from the library and practised in his bedroom each night for months. It meant that he had to pay a £1.50 fine on the library book, but it was well worth it.

Tommy arrived at Bill's house straight from the Cadets one evening, and proceeded to show Bill his new skill of sending messages by semaphore. He gave a masterly demonstration in the kitchen using two of Bill's mother's dishcloths. Bill, the poor lad, had had quite enough of Admiral bloody Duckinfield by this time, and challenged him to a knot tying competition. Tommy had never heard of a carrick bend or a buntline hitch, let alone being able to tie them. A deflated Admiral Duckinfield withdrew shortly after that and the Smith family's honour had been restored.

Bill and Janice lived a mundanely clockwork existence. Tuesday and Friday was Tesco supermarket day, and Sunday was mostly visiting-her-parents day. Much less frequently, they would travel across town to call in on Bill's parents.

It was on one such visit to Tesco that they bumped into an old classmate of Janice's, Doreen Parker. In the supermarket café, Doreen unfolded the horrendous tale of her experience earlier in that week.

'I'd been down to the benefits office and I was walking back alone alongside the canal, when all of a sudden, up from the water popped one of those frogmen fellers! He gave me the shock of my life. The next thing nearly made me sick! A dead body appeared next to him. Its eyes were wide open and its face was all white with weeds sticking out of its mouth. Honest to God, Janice, it was the most horrible, scary thing I'd ever seen. It's nothing like you see on the movies. Then a policeman on the other bank appeared with a sort of stretcher thing, which he lowered into the water. And you won't believe this: they tied a Tesco bag over its head before dragging it out on the stretcher! I'll be haunted by that ugly dead face for the rest of my life.'

Bill and Janice trudged home laden with their shopping. Doreen's tale was sufficiently interesting for them to engage in a conversation en route; usually the journey would be conducted in total silence. As they turned the corner, a police car was parked outside their house. Bill's father had been missing for three days. It was nothing unusual for him not to turn up for days on end, and so Bill's mother had felt no compulsion of concern. Apparently, he was returning home, drunk as always, when he suffered a massive heart attack and fell off the towpath into the water.

At the funeral in the crematorium, Bill's mother and Janice wept uncontrollably, while Bill struggled to muster a moistened eye. Several of his father's drinking partners turned up, and proceeded to pass cans of beer around to each other in the church during the eulogy. The local betting shop bookie came along to mourn the loss of his income.

After the service, a modest offering of refreshments was made available at the Bull's Head pub. The mourners attacked the food like a cackle of hungry hyenas that had just discovered a fresh kill. Bill held back until the queue had subsided, but all that was left was half a sandwich which had been on the floor and a mushroom pastry vol-au-vent. On closer examination, he observed that someone had left a stubbed-out cigarette in the middle of the mushroom.

It wasn't long before a fight broke out, and panic and chaos ensued with tables, chairs and beer glasses flying in all directions. The police were called and five of the mourners were carted off in a Paddy-wagon.

Bill's mother had had the good sense to secretly put aside a Co-op insurance policy to cover the cost of both of their funerals. Goodness knows what she would have done without it, although Bill would have been quite content to see his father receive a pauper's farewell at the expense of the state.

All in all, it was a most fitting end to an unremarkable man who spent all of his violent, miserable life pickled in alcohol.

Following the death of his father, life became a totally liberating experience for Bill's mother. She moved into a new place closer to the church, where she became highly active in the Union of Catholic Mothers. Her goodly nature allowed her to dedicate more time to local charities, and she was able to freely lavish her affections on her only grandson, Jack. She became a joy to be with, and Bill and Janice began to include her in their Sunday outings to Janice's parents.

The time was drawing ever closer for Bill to reveal the 'secret of his dreams' which lay behind the closed doors of his garden shed. He decided that an appropriate time would be his birthday, May 3rd, because this year it was due to fall on a Saturday, and so he was sure that everyone could attend. The weather was predicted to be fine with sunny spells, and on the Wednesday a much bewildered Janice watched as Bill started to hang Union flag bunting from the house to the shed. Bill thought that an afternoon barbecue would be most suitable for the occasion.

At midday on Saturday, his mother, Janice, Jack, Tommy, Les and an assortment of friends and workmates all crowded into the small garden at the back of the house. Bill couldn't contain his excitement and he was so relieved that he no longer had the possibility of his father ruining it for him. He had spent two years of his life working on this project, along with every penny of spare money he could get his hands on.

The birthday festivities continued for much of the afternoon, and around 4pm, Tommy reminded Bill that now was as good a time as any. Bill puffed himself up to make his grand announcement.

'Ladies and gentlemen, could I please have your attention for a moment? Would you all make your way to the front of the shed and gather round in a semicircle? Mum, I need you to come with me because I've got a little job for you to do.'

Tommy stood on one side of the double doors and Bill on the other. Again, Bill raised his voice as the doors slowly opened.

'Ladies and gentlemen, I give you … *Arthurian*.'

For several seconds there was silence, followed by a chorus of *ooohs* and *aaahs*. Janice made the first comment. 'What the bloody hell is it?'

'A boat!' snapped Bill.

'I can see that! I've seen one just like it on a *Captain Pugwash* cartoon. But what the hell are you going to do with it?' she said.

'Sail the Atlantic in it! That's what I'm going to do.' Bill was slightly deflated by the laughter that ensued, but nothing was going to stop him now.

'You've never been sailing in your entire life! No, I tell a lie. You and I did go sailing on the swan ride at Alton Towers lake!' mocked Janice.

Uncle Arthur would never have laughed, had he been alive. He would have been filled with pride and encouragement. He would have marvelled at Bill's ingenuity and the fact that he had built the *Arthurian* with no prior knowledge and designed his own style of rigging. That was why Bill had decided at the very start to bestow the greatest honour a seafaring man could have: to have a ship named after him.

The laughter changed to curiosity, and the men in particular were fascinated to know what she was made of and how Bill had come to make her in that particular shape. But the proceedings had not reached their conclusion just yet, and Bill called everyone to order once more. 'Come on, Mum! You stand here.' A bottle of cava sparkling wine hung from the ceiling of the shed on a length of string. 'I want you to name the ship and bless her. You're the Queen today, Mum!'

Mother rose to the occasion; she'd never felt this important or proud in the whole of her life. 'I name this ship *Arthurian*. May God bless her and all who sail in her.' The bottle exploded against the bow first time and there was a great uproar of applause and cheering from everyone there.

Tommy stepped forward with his birthday gift for Bill, which was a beautiful red, white and blue box tied up with string. Bill burst out laughing when he saw that Tommy had tied the string into a Celtic rope knot, one of the most complex and difficult knots you can possibly learn to tie. Inside the box was a Red Ensign, the one thing Bill had forgotten to get. He was tearfully moved by his friend's thoughtfulness.

As the festivities subsided and the guests filtered away, Bill's mother was in the kitchen tidying up. It was very evident that she was upset. Bill walked in carrying a tray of dirty glasses and empty bottles.

'You are not serious about sailing that tiny little boat in the ocean, are you, son?' she enquired.

'Don't worry, Mum, I'll survive! There's all sorts of survival equipment you can have with you nowadays. It's not as if I'm going to be clinging to a piece of wood after a shipwreck. People have survived for incredible amounts of time. Did you know that there was a bloke called Poon Lim who lasted for 133 days in a raft after his ship was blown up in 1942? I'm going to be totally prepared. Stop worrying, Mum.'

'But Janice was right, you've never been out in the sea before. How will you know how to cope?' she persisted.

Janice shouted from another room, 'It's because he was just born selfish, all he ever thinks about is himself and what he wants. He's not given a single thought as to what's going to happen to me and Jack after he gets eaten by a bloody jellyfish!'

Bill chose to ignore Janice's silly remarks. He was determined not to be lured into a blazing row with her; after all, it was his birthday.

His mother continued to press the subject. 'What made you think of such a crazy thing to do? You're going to kill yourself, son!'

'It's the fulfilment of a dream, Mum. I couldn't let myself get old and end my working days in a dead-end job like Rawley's, and, who knows, probably end up in the canal like my dad. My father spent sixty years on this planet, and in another few years nobody will know that he ever existed. And neither will anyone give a shit. Nobody's going to be writing books and making documentaries about Freddie Smith, the great alcoholic canal diver!'

'Don't you be disrespectful to your father's memory, God rest his soul in heaven,' said his mother.

'I want more out of life than that, Mum. I want Jack's grandchildren to be able to talk about me and say that their great-grandfather was a man who fulfilled his dreams. I hope that someday I'll be an inspiration to them to follow their own dreams.'

'It sounds good, son, but swanning around the world fulfilling dreams is only for rich people, not for the likes of us,' said his mother, wistfully.

Bill insisted, 'You are wrong, Mum, and I'll prove how wrong you are!'

Again, Janice shouted from the other room. 'He needs his bloody head examining. What idiot thinks he can sail the Atlantic Ocean in a sodding bathtub? I'll bet they're all going to be having a right laugh about it in Rawley's on Monday, once the word begins to spread. And what about poor Jack? He's going to be teased and bullied when his classmates get to know that Jack Smith's dad is the famous Captain bloody Birdbrain, the bathtub sailor! You're just downright thoughtless if you ask my opinion, Bill Smith!'

'Nobody is asking for your opinion,' replied Bill.

He was totally focused. He had spent years reading about great survivors of ocean crossings: the likes of Tom McNally, Hugo Vihlen, and many more.

Most inspiring of all was Dr Alain Bombard, a French biologist and politician, who in the 1950s set out to prove that people set adrift after escaping sinking ships died very quickly from fear, and a firm belief that they were going to die. In those circumstances, stress was a far more efficient killer than anything that the elements could throw at them. Dr Bombard intentionally placed himself in the position of a castaway. He carried a sealed container of survival rations on board the raft, which was still unopened when he reached Barbados. He proved that mental preparation was far more important than any physical ability or sailing experience when attempting to cross the ocean in a tiny boat alone. If he could do it, then so could Bill.

Chapter Two

There was an element of *Captain Pugwash* about the design of Bill's boat, but behind her slightly comical façade lay some ingenious features. The structure and outer skin were fibreglass with a three-inch inner skin which was filled with a high-density foam. In addition, he had built in plastic tube ribs which could be filled with fresh drinking water, which would only be used as a last-resort backup when his onboard supply had gone. He had originally hoped to make the boat out of Kevlar, but that was well beyond budget. Bill had meticulously calculated the weight ratio of provisions and his body weight against the buoyancy factor. Theoretically, even when fully laden and filled with seawater, the boat shouldn't sink!

The nine-foot mast was made from a scaffolding pole with two similar booms connected by modified gooseneck joints at the mast, one slightly above the other. By pulleys, the booms could close up to the mast in the same way that you close an upside-down umbrella, and so it was rarely necessary to physically hand-lower the sails. The wind could be removed from the sail with a quick, almost effortless action. He had got that idea from a garden pole washing line. In order to tidy the sails when both booms were closed, he had designed a highly luminous skirt which could be raised up from the bottom of the mast. He thought that when he was asleep at night and drifting, this bobbing luminous pole would be visible to passing ships from miles away.

The batten-down hatch was made from the door of a spin dryer, which provided the perfect porthole. It could be sealed watertight.

The vessel was professionally painted in the Union flag

colours and the proud name *Arthurian* was painted on both sides of her bow, in two-tone blue. There was a sturdy rudder, and a saddle for a small outboard motor, although on the crossing he would rely entirely on sail.

Bill was totally confident that he had left nothing unchecked nor uncalculated. All he needed now was to save a little more money and embark upon the first of the sea trials. He thought that he would conduct a coast-hugging sea trial between Liverpool and Bristol at first, in order to get his sea legs and iron out any minor problems which might occur.

The idea of attempting to achieve his goal with the aid of sponsorship had never entered Bill's head. It was his good friend Les, the owner of Cohen's Emporium, purveyors of high-class pre-owned furnishings and objets d'art, who told him that companies would just love to have their names plastered all over Bill's boat, and they would pay heavily for the privilege.

'After all, Bill, let's not forget that it was me who supplied you with those scaffolding poles, and the door to the spin dryer, at a very reasonable knock-down price,' said Les. 'Cohen's Emporium helped make all this possible in the first place. It's only right that it should be the first corporate name to appear on the hull of such an illustrious vessel, at no additional cost.'

Naturally, Bill agreed.

Nothing in Les's junk shop was ever referred to as 'second-hand'; it was always 'pre-owned' or 'pre-loved', and every piece of worthless tat had been previously owned by an obscure celebrity or a long-forgotten Lady Mayoress.

Bill's arrival at work on Monday, as predicted by Janice, was met with derision and a chorus of whistles to the tune of 'Popeye the Sailor Man'. Bill chose to ignore them. A parcel was left at the window of the Goods Inwards department addressed to him; it contained a bag of supermarket spinach.

By mid-afternoon, word came down from on high that he was to report to the office of Mr Rawley himself. In all the years he had worked there, he had never set foot into the inner sanctum of the directors' offices, let alone the office of the chairman. He was led through a labyrinth of corridors, each one becoming more grand. The walls went from being painted to having wallpaper, and then, eventually, rich mahogany panelling. Black-background portraits in heavy gilt frames, showing five generations of previous Mr Rawleys, lined the walls. The secretary led the way to a massive pair of double doors at the end of the final corridor. She gave a gentle knock, and entered.

'Do come in, please. How lovely to see you, Mr Smith,' boomed a very distinguished and white-haired Mr Rawley. 'Please, take a seat. Do you mind if I call you Bill?'

'No, sir, please do,' said Bill.

'Miss Knowles, would you be kind enough to bring us tea and a nice assortment of biscuits?'

Bill sat in the chair in front of Mr Rawley's enormous Napoleonic desk. His nerves got the better of him, and his right leg started to bounce up and down by itself. Miss Knowles arrived with the tea and was instructed not to let any calls interrupt Mr Rawley's meeting with Mr Smith.

'Now, Bill,' said Mr Rawley, as he poured the tea. 'I want to hear all about this boat that you've been building. Who are your sail makers? Jeckells of Norfolk make all of mine when I need them.'

'Oh, so you're a sailing man, then, sir,' said Bill.

'Yes, indeed,' came the reply. 'My grandfather, on my mother's side, sailed with Shackleton on the *Endurance* when they were trying to explore new routes through to Antarctica. Our family has always had an insatiable appetite for adventure.'

Bill couldn't believe what he was hearing. Not only was he sitting chatting with the chairman of the company, but he was also in the presence of someone whose relative had actually shared a close friendship with Shackleton! A great national hero, and an absolute idol for Bill. Uncle Arthur had told him everything there was to know about Shackleton. Bill could have picked him as his specialist subject on TV's *Mastermind*.

Before long, the two men were laughing together as if they had known each other on an equal footing for years. Bill found himself pouring out all of his dreams and ambitions and Mr Rawley listened most attentively.

All of a sudden, the works bell rang out. They had been talking together for nearly two and a half hours!

As they got up, Mr Rawley put his hand on Bill's shoulder. 'I want to help you, Bill. I'd like to contribute a thousand pounds to your Atlantic project.'

Bill was overwhelmed with emotion. 'I just don't know how to thank you, sir.'

'You don't have to thank me at all. It is men with guts and determination like yours, my grandfather's and Shackleton's that made this country what it is. That fearless conviction to achieve is a rare thing, Bill.'

'Perhaps I could put "Rawley's Brake Linings" on the side of the boat, sir,' said Bill.

'No, that's really not necessary. After all, if it all goes pear-shaped we don't want bits of your boat washed up on some beach with our name stuck all over it, now do we?' joked Mr Rawley.

As the two men shook hands to say goodbye, Mr Rawley said, 'Godspeed, Bill. And always remember that the door to your employment is forever open here at Rawley's, should you ever run out of dreams.'

'Thank you, sir. Thank you for everything,' said Bill.

'Please, call me Marcus,' came the reply, 'but never in front of the staff!'

Miss Knowles showed him the way out, but not before handing him an envelope. 'I believe Mr Rawley wishes you to have this, Mr Smith.'

It contained a cheque for one thousand pounds.

Bill had never felt this level of elation before in his entire life. Not only was he a thousand pounds richer, but a man as eminent as Marcus Rawley had shown so much faith and respect for him. Bill had spent enough time being dismissed as the village idiot and the butt of everyone's jokes. Things were going to change from now on. *He even included my name in the same sentence as his grandfather and Sir Ernest Shackleton,* mused Bill.

His workmates were keen to enquire about the meeting. 'Hey, Popeye, have you been fired yet? What did the big boss want to see you for?' came the chants from the loaders in the Goods Inwards department.

'If you must know, Mr Rawley is a very keen and experienced sailing man, and he kindly offered to give me some sailing advice,' said Bill, nonchalantly.

Bill's street credibility was raised above the stratosphere at this point in the conversation. 'What's his office like? I'll bet he's got a really fit secretary!' There came a volley of similar questions, but Bill was having none of it.

'What Mr Rawley and I happen to discuss behind the closed doors of his office is strictly between him and me, and it's bugger all to do with you lot! Now piss off.'

As of that moment, things really did change for Bill, and he finally started to get the long-overdue respect that he rightly deserved.

*

Understandably, Bill arrived home that evening in a more than jubilant mood; he had a permanent grin on his face. However, he decided not to mention his newfound fortune to Janice at this stage, but to savour it all for himself for just a little while longer. He was humorous and light-hearted. He had a spring in his step each morning as he left for work.

After nearly a week of this, Janice suspected that he had met another woman. All sorts of things were going through her head, and when Bill came home on the Friday evening he found her in the kitchen sobbing her heart out.

Seeing her in that state suddenly aroused a flame of compassion and love from the embers of what he thought had long been extinguished. He couldn't remember the last time he had told her that he loved her. But even now, he still couldn't quite utter the three most important words in the English language. The treadmill of their lives had brought them to take each other for granted. The knowledge that the other one will always be there is a better option than the fear of the unknown when they are not.

Bill put his arm around her. 'Come on, girl, get some decent clothes on. We are going out to the swankiest restaurant in town tonight!' he declared. 'And you, Jack! Go and get yourself smartened up, you're coming with us.'

Janice was all a fluster. Her life wasn't used to impromptu decisions or events; everything had to be orderly and predictable.

Bill held her face in his cupped hands and kissed her on her lips. 'Now do as you are told and go and get ready. I'll tell you everything over dinner,' he said, lovingly.

At the restaurant, Bill relayed the events of his meeting with Mr Rawley in detail.

Marcus Rawley was considered to be the head of local royalty. His family had been the principal employers in the town for the past one hundred and thirty years. All of the Rawley family were treated with reverential respect, and it was only with the fairly recent succession of Marcus that men had stopped doffing their caps and women factory workers no longer gave a curtsy as a family member passed them by.

Finally, Janice started to understand her husband's passion to do something different with his life. If Bill's crazy dream had met with the approval of Marcus Rawley, then maybe it wasn't as crackpot an idea as she had first thought. What was it that Marcus had seen in her husband that she hadn't? She was still deeply concerned that he would kill himself, though.

They made love that night for the first time in over a year. Poor Jack had to endure the embarrassment of listening to his parents' headboard banging against his bedroom wall, and his mother's ecstatic yodelling long into the night.

The weeks passed.

It was 5am, and Bill was wide awake. Today was the first day of the long-awaited sea trials, and he had mixed feelings of excitement and nervous apprehension. Janice had chosen not to attend the launch.

What if he'd got the design completely wrong, what if the closed booms were too top-heavy? Question after question ran through his mind. If she didn't sail properly, then it would be a proven fact that he really was the idiot that everyone thought he was! He'd have to give Marcus the thousand pounds back! Oh, the humiliation of it all. There would be no solution other than to kill himself, he thought.

Les supplied the transport to Liverpool in the form of his open flat-back Transit van. *Arthurian* was only seven feet eight inches from stem to stern with a four-foot beam and she was not that difficult for three or four men to manoeuvre.

As they drove into Albert Dock, Bill was having second

thoughts about launching her in Liverpool. He had not taken into account that the place would be full of gawping tourists.

His protests were ignored and Les backed the Transit down the slipway, up to its back axles. A crowd gathered round, with American tourists wanting to know all about this 'cute little ship'. At this point in the proceedings Bill was in no mood to be affable.

With Tommy on one side and Bill on the other, they synchronised the release of the guy ropes and the 'cute little ship' crashed unceremoniously into the water. Immediately afterwards, Tommy and Bill almost came to blows and embarked upon a tirade of expletives at each other, many of which the Americans had never heard before. Neither one of them had remembered to keep hold of the guys, and the *Arthurian* sailed happily off into the middle of the dock by herself. The driver of the yellow Wacker Quacker Landing Duck came to the rescue, with onboard tourists helping to tow her back to the slipway.

The Americans just loved it, and thought it was all part of the Liverpool tour entertainment. Tommy and Bill's performance compared favourably with any done previously by Laurel and Hardy and they got enthusiastic applause from some of the people standing along the quayside. Quick-thinking Les immediately went round with a hat and collected a total of £7.59.

Bill managed to get the outboard motor going and he put-putted the *Arthurian* around the enclosed dock while Tommy and Les watched in admiration from the quay. 'She looks good, and she sits well in the water,' commented Tommy, sounding all knowledgeable and nautical. All three of the world's most inexperienced marine engineers were feeling pretty pleased with themselves.

But that was to be short-lived and rudely interrupted by the arrival of two police cars and the harbour master.

'What the hell are you lot playing at?' enquired the first policeman.

'We are launching this vessel on her very first sea trial, and you are among the privileged few to witness it,' said Tommy, somewhat defensively.

'Not here, you're not,' said the harbour master. 'You've got one hour to get that floating bathtub out of my dock, and for it and you to be off on your merry way.'

'Well, where can we launch it?' asked Bill, speaking from the bridge-on-board, so to speak. It was the second time the *Arthurian* had been referred to as a 'bathtub' and Bill was already getting a bit sick of it.

'Try someone's swimming pool,' came the reply.

It wasn't as difficult to get her back onto the Transit as they first expected, and they then sped off through the Mersey Tunnel and over to New Brighton. Again they attracted a small crowd of onlookers, but this time it all went smoothly and without interruptions. They loaded the minimal amount of essential provisions that Bill was going to need to get him to Bristol, and after a hearty farewell, *Arthurian* proudly made her way from the mouth of the river Mersey on her maiden voyage. Bill certainly wasn't going to chance setting the sails while there was still an audience watching, that was for sure! But he did tie the Red Ensign and give a thumbs-up sign back to Tommy, who was still waving from the promenade.

The two friends stayed to observe Bill's first slightly uncomfortable moment, as the wake of the incoming Isle of Man ferry swept him aside at the same moment that she blasted her foghorn. Bill assumed it had been a fearsome warning to him, but the big ship was merely announcing her own arrival. Close to her bow, Bill realised just how dangerous the ocean could be and how insignificantly small he had become.

The weather was fair and the seas were calm as Bill made his way through the maze of giant offshore wind turbines. He passed Hoylake and headed on down toward Rhyl. He was savouring every moment of his newfound freedom. It was a feeling of absolute joy, the like of which he had never quite felt before.

Remarkably, by nightfall, he had chugged all the way to Conwy, where he moored up and managed to get onshore for a well-deserved feast of fish and chips, and a visit to the pub. Before retiring, he filled his petrol cans ready for his onward journey. Bill slept like a log on board his new little home and by 6am he was up and ready to pull out of the estuary in preparation to fill the sails for the first time.

Ahead of him to the right, he could see Puffin Island. There was a light westerly wind and Bill felt brave enough to simultaneously drop both booms and allow the pair of sails to billow out.

All went well for the first few minutes until there was a slight change of wind direction. All of a sudden, she tipped over quite violently and a cascade of water flooded into his cab. She was leaning right over at forty degrees and the water just kept flooding in. In absolute panic, Bill frantically yanked one of the booms up. The boat righted herself while the other boom lashed around wildly. He managed to get control, but even with a single full sail she would bank over and take on more water. Something was dramatically wrong!

As he grappled with the sails and finally got them safely put away, he was relieved to see that he had passed Beaumaris and was heading into the Menai Strait. There was no way he was going to risk sailing round the Irish side of Anglesey.

When his palpitations had finally subsided and all was calm again, he noticed that without the engine the tide was drawing him into the straits quite quickly. He managed to bail out much of the two feet of water which was swishing around below deck, and he hoisted his inside-out sleeping bag up to the mast in the vain hope that it might dry. Eventually, he was able to hold the rudder on an even keel, sit back and relax. With no effort whatsoever, he was moving along quite nicely. He even felt the compulsion to wave at people on the shoreline, who returned his wave.

Ahead, he could see the magnificent structure of Thomas Telford's suspension bridge. Built in 1826, it was made so high as to accommodate the sailing ships of the day, and allow them to pass below it in full sail without hindrance. At this point Bill felt he had a kinship with those earlier mariners who had sailed this way before him.

No sooner had he passed beneath this great colossus of stone and steel than he noted that the boat began to change direction entirely by herself! Movement of the rudder in any direction made no difference at all. Suddenly, the *Arthurian* had a mind of her own! 'What the bloody hell is going on here?' said Bill to himself.

The little craft began to move round and round in ever-decreasing circles. Faster and faster she went. Bill unsuccessfully tugged at the starter cord to the engine, but the damned thing wouldn't start. All too soon he found himself staring down into a giant gaping vortex in the centre of a whirlpool.

His dormant Catholicism suddenly reappeared, and he started to shout at the top of his voice, 'Hail Mary, full of grace, the Lord is with thee, blessed art thou amongst women, and blessed is the fruit of thy womb, Jesus. Holy Mary, Mother of God.' If he shouted loud enough, perhaps the Blessed Virgin, or anyone else in heaven for that matter, would hear his desperate prayers and save his life.

Cars on the bridge slowed down and stopped to watch, as

the little boat spun helplessly round and round. People on the banks stared and pointed, but there was nothing anyone could do.

As if by some celestial intervention, the vortex suddenly disappeared, and the little boat continued her journey unaided. Bill had been totally unaware that during a high tide, the rising sea pushes in at both ends of the Menai Straits between the mainland and Anglesey. Where it meets in the middle, it creates the most dangerous mass of swirling waters.

It took Bill quite some time to recover from that little interlude. This sailing the ocean business was a lot more challenging than he had first anticipated, and he'd not even left the shallow waters of home yet.

Undeterred, he chugged on down the coast and eventually moored up by the old Ty Coch Inn at Morfa Nefyn. There he met an old sea dog called Barny Watson, or 'Barnacle', as he was affectionately known. After a few beers together, Barnacle asked to see the *Arthurian*, and look her over.

Barnacle shook his head when he saw her. 'You'll never sail that in the open sea,' said the true voice of experience. 'She's got the wrong keel, and not a scrap of ballast in there either. You'll kill yourself, lad. She's fine if you want to take her for a picnic on the Norfolk Broads, but you put her in a slight swell and she'll flip upside down straight away. I'll draw you a picture of exactly what you need.'

It was time for that 'come and get me' phone call to Tommy and Les!

Bill shivered through a miserable sleepless night of deflated expectation. It would be a pointless exercise to continue on to Bristol at Avonmouth. He lay on top of his sodden sleeping bag, with six inches of water still swishing around in the bottom of the boat. Everything he touched was cold and wet, and it rained incessantly throughout the night. But this trivial setback was in no way going to dampen the ardour of our intrepid sailor; he was made of sterner stuff!

Tommy and Les had agreed to arrive with the Transit by lunchtime the following day. It was back to the shed, and back to the drawing board.

Janice and Jack were greatly relieved to see Bill in one piece, and to hear in fine detail the news of his adventure. Jack listened intently, and for the first time in Bill's life, he could see a reflection of himself with that of his uncle Arthur. It felt so good to be the storyteller for a change!

Chapter Three

Bill returned to work with a new title. 'Popeye' had been dropped by his workmates and replaced with 'Captain Bill'. He still had to save face, though, and he explained to them that he needed to make a few alterations to his boat, in order to comply fully with the international law on maritime health and safety. They were all happy to swallow that load of old bullshit, hook, line and sinker.

Marcus was keen to be updated on the progress of things. He always encouraged Bill with sound counselling, and never condescension. Bill found it very easy to tell him the whole truth.

One Saturday afternoon, Bill was busy in the shed as usual. Curtains twitched on the council estate as a new maroon Bentley glided to a standstill at their front gate. Spotting its arrival, Janice flew into a panic, desperately trying to hide discarded clothing and half-empty cups left lying around in the sitting room.

'Please, come in, Mr Rawley. Bill is out in the back, sir!' said Janice. Although she had never met Marcus Rawley before, with a car like that, she knew precisely who he was, and she was unsure as to whether a slight genuflection might be in order. 'Would you like a cup of tea, sir? I've got some Swiss roll,' she said nervously.

'I'd love that, thank you so much, Mrs Smith,' came the reply.

'Oh, please, you must call me Janice.' With that, she screamed Bill's name from the kitchen window.

Bill approached with an outstretched hand. 'Marcus! What a lovely surprise.'

'I've brought you a little something that I thought you might find useful; it's out in the car,' said Marcus.

The boot of the Bentley opened automatically as they got close. Inside, there was a top-of-the-range hand-operated bilge pump.

'You'll have to fit it properly to the bulkhead. I just couldn't imagine you having to bail out a cabin full of water with a baked bean tin,' said Marcus, with a laugh. 'Oh, and I also thought you might find these useful!' He pulled out a large plastic box filled with all kinds of sea fishing equipment. 'You can bait several lines and let them trail behind the boat when you are sailing. That means dinner is never far away.'

'Marcus, you really are too kind to me,' said Bill.

'Think nothing of it; they're just a few things we had lying around in our old boathouse. If I see anything else that I think might be of use, I'll get it to you.'

Marcus immediately spotted Bill's design fault in the keel, but he was gentle with his criticism. He finished his tea, bade farewell to Janice, and took an extra piece of Swiss roll as he was leaving.

Janice couldn't wait to get on the phone to her parents to tell them that a genuine millionaire had just called round for tea. Jack was with them at the time. He spent more time with Janice's parents and Bill's mother these days than at home. Bill still didn't offer to include Jack in any part of his Atlantic adventure, dismissing it as being a clash of personalities.

Jack was deep and introverted. He hardly spoke, and he didn't seem to have friends. He rarely went out, preferring to stay in his room with his computer. Janice was concerned that he might be being bullied at school, but whenever the subject would come up, Bill would say, 'Oh, he'll grow out of it. That lad needs to toughen up; he's too bloody soft. You've got to learn to take the knocks in this life.' Even Don Wilson had tried his best to help. He'd called round to their house several times to try and include Jack in some of his outings with his own son, Mark, but Jack always found an excuse not to go with them.

Don Wilson had never been a member of Bill's innermost circle of friends, but they had grown up together attending St Bernadette's youth club, even though Don wasn't a Catholic. St B's was the only focal meeting place for all the kids in the area, regardless of their faith. Janice and Bill had always greatly appreciated Don's kindness toward them, and in particular his considerable concern for Jack. Don knew only too well how important it was for people of Jack's age to engage in sporting activities and to create bonds of friendship. He ran the local youth football team, and he was forever trying to encourage Jack to join in, at the same time being careful not to bully him.

Bill spent the winter months fitting a new keel and putting an appropriately weighted concrete ballast in the bottom of the boat. If nothing else he was a stickler for detail and, thanks to that chance meeting with Barnacle, this time he was not going to get it wrong. His new hand-cranked bilge pump worked perfectly, and by March all that was needed was to finish the exterior paintwork and add 'Cohen's Emporium', painted in black to exactly match the sign over the shop. As promised, it was written in a prominent position on both the port and the starboard side. Thus far, there had been a distinct lack of enthusiasm from the local corporate world to associate itself with what was considered to be a somewhat dangerous and eccentric enterprise.

The next sea trial was going to have to be fully laden with all of his kit in readiness for the big journey. All of Bill's meticulous calculations of weight versus water displacement and so on got thrown out with the bilge water. He thought that

April would be a good time for the sea trial, leaving the final journey until May, just after his birthday.

April 1st was to be avoided, and by April 5th Bill was all set to go. He had incorporated two heavy-duty car batteries encased in fibreglass pockets in the cab, and in addition to them there was a single solar panel built into the forward deck area. He reckoned that should be sufficient to provide him with a ship-to-shore radio and minimal lighting, and he would be able to charge a GPS. He also built two good old-fashioned needle compasses into the bulkhead and had all the appropriate paper charts to take him to the Americas. Bill was trying his best to minimise the risk of getting lost in a very lonely ocean and losing contact, given that he had a limited budget of cash and an even smaller budget of experience.

The weather on the morning of the second sea trial was horrendous. The driven sleet and biting winds were as sharp as a whetted knife. The boys wondered if it could be a bad omen to leave on such an awful day.

At Bill's insistence the *Arthurian* was loaded onto the van. After all, 'Fortune favours the bold,' said Bill, confidently.

Their arrival at New Brighton attracted no attention whatsoever. The sea was fiercely angry and grey, and when the Irish Sea gets in a bad mood it becomes the devil itself. There was hardly a vehicle or a living soul in sight, and even the gulls felt wise enough to sit in rows along the promenade walls rather than venture into the skies.

Tommy and Les were not happy with the situation.

'This is total bloody madness,' said Les, as a massive wave crashed over the walls, flooding the entire road. The startled gulls scattered into the air, calling out with their familiar distressful cries.

'Come on, you two, stop whingeing and sounding like a pair

of soppy schoolgirls. Help me get this bloody ship in the water,' said Bill.

With much huffing and puffing, heaving, shoving and cajoling, the *Arthurian* made another undignified entrance into the water and she bobbed around like a cork. This time they remembered to hold on to the guys.

The feeling of achievement was short-lived. Tommy and Les kept moaning about how wet they were, and that they would have to drive all the way back home in the van wearing sodden clothes. Bill secured the boat and got himself properly organised, while at the same time struggling against the winds to try and stand up straight.

Tommy was the first to embrace Bill with a farewell hug. 'I'm still trying to figure out whether you're incredibly brave or just incredibly stupid, but either way, I'll worry about you until I see that ugly face of yours back on dry land.'

Les was not one for man-hugs and gave Bill a firm handshake. 'Stay safe, Bill. I think you're bloody crackers sailing in this weather!'

'Let's just call it my baptism of fire,' said Bill. 'If I can't survive this kind of weather when I'm yards from home and five minutes from a lifeboat, how will I deal with it in the middle of the Atlantic? No, this weather is just perfect.' With a single pull of the cord, the engine fired up. 'I'll see you two bozos in Bristol!' he shouted.

Bill was very aware that he had to get out to sea as quickly as possible. In a heavy squall such as this, and with such an underpowered motor, it would be so easy to get swept back to shore and smashed against the rocks. Contrary to general thought, the open sea is more likely to be your friend than the treacherous shoreline.

As if on a rollercoaster, the tiny craft rode the giant swell and headed directly westward. Bill's hand was frozen and fused to the arm of the rudder, and he contemplated whether to be brave enough to lower a single boom. *It's now or never,* he thought.

'Set the jib, Mr Bosun!' he shouted, as if giving orders to an invisible crew. The boom lowered and the little triangular sail billowed out. The boat tilted slightly and began to cut through the water by herself. All his hard work and his modifications to the keel proved to be a perfect success. 'Mr Bosun, tell the engine room to cut all engines!' he yelled, as he silenced the little outboard motor. For the first time in his life he really was 'sailing' and he was now the master of his very own vessel.

A seagull passed close by in its battle against the winds. Bill waved at it and yelled, 'Now I'm free, just as you are, my friend!'

To that, the bird responded by dropping a substantial fish-smelling splat all down Bill's shoulder and onto his sleeve.

'Thanks a bunch,' said Bill.

Within a few hours the inclement weather had begun to subside. Bill had battled his first storm, and won. His feeling of self-satisfaction was immeasurable, but as he sat back, totally exhausted, he experienced his first ever bout of seasickness. While he hung over the side, an unexpected mouthful of seawater helped it on its way.

It was back to Conwy for a well-deserved rest, and a few days later Bill found he just couldn't pass Morfa Nefyn without calling in at the old Ty Coch Inn to meet up with Barnacle one more time. Barnacle was most impressed with the quality of Bill's work, and early the following morning, as he was preparing to set sail again, there was a knock on the side of the boat. It was Barnacle and his wife, Mrs Watson. Barnacle handed Bill a bottle of Old Jamaica Rum.

'Wow! Thank you so much,' said Bill.

'Nelson's orders! You can't go to sea without a daily tot, you know,' replied Barnacle.

Mrs Watson stepped forward and introduced herself. 'Hi, I'm Maggie.' She had baked him the most enormous cream and jam sponge cake. It was so big it hardly fitted through the boat's spin dryer door hatch. Bill had to get out and then lower it in.

Following a series of affectionate goodbyes, Bill clambered back on board. As he jumped in, he felt the warm cream squeeze up between the toes of his bare feet. He continued to shout his farewells and wave enthusiastically as if nothing was amiss until they were out of sight. Sadly, most of the cake ended up being dumped overboard.

The days passed quickly with no major catastrophes to mention. Bill had successfully avoided all general marine traffic, including several container ships heading up toward Liverpool and Belfast, and the fine weather had followed him much of the way down the Welsh coast. He'd got used to having regular catnaps rather than a full night's sleep.

But what he enjoyed most was the clear firmament of creation. The black night and the Milky Way. He had never had the experience of being utterly alone before, and he witnessed his very first shooting star. The craters of the moon were so much clearer than could be seen in the hazy suburban light. Absolute solitude was no menace to him at all; it was both exhilarating and contemplative. Many of the old friends he had grown up with had turned to drugs to escape their misfortunes of domestic violence and poverty. Bill had found his drug, alone in the open sea.

As he turned the corner into the Bristol Channel, passing Barry on his port side, Bill took the final swig of Barnacle's bottle of

Jamaica rum. He tossed it overboard, but not before leaving a note in it, which read, 'William Smith Esquire launched this bottle in the Bristol Channel on the trial voyage of his boat, the *Arthurian.*' He added his telephone number and address in the hope that it would survive the journey of the Atlantic Gulf Stream and end up being discovered in the Caribbean or up on the eastern American coast somewhere.

As Portbury dock by Avonmouth came in sight, Bill noticed two tiny figures standing together on the long outstretched quay wall. It was Tommy and Les, loyal as ever. Bill could see Tommy jumping up and down, frantically waving his arms in the air, and he responded with a Morse code flashlight message: 'Ahoy there, all's well, good to see you two landlubbers!' Of course, only former Sea Cadet Tommy Duckinfield was able to translate the message, and he relayed it to Les as each torch flash was received.

Chapter Four

Back at home, Bill's first port of call was the luxury of a long soak in the bath and a shave with a brand new razorblade. In his short trip at sea, items of personal hygiene had been pretty low on his list of priorities. In short, he'd forgotten to take any.

Janice was relieved to see him and she was genuinely excited to hear all of his news. For the first time in their marriage she told him that she was proud of him. Janice could never know how much those words would mean to Bill. Marcus Rawley was the only person in Bill's life to have ever made him feel more than a complete failure. Things were improving.

The following day, as Bill and Janice sat at the kitchen table chatting, they heard a key turn in the front door; it was Jack. He quietly went up to his room, unaware of his father's return.

Janice crept over to the kitchen door and closed it. 'I've got a bit of news for you. I think Jack has gone and got himself a girlfriend,' she said in a whisper.

'Thank God for that,' said Bill.

'She's a lovely girl, she's from a very good Catholic family. She's a proper young lady,' said Janice. 'Oh, and she's black.'

'Black!' yelled Bill. 'How bloody black are we talking about?'

Bill was unable to hide a deeply ingrained prejudice. His father had taught him from the very start to be suspicious of black people, despite giving him such a strict Catholic upbringing. It all began in 1948 when the government first brought over Caribbean people on a ship called the *Empire Windrush* to help replenish Britain's much-depleted labour force after the losses of the Second World War. There were no immigration restrictions preventing any member of the British

Empire from moving to another part of the Empire. Theoretically, all of Her Majesty's subjects could have chosen to come to live in Britain at that time: all two billion of them. An Act of Parliament controlling immigration only came into being in 1962. Many of the poorest white working-class men deeply resented those few that did come, fearing they would take their jobs or, worse still, take their women.

'Her name is Sophie, and she and Jack have been helping each other do their GCSE homework together. I'm not saying that it will amount to anything; it's just that my woman's intuition tells me there might be a bit of lovey-dovey going on,' said Janice.

Already, in his mind's eye Bill could see, with horror, coffee-coloured grandchildren with enormous football-shaped Afro hairdos running round his kitchen.

Janice continued, 'Her father is white, and I think he was something to do with the government in Jamaica, and her mother is black and she's a music teacher. And that's all I know about her.'

Just then, the kitchen door opened. Jack walked in and went straight to the biscuit tin, removed a handful of chocolate McVitie's and tried to put a whole one in his mouth.

'Aren't you going to say hello to your father?' said Janice impatiently.

'Oh, yeah. Hi, Dad, how did it go?' replied Jack, in mid-mouthful.

Bill couldn't contain himself. 'Fine, just fine, thank you very much. Now, what's going on with this black girl I'm hearing about? I hope you are using French letters and not being stupid and reckless.'

'We're not doing French, Dad, we're doing English Literature and Media Studies,' came Jack's reply.

Bill quickly realised that Jack hadn't the faintest idea what a

French letter was. 'Come on, then, is it serious with you two or what?'

'There's nothing going on, Dad. We're really good friends, that's all. She's not been at our school for very long,' said Jack.

Janice interrupted. 'You'll have plenty of opportunity to find out for yourself, Bill, because I've invited her round for tea this evening.'

'Well, we'd better get a couple of tins of pineapple chunks in from the Co-op; they like that kind of thing, do those Jamaicans,' said Bill in all seriousness.

'Don't be stupid,' said Janice. 'Go upstairs and get a clean shirt on, you look a mess.'

Bill dutifully obeyed.

At six o'clock precisely, the doorbell rang and Janice was first to open it. 'Hello, Sophie, love, come in. It's so lovely to see you again. Go into the sitting room, Jack should be down in a few minutes.'

Janice steered her into the room where Bill was sitting in his favourite armchair pretending to read the newspaper. 'Sophie, this is my husband, Bill.'

Sophie offered an outstretched hand. 'It's a pleasure to meet you, Mr Smith. Jack has been telling me what a remarkably talented and brave man you are, and that you are about to single-handedly sail the Atlantic Ocean.'

Bill was unable to answer her, and remained motionless with his hand still attached to hers. Sophie was nothing less than the female form in absolute perfection. He stared at her, his mouth slightly open, totally intoxicated by her sensual nubility and her beauty.

Janice broke the awkward silence. 'Aren't you going to say anything, then?'

'Oh, yes, yes, sit down, Sophie, please.' Bill stumbled over his words. He struggled to suppress this sudden surge of inner passion and turmoil. He'd never experienced such an instant and overwhelming feeling before. This was the girlfriend of his teenage son, for God's sake! He shouldn't be thinking such thoughts. He kept repeating it to himself over and over again.

Before him was nothing more, and nothing less, than a staggeringly beautiful woman.

Sophie appeared to be more southern Mediterranean than Afro-Caribbean. Her skin was olive, silken and tanned. Her hair, loosely tied back, was as straight and as black as a raven's wing, and her eyes appeared to be almost mahogany. Bill averted his own eyes from gazing at her full and beautiful pert breasts. He could feel Janice's laser vision boring a hole in the side of his head. Sophie sat neatly upright on the chair opposite him, making sure not to look too brazen or relaxed.

Bill continued to blunder from one social gaffe to the next.

'Well, Sophie, I believe your mother plays in a Caribbean band, or something?' he said confidently.

Sophie coyly smiled. 'No, she doesn't, no, I'm afraid not. My mum is a teacher of classical music; she's a cellist principally, but she mostly teaches violin. I'm trying to get Jack to start to learn an instrument. I'm so pleased because he seems really keen. A few nights ago I took him to see my mum and her student choir perform Schubert's Latin Mass No. 2 in G Major, and then they did Mozart's Requiem. To my surprise, Jack was really quite moved by it all. It was just wonderful,' she said with a girlish enthusiasm.

Bill was totally out of his depth by this time, but he muddled on. 'Oh, that's lovely, and what do you do, Sophie?'

'I play violin, piano, and I sing a little, but not very well,' was her modest reply.

'Sing me a bit of that first one you mentioned, the Schubert one!' said Bill, trying to sound knowledgeable and sophisticated.

Sophie cleared her throat. With the almost whispering dulcet tones of an angel, she started to sing the Latin Credo. '*Credo in unum Deum, Patrem omnipotentem.*'

Within a couple of minutes, Bill could feel the tears welling up in his eyes. There was something going on in his head, his heart and his loins that had thus far eluded him in his life.

'That was just about the most beautiful sound I've ever heard, Sophie,' said Bill as she finished. 'Wasn't it, Janice?'

Just then Jack walked in. 'Hi, Sophie. I see you've met my father, then,' he declared.

'Yes, you never told me that your dad was such a fan of classical music!' said Sophie.

'Oh yes indeed. Dad's got a cockney pal down at the pub and they are always saying that they want to be Brahms and Liszt,' said Jack sarcastically.

The cockney rhyming slang completely passed over Sophie's head and the conversation changed to other things.

Janice's dinner was a great success. The prawn cocktail starter, followed by roast chicken, assorted vegetables and roast potatoes, was not adventurous, but it was safe. Jack and Sophie were not excluded from partaking of a glass of white wine each, which made them feel that they had been fully accepted into the world of grown-ups. Janice had been told by the local supermarket manager that white wine went with chicken.

'So, Jack, you'd like to become a musician?' enquired Bill.

'Yes, Dad, I think I'd like to learn to play the cello like Sophie's mum.'

Bill leaned back in his chair and took a long slow sip of his wine. 'Well then, we'd better start to see about buying one for you, son. It's quite some time now since I last priced a cello. What sort of money are they nowadays?'

Sophie jumped into the conversation. 'Oh, that would be just sensational, Mr Smith! You should be able to get a reasonable one for about five thousand pounds.'

Bill nearly choked on his wine. 'Are you sure you wouldn't prefer to take up the harmonica instead, son? It would be a lot less carrying around. Think about it!' He set his glass down. 'Joking aside, why don't you take some lessons from Sophie's mother and see if you really do want to learn to play the cello, or perhaps some other instrument?'

Inwardly, Janice questioned Bill's motive for such warmth and generosity toward Jack. He was obviously trying to make a seriously good impression for Sophie's benefit, but Janice could see right through him.

At 9.30pm, Jack insisted on escorting Sophie back home safely to her parents. It had been a wonderful evening. At the door, Sophie put her arms around Bill, thanked him, and kissed him goodbye on both cheeks. Her hair brushed against his face and he could smell the cleanliness and sweet perfume of the soap on her soft skin. He desperately wanted that embrace to last so much longer than the millisecond that it took.

The front door had no sooner closed than Janice thrust her forefinger in his face, with all the menace she could muster. 'I know exactly what's been in your dirty little mind, Bill Smith. This entire evening you have been behaving like some bloody lovesick puppy dog. I've had my eye on you; it's pathetic!'

'What the hell are you talking about, woman?' growled Bill. 'I'm thrilled to bits that Jack has found himself a lovely sensible girl. She's going to be really good for that lad. I'm just relieved that he hasn't got himself mixed up with one of those little scrubbers that hang around outside the football stadium every evening. Don't be so damned ridiculous, woman, that girl is nearly half my age; she's seventeen, for God's sake! Yes, of course she's a pretty girl, but there's no law in any land that says that a frog can't look at a princess, now is there? My love, oh light of my life!'

'You've got a bloody smooth-talking answer for everything, Bill Smith,' snarled Janice. He was always referred to as 'Bill Smith' when she was angry with him.

Thankfully, she didn't take too much convincing, and they decided to leave the dirty dishes until morning and retire early to bed. Not surprisingly they made love that night, during which Bill's mind was definitely floating off within the realms of his newfound fantasy.

Two days later, a letter arrived. It was a thank-you letter from Sophie. Janice waved it at Bill. 'That, Bill Smith, is class! Upper-class people always send thank-you letters. See, I told you she was a proper lady, didn't I?' she declared triumphantly.

Bill had to concede fully to his previous errors of judgement and his long-standing prejudice.

Over the coming weeks Sophie visited them regularly. Sometimes she would join Bill in his shed as he busied himself with cleaning and preparing the boat. She would always sit on his workbench and swing her shapely tanned legs back and forth as she chatted twenty to the dozen, firing endless volleys of questions at him.

Bill rather naively believed that Sophie was completely oblivious to the extent of his infatuation with her. But one thing was for sure: Sophie was very aware of the power of her own sexuality. She would always slightly open her legs as she jumped off the bench, which she did only when Bill's gaze was in her direction. She was teasing and goading him to dare to make his move. But the truth of the matter was that the sheer terror of the consequences was preventing him from tasting this forbidden fruit. Bill was too insecure to try it on, and Sophie knew it; she was just having fun with him.

Jack had more reason to stay at home these days, rather than spend his time with his grandparents. His relationship with Sophie was the dream of every sexually inexperienced spotty-faced youth, and every grown man, for that matter. For although Jack and she were of similar age, Sophie had all the countenance and experience of a woman of thirty, and she obviously enjoyed being in charge. She also seemed to have all the qualifications needed to partner any English gentleman. Behave as a lady by day, but as a whore in the bed by night. Perfect!

Janice tolerated Bill's silly childlike indiscretions with Sophie, and as long as he stayed within the bounds of his tether, it was harmless enough. Sometimes, it was difficult to distinguish which one was more the puppy dog: Jack or Bill. Janice would jest with her husband, announcing, 'Your girlfriend is coming round tonight, Bill,' to which he would snap at her, 'For God's sake, woman, stop being so bloody stupid.' Janice would always scurry off giggling to herself.

Chapter Five

The first week in May came all too soon.

Bill, meticulous as always, checked his list of supplies at least half a dozen times. His birthday came and went, with people kindly offering him presents of all sorts of useless keepsakes, including a large Captain Birdseye doll. They had little thought for the fact that every square inch of space in the *Arthurian* was precious.

It was decided that this time he would set sail from St Ives in Cornwall. They would make it a special weekend treat and stay at the Old Sloop Inn, which had been an inn since AD 1312. Mini holidays were a rare thing for Janice and she was really looking forward to it. As there was little room for four of them in Les's uncomfortable Transit van, Don Wilson kindly offered to drive Janice there in the comfort of his car, along with his son, Mark.

On the Friday morning preparations were underway. Jack and Sophie had decided to stay at home for the weekend, allowing them the run of the house. During the last hour, whilst waiting for Tommy and Les to arrive with the van, Bill remained alone in his shed with his boat and he contemplated all the hard work that had gone into arriving at this moment.

The door to the shed creaked open. It was Sophie.

'Hi, I've only got a couple of minutes. I just thought I'd pop over to see you and say goodbye and safe journey,' she said.

'Ah, that's really nice of you, Sophie. Thank you,' said Bill.

Sophie moved rapidly toward him and put her arms around his neck. She kissed him full on the lips; her tongue began exploring his mouth, his neck and his ear. Almost immediately, she forcibly removed his hands from around her waist and put one firmly between her legs and the other on her breast. Bill had suddenly gone well beyond the bounds of his allotted tether, and there was no turning back now.

Not two minutes had passed when Sophie jumped back from their embrace, smiled at him and said, 'Have a safe journey, big boy. Until we meet again!' She turned and ran out of the door.

It took Bill several minutes to recover and allow his heart to stop racing. *Did that really happen to me, or did I just dream it?* he thought.

Don and Mark were the first to arrive, whilst Janice was still frantically packing her things. With so much manpower around, the boat was quickly secured on the Transit and all last-minute checks were made. Jack and Sophie stood on the pavement holding hands; they said a quick goodbye, turned and went straight into the house together. For that fleeting second Bill felt a twinge of jealousy, knowing full well that the minute they had all gone, Sophie and Jack would be rolling around on his and Janice's king-sized bed.

Janice leaned over and whispered in Bill's ear, 'Ah, that's a shame, you didn't get a little goodbye kiss from your girlfriend!'

'That joke is wearing a bit thin now, Janice,' Bill snapped back at her.

Les intervened. 'We'll go in convoy, but if we get split up, then we'll all meet at the Sloop this evening.'

The van was far too slow and Don, Janice and Mark were quick to lose it.

By evening time the boys found them at the inn as planned. Janice had already got into the holiday mood and was moderately amusing and slightly tipsy. She was always a happy drunk, and rarely a nasty one.

That night in bed, Bill and Janice talked almost incessantly. She had come to terms with his determination to break free from their mundane life and seek adventure while he still had the energy and strength to do it. She was sure that this trip would get it out of his system, and that he would come back home to roost any time soon. Bill had estimated about four to six months overall, taking into account stopovers in Portugal, Madeira or the Canaries. But he was free and not subjected to any strict time schedule.

The following morning everyone enjoyed a hearty breakfast and headed over to the quay where they had moored the boat. As everyone milled around talking and making a fuss, Bill noticed a familiar sight gliding toward them. It was Marcus Rawley's maroon Bentley.

'What a wonderful surprise!' shouted Bill, as Marcus stepped out of the car.

'I didn't want to miss out on all the fun and excitement,' said Marcus, and he handed Bill an envelope for him to open later when on board.

They were all busy taking volumes of photographs when Marcus reminded everyone that the tide was on the turn. Bill needed to get out of the little St Ives harbour quickly or suffer the indignity of being left high and dry.

With a tug on the engine cord, the little motor signalled that it was time for his departure. Janice kissed him and squeezed him tightly. 'You'd better get back here in one piece, Bill Smith,' she commanded.

There were glazed eyes all round, and even Marcus looked a little upset. Perhaps his innermost thoughts were, *I hope I haven't played a part in sending this man to his death.*

The receding tide rapidly swept the *Arthurian* out of the harbour and into the open sea. The little band of people still waving and shouting from the quayside quickly became a tiny speck on the horizon. At this point Bill cut the engine and decided to take time to rearrange the interior of his little floating home.

He opened Marcus's letter. It contained five hundred dollars in ten- and twenty-dollar bills. The letter just said, 'Dear Bill, I'll bet that you forgot to change some money into US dollars. That's what they like best in the Caribbean. Good luck. Call me if you ever need me. Best wishes, Marcus.'

In the early days of Bill's infatuation with Sophie his curiosity had got the better of him. One afternoon, he had secretly checked her social media pages on Jack's computer. As with so many teenagers, she had foolishly included several semi-naked pictures of herself, along with the usual photos of her family and friends. Bill had had no hesitation in downloading the juicy ones and printing them off for himself. They were among the first to be gaffer-taped to the wall next to his pillow. She would be the last thing he would see at night, and the first thing he would wake up to in the morning.

Also included in his little picture gallery were three early photographs of Uncle Arthur. He knew that times could become seriously difficult, and Uncle Arthur would be there to guide him and protect him.

Over the next few days he successfully journeyed past the Scilly Isles, and avoided any collisions with incoming maritime traffic. The gateway leading from the Celtic Sea into the English Channel was one of the busiest and most congested shipping lanes in the world. Giant tankers could run him down and nobody would be any the wiser. It was a great relief to spot Europe's tallest lighthouse at Phare de L'Ile Vierge off the coast of Brittany.

From there on, his course was a straight line across the Bay of Biscay, almost touching the northwest coast of Spain, and then on down to Madeira.

With each passing day Bill rapidly grew in confidence, knowledge and experience. In his second week at sea he had mistaken some inquisitive dolphins for sharks. Only when one came right up to the boat and gave him a big dolphin smile did he realise he was among friends. These highly intelligent and friendly animals quickly understood not to take any of the fish from Bill's trailing bait lines. They would circle the boat to tell him when he had sufficient catches on the lines. Bill recognised that the dolphins knew that the fish were all caught with hooks in their mouths. Rather than risk damaging themselves by attempting to steal them, they would wait until Bill hauled them all in. They seemed to know that he would keep one for himself and share the rest with them. It was a reciprocated friendship.

A couple of days before reaching Madeira, Bill was to encounter a very different set of sea companions. He was rudely awakened early one morning by the most enormous bang on the side of the boat and he felt the boat being pushed sideways. This was followed by a second bang in another direction. *Surely I couldn't have drifted aground* was his immediate thought.

As he opened the spin dryer door hatch he was introduced to the most vomit-wrenching stench of putrefying flesh. There floating beside him, not more than ten feet away, was the enormous rotting carcass of a sperm whale. Around it was a frenzy of maybe thirty to fifty blue sharks tearing at its blubber. Many of them were more than three metres in length.

Frantically, he tugged at the engine cord, but the more he tugged the more he flooded the motor and the damned thing wouldn't start. His little boat was being bashed and cajoled ever further into the midst of this unsavoury banquet. He could see down into the abyss below him, layer upon layer of circling sharks awaiting their turn. His greatest fear was that he would be tipped over and end up as a side dish for some of the guests. In a state of sheer panic, he began lashing out at them with his paddle, aiming mainly at their eyes. Eventually, he was freed by enough distance to open and fill the sails and return safely to his course of south-southwest.

The distant hills of Madeira were a most welcoming sight. Bill was very aware that although he had sufficient food, drink and supplemental nutrients in tablet form on board, he had already lost a considerable amount of weight. He'd quickly got used to eating a fraction of the amount of food he would normally eat at home. He'd learnt to consume tiny amounts, little and often, as our early hunter-gatherer ancestors would have done, with few sugars and very few carbohydrates. He couldn't wait to get on land and tuck into a big plate of steak and chips.

His arrival caused some interest and general amusement amongst the tourists. As he stepped ashore by the Royal Savoy Hotel, he staggered all over the place, and for the first hour he walked around like a severely drunken man. He'd not shaved in over a month and neither had he been able to bathe properly. The first bar he tried to order a beer from, they not-so-politely removed him from the premises. He returned to the boat and did his best to clean himself up.

Down in the town of Funchal, Bill eventually found a Turkish barber shop and thought that it was time to treat himself to a haircut and the luxury of a hot towel shave. In light-hearted banter with the barber, he was persuaded to keep the bushy moustache. Those Turks just love their handlebar moustaches and by the time the barber had finished with Bill, he looked like he'd stepped straight out of the Ottoman Empire.

Bill quickly started to thoroughly enjoy himself. He decided to stay for at least a week, recharge his batteries and kit out the boat ready for the very long journey ahead.

His first telephone call to Janice didn't quite go as expected. Bill had thought that the news of his safe arrival in Madeira would be met with a lot more enthusiasm and relief. Janice seemed a little subdued and somewhat distant. We all have our off days, and Bill put it down to the fact that without him there Janice's routine had been upset; he knew only too well that Janice didn't like change. He promised to phone her again before he left.

Several days passed and all was going swimmingly. Bill had everything set and prepared for his big journey ahead. All his kit and food supplies were neatly folded and appropriately placed in his cabin. But as Robbie Burns once said, 'The best-laid plans of mice and men often go awry,' or, to put an Elizabethan proverbial spin on it, 'There be many a slip betwixt the cup and the lip.'

The night before he was due to leave he had the misfortune to acquaint himself with a Glaswegian hen party, in full swing. The not-so-blushing, corpulently well-upholstered bride and around twelve of her entourage had been drinking almost non-stop for three days. They were uniformly dressed in white low-cut T-shirts, black tight-fitting miniskirts and white stiletto-heeled shoes. Many of them had the complexion of ripe tomatoes. In order to signify their rank within this motley troop, they each wore a pink sash emblazoned with 'Mother of the Bride', 'Friend of the Bride' and so on.

They took a shine to Bill and in a semi-drunken state he joined in with their revelry. He decided to invite them to inspect his boat, which seemed a jolly good idea at the time.

The fat bride, and her even fatter sister, were the first to climb on board for an inspection. The pair of them were precariously hanging onto the mast. As the boat began to sway back and forth there was an almighty crack when a stiletto heel went through Bill's inbuilt solar panelling. The heel snapped off the shoe and unbalanced its owner. Holding tight onto the mast, the two of them crashed unceremoniously into the dock. With the hatch open, the boat instantly filled with water and anything that could float left the cabin. *Arthurian* bobbed up and down inches below the surface, whilst the two lumps floundered in the water. If nothing else, it proved that Bill's meticulous calculations were correct. The fully laden boat would still float even when completely submerged.

Naturally, Bill flew into an almighty rage, but he was met by a full volley of drunken Glaswegian expletives from the entire troop. The mother of the bride attacked him, bashing him several times with her handbag, and another one struck him with her shoe. As the two sopping wet 'ladies' hauled themselves out of the dock, the bride declared, 'Ah, fuck 'im. Come on, lassies, we've got some serious drinkin' tae do!'

Bill was left sitting alone on the quayside; all he could do was weep.

In the heat of the night, Bill slept on the quayside under a tarpaulin with only feral cats for company. As the dawn broke, he began the task of putting Marcus's bilge pump to work and laying the entire contents of the boat on the dockside. It was a sorry sight indeed.

This wasn't to be his most challenging problem; more was yet to come! His corner of the dock looked a bit like a jumble sale, with his clothes hanging out to dry and all manner of things strewn everywhere. Predictably, this attracted the attention of the Portuguese harbour master, who sauntered over to see him. So far, he had managed to avoid the authorities as he had moored amidst a handful of non-paying rowing boats.

'What are you doing here and where has this boat come from?' he was asked.

'I've sailed it from England,' was Bill's rather cocky reply.

The harbour master was not impressed. 'Really? Then where is your UK safety permit?'

What the hell is that? thought Bill.

'This vessel is not permitted to leave this port without the correct safety certificates,' said the master.

Bill began to plead with him. He said he must have left his permit at home. He was told that in that case, he was going to have to fly home and leave the boat there. Bill told the master that he was hoping to sail it back to Gibraltar, but that was only to throw him off the scent of his real plan.

'If I have to fly back to England, where can I put all of my stuff for safe keeping?' asked Bill.

'You can box it all up and it will be locked in our storage room until you come back. If you don't pay the storage within a month, then it and the boat will be sold. You have got two days to get your things sorted out,' said the master.

Bill had to think fast!

He headed straight for the local supermarket. Earlier that day, he'd noticed a pile of cardboard boxes stacked up behind the rubbish bins. As nightfall came, he returned. Armed with a roll of gaffer tape and a felt tip pen, he began to fill each box with supermarket rubbish: old fruit, vegetables, paper bags, plastic, you name it. When each box was full, he neatly sealed it and marked it accordingly: clothing, first aid supplies, fishing tackle and so on. All of his boat's real contents were piled into the rowing boat moored next door and covered over with a tarpaulin.

The following morning, the harbour master paid him a visit. He was terribly impressed by how quickly Bill had organised himself, and he even helped him to carry some of the boxes to the storehouse.

Bill spent the following day preparing for his great escape. He replenished lost goods as best he could, and stocked up on food supplies. He had to get well away from the island before the storage room began to stink to high heaven and the full measure of his deception was discovered. He hoped that if the coast guard were instructed to bring him back, they would start by looking for him en route north-northeast to Gibraltar. Instead, Bill was to turn right out of the port entrance and head south-southwest for the open Atlantic. The Gulf Stream, that great Atlantic conveyance, would help drive him down toward the Equator and then over to the Caribbean.

At midnight, he pulled the engine cord, and as silently as possible he chugged his way past the lines of moored yachts. He could hear the laughter and raised voices coming from the people in the taverns and restaurants nearby. Slowly and unnoticed, he made his exit out into the open seas where he cut the motor and filled the sails.

Chapter Six

It was the following midday before he felt that he'd covered a safe enough distance to raise the booms and to get a little afternoon shuteye.

In the intense heat, and with the hatch closed, Bill found it impossible to sleep comfortably. The sweat just poured off him, and he had not bargained for the fact that his little floating home would turn into a roasting hot greenhouse the minute he closed the hatch. Sleeping in the cool of the night was his only option, but as he got closer to the Equator, even that became more uncomfortable.

The weeks passed, and he had been blessed with favourable weather and light winds for much of the way. He was confident that he was making really good progress. The last time he had checked, he had dropped down past the Tropic of Cancer and was heading about W30 degrees just south of Santiago and Cape Verde. However, with his solar panel destroyed by you-know-who, and his lighting system failed, fortune's little favours began to turn for the worse.

In addition to a dramatic weight loss, the flesh between his toes had begun to split, bleed and pustulate. Invariably, there were always several inches of salt water swishing around in the bottom of the boat. What he'd not realised was that during his encounter with the Glaswegian hens in Madeira, after the boat had capsized, the battery acid had seeped out from one of the car batteries. His feet were slowly being eaten away.

Additionally, when he turned the electrics on, salt water electroplated the salt throughout his copper wiring system. He noticed that the wires quickly turned green and fuzzy and crumbled into powder in his hands. All systems were down and all he had for navigation were his two needle compasses. He'd lost any sense of where he was, except that he was pointing in the right direction: west.

Bill had not washed in fresh water for several weeks. The last time had been during a brief monsoon storm when he had stood naked on the deck and washed himself down with soap in the torrential rain. The salt and the baking sun were taking their toll. Sleeping each night in his little greenhouse had created serious fungal problems, and his groin and armpits were particularly sore. He resorted to caking his genitals and underarms with black axle grease. He'd brought it along in order to lubricate some of the moving parts in the engine. He'd long since run out of cortisone and antiseptic creams, and as part of his sleeping arrangements he had made two hammocks, one for each leg. This meant that he could sleep with his legs wide apart and suspended in the air. It was the only way he could get relief from the excruciating pain in preventing his genitalia from flopping from side to side with the movement of the boat.

His mouth and lips had also become severely blistered and eating was beginning to be a problem. Bill tried to liquefy much of his food, including mashed-up fish. Everything seemed to end up as a kind of revolting soup. There were no bounds to his culinary creativity. Last week's half-eaten tin of chopped tomatoes mixed with a couple of pineapple chunks and some fish giblets was breakfast and dinner. He was aware that he was suffering malnutrition and possible scurvy. His reasoning and common sense were becoming confused and he was about to make a careless mistake that could take his life.

He was living on a diet of almost no carbohydrates. Everything went in as a liquid, and, very quickly, it came out as a liquid. His toilet seat contraption was mounted at the back of the boat, and many an hour was spent enthroned there in contemplation.

This particular day was fairly calm, but there was a light wind with a gentle undulating swell. Bill was seated on his throne. In an unguarded moment, the bow suddenly climbed a rogue wave. Bill was flipped into a somersault off the back. He had never really learnt to swim properly and he embarked upon a panic-ridden thrashing of arms and legs. Seawater flushed down his nose and he took in great gulps of the stuff. He was breathing, gagging, coughing and vomiting all at the same time. The more he panicked, the more he sank and rose again. Each time he surfaced he looked for the boat, but it was nowhere to be seen. 'Sweet Jesus, help me!' he pleaded.

He also knew that panic alerted sharks, and he could only hope that none were in the immediate neighbourhood. First things first: stop panicking! He started to think rationally again. *Stay calm, and try to swim like a frog,* he thought. It worked. Suddenly, and with his head above water, the boat came into view again.

It was only yards away, but as a non-swimmer he might as well be swimming the English Channel. Every time he rose on a swell, the boat seemed to go just that bit further away. In desperation he screamed out, 'Uncle Arthur, for God's sake, where are you?'

No sooner had he uttered Arthur's name than he felt the baited fishing line in his hand. He never felt the hook embed itself deeply into his palm as he grasped it. Carefully, he hauled himself toward the boat. He was unsure of the strength of poundage on the line, and at this point he was not going to risk snapping it.

Only when he got back on board did he see the full extent of his injury. The large sea hook had gone completely through his palm and come out through the back of his hand. With a pair of pliers he managed to cut the barb and pull it back out the way it went in.

Minutes later, he received a visit from one of his neighbours from hell. A great white shark had rushed to the scene and was circling the boat. Sure enough, Bill's thrashing and panicking, along with the loss of blood from his hand, had invited Whitey to dinner. But this time he was to be disappointed and Bill just glared at him from the safety of his hatch.

Never again would he risk being dethroned or separated from the boat. From now on he would only go outside his cabin with a rope tethered to his ankle.

Since Madeira, he'd been saving a half-bottle of rum for when he sighted the land of the Americas, but now he had a more pressing use for the alcohol. He poured it into the gaping hole in his hand and wrapped the wound in an old shirtsleeve bandage.

Fortunately, he'd not severed any tendons or any of the larger veins and it managed to avoid becoming septic. Most remarkably, it healed quite quickly, within a couple of weeks or so, and he didn't lose any of the function of his hand either.

With his own religious fervour, he was able to endure that initial excruciating pain by likening it to Christ's stigmata. If the good Lord had to put up with nails hammered through his hands and his feet, then Bill could cope with a single five-inch fishing hook through his palm. He just accepted it as his penance and atonement for all his sins in the sight of God. Bill's lengthy solitude had made him a far more spiritual kind of fellow. He was convinced that Uncle Arthur's guiding spirit had been responsible for saving his life.

His main problem was that he had run out of any kind of variable diet. He had long since exhausted his supply of vitamin tablets and tinned provisions, and all he had to sustain him was fresh water, sugar and salt. He knew that the body could survive for quite a long time as long as it had those three ingredients. But he had lost far too much weight and his health was finally failing him. The weaker he became, the less he wanted to eat. The less he wanted to eat, the more he wanted to sleep. He had stopped sailing the boat, and for several days he just drifted and dozed with the hatch door fully open.

Bill had finally reached the point of inviting death to join his gentle slumber. He had done his best. He'd broken the mould and followed his dream. He knew that people would remember him and talk about him for years to come.

Bill raised a single eyelid and surveyed the picture gallery that surrounded the area of his pillow. Amidst the faded photos of Uncle Arthur and the semi-naked pictures of Sophie was a single photograph of him and Janice. It had been taken at St Bernadette's youth club on the night of their first kiss.

He remembered the tenderness of that kiss as if it were yesterday. Tears clouded his eyes as his thoughts drifted back over the years of his life spent with Janice. She had been the one and only love of his life, his companion, his confidante, his rod and his rock. Oh, what he wouldn't give to be with her now!

A becalmed sea hailed the break of dawn. Bill was fading fast and silently drifting in and out of consciousness.

Suddenly, startled and confused, he heard a knocking on the side of his boat. A booming voice cried out, 'Hello there! Is anybody home?'

Bill snapped to attention, and then feebly emerged from his open hatch.

'Holy Christ! You look like a bag of shit, old buddy,' said a tall, middle-aged American with a Texas drawl.

Bill struggled to focus. Beside him loomed a beautiful seventy-foot gaff-rigged ketch.

'Where the hell were you planning on going in that little bathtub?' said the Yank.

'America,' replied Bill.

'America! Do you have any idea where you are?'

'Not the foggiest,' came Bill's reply.

'Where did you sail from?'

'England, of course,' was Bill's response.

'Holy camoly!' said the Yank. 'Only a wacko Limey would think of sailing the ocean in his own bathtub.'

'We Brits are a seafaring nation. If it floats, we'll sail it,' said Bill.

Two of the American crew hoisted Bill's frail little skeletal frame up by his arms and on to the deck of the ketch. The sight of Bill, heavily bearded, completely naked and struggling to stand up, was too pitiful for any of them to find it amusing.

'Come on, my friend. You look as if you could use a beer and a burger,' said the Yank.

The Americans had spotted Bill's luminous mast wagging back and forth in the dark from miles away, and they had wondered what on earth it was. It looked just like someone waving for help. They'd set sail from Florida and were heading all the way down to Montevideo and Buenos Aires.

Bill managed to eat half a hamburger and drink a full tin of Bud. He felt alive again! On checking their maps, he could see that he had been swept much further south than he'd anticipated. He had crossed most of the Atlantic down at the Equator, and the Gulf Stream had then pushed him back up to about three hundred miles off the South American coast. He was now positioned N10 degrees, W57.30 degrees. He was not far from the coast of Trinidad and Tobago and from Port of Spain.

At this stage of the game, Bill could have just landed in Trinidad and called it a day. He would have achieved what he'd set out to do, and that would have been fine. But Bill was made of sterner stuff and he was determined to carry on regardless. He planned to enter the Caribbean Sea, make for

Jamaica, and then possibly head up into the Gulf of Mexico and the Mississippi Delta. He had wanted to visit New Orleans from being a boy. Maybe he could now add that to his list of ticked-off dreams.

The Americans were as kind as it is humanly possible to be. One of the crew cut Bill's hair and gave him a shave and a proper shower. Bill insisted on keeping his handlebar moustache, though; he wanted to look as British and as eccentric as possible, so that people would recognise him and remember him. The crew gave him Hawaiian shirts, shorts and a bright red baseball cap. They stocked his galley with everything from corned beef, beer and lime fruit drinks to razors, shaving foam and medical supplies. Bill remained moored to the ketch and he slept in a real bed that night.

The following day the Americans were due to continue their journey south and the time had come for them to part company. They couldn't do enough to make sure that Bill was going to be safe for his onward journey. The goodbyes were an emotional affair. Americans have a propensity to get all teary-eyed at such occasions, and this was no exception. Big burly men welling up and blubbering is a very un-British thing to participate in. There were lots of man hugs, farewell messages, email address exchanges and promises to keep in touch.

Bill waved goodbye and watched the sails on the two masts of the ketch billow out in all their magnificence as she sailed off toward the south. By sundown, he was alone again.

That little interlude of human contact and kindness had invigorated him, rejuvenated him and recharged his batteries. He was back on form and ready for whatever nature and the elements could throw at him. There was no doubt that the Americans had saved him from a slow and unspectacular death, but *I'll bet that Uncle Arthur had a hand in steering them my way,* thought Bill.

Chapter Seven

For the next few days Bill dined well and slept well. He needed to acclimatise to his new luxurious onboard diet, but his digestive system was struggling and somewhat confused. There were many visits to his throne during those days.

He had entered the Caribbean Sea and decided to turn right at Grenada rather than travel diagonally across the large expanse of water in the direction of Jamaica. Bill was very aware that he had just entered serious hurricane territory and so he thought it prudent not to stray too far from the land until he reached the relative safety of Kingston. He felt that he would be safer with a lot more small craft traffic about, should he run into trouble. He had thus far managed to avoid the main shipping lanes, although that was more by accident than design. Bill's plan was to hug the archipelago of islands to include St Lucia, Martinique, Antigua, Puerto Rico, the Dominican Republic and Haiti.

His downfall was that he had no radio or ship-to-shore communication system, which was the one thing the Americans had been unable to help him with. He had his trusty sextant, his two needle compasses and some badly disintegrated charts. The first he would learn of an incoming storm would be in visually witnessing its approach or awaking to its arrival.

Bill felt altogether more at ease over the following weeks. He had a fleeting contact with several yachts and cruisers which would signal or call out to him to check that he was OK. Usually, their crews were intrigued at seeing such a tiny craft, the size of a rowing boat, out in the midst of the ocean. They were also drawn to the fact that it looked like a ridiculous floating washing line. Bill would hoist his shirts, pants, rags, towels and so on from guy ropes that stretched stem to stern from the top of his scaffold-pole mast. Although a little worse for wear, Tommy Duckinfield's Red Ensign still fluttered proudly, never to be lowered in foreign waters except in surrender. Although much of the time Bill felt far more comfortable being completely naked, occasionally, even in the Caribbean, a chill wind would make him put some clothes on.

Bill was up and about at first light when he spotted an unwelcome sight on the horizon, and it was bearing down fast in his direction. It looked remarkably like a gunboat.

He had absolutely no idea of the origin of the flag she was flying, but, to err on the side of caution, he quickly clothed himself and counted out the five hundred US dollars given to him by Marcus. He placed two hundred and fifty dollars under the inner soles of each of his deck shoes and put them on his feet. In these waters, if it wasn't American or British, then expect the worst.

A painted grey rust-bucket pulled alongside. On her bow was a mounted heavy machine gun. A crew member climbed onto the gun seat and swung it round, pointing it directly down at Bill.

There was silence for several minutes and then the captain appeared at the guardrail. He was a thoroughly disgusting-looking fellow, unshaven, heavily sweat-stained with an overhanging beer belly. His sinister smile revealed a row of brown teeth.

'American?' he called down to Bill.

'No! I'm English,' replied Bill.

'Why are you here in Haitian waters?'

'I'm so sorry, sir, I had no idea, I've lost my bearings. I'm on my way to Jamaica,' said Bill nervously. He could see that this was going to become quite unpleasant; the captain's demeanour was seriously threatening.

'You Americans think you are very smart, but we are not afraid of you.'

'No, honestly, sir, I'm not American.' Bill scrambled to show him the Red Ensign. 'Look, I'm British, sir.'

The captain cleared the contents of his nose and spat them down at Bill. 'British, American, you are brothers together, you are both just the same. You come to spy on the people of Haiti!'

'Spy! No, sir, I'm not a spy, I make brake linings. I work in the Goods Inwards department! I wouldn't know what to do as a spy, sir,' pleaded Bill.

'You look like a spy to me!' said the captain with a leer. The entire crew, who had joined him at the guardrail, burst into uproarious laughter.

'I'm not a spy!' shouted Bill at the top of his voice.

With that, the captain withdrew the revolver from his side holster, cocked the trigger hammer and pointed it directly at him. At the same time, the machine gunner cranked his gun in readiness to fire.

Bill raised his hands in the air and began to tremble uncontrollably. 'I'm so sorry, sir, I had no idea that I'd entered Haitian waters. I don't have any navigation equipment, you see. It all started because a fat Glaswegian woman wrecked it in Madeira!' He then began a long, rambling explanation as to how he'd been drunk and had met this Scottish hen party.

The captain remained silent and motionless except for a slight tilting of his head, back and forth, as if deciding whether to pull the trigger or not.

The gunner addressed the captain and they began a conversation with each other in French, with seriously raised voices.

'My gunner wants to kill you, Mr British Spy! He wants to use your little boat for target practice. He says his shooting skills are getting very, very rusty and he's not killed anyone in weeks! What do you think about that, Mr British Spy?'

'No, please, sir, I've got a wife and family in England.' Bill blessed himself with the sign of the cross and began to recite the Lord's Prayer out loud.

'So, you are a Christian man, Mr British Spy!' said the Captain.

'Yes, I once met His Holiness the Pope, when he came to Heaton Park in Manchester.'

'That's good! Then you have nothing to worry about. You'll go straight to heaven because you have friends in high places! Yes?'

'I don't want to go to heaven just yet, sir!' pleaded Bill. Again, the crew burst into laughter whilst the captain remained completely stone-faced.

'Enough talk!' shouted the captain. His patience was finally running out. 'You have to come with us, we need to take you back for questioning.'

A line was thrown down, and Bill obediently attached it to his boat and lowered his Red Ensign, which he carefully folded and put into his cabin.

The gunboat took off with such rapid speed that it first dragged the *Arthurian* under, and then bounced her along on the surface. Bill had to cling on for dear life and decided that all he could do was close the hatch and stay inside. It was a thoroughly unpleasant and severely bruising experience. Any damage to the boat was secondary to whether he would be shot dead, or spend the rest of his life rotting in a Haitian prison.

*

Life is very cheap in Haiti. Street killings and political assassinations are commonplace. It is a country with the most gruesome history right from the start.

After the island of Hispaniola was discovered in 1492 by Christopher Columbus, incoming Europeans brought with them disease and slaves from Africa. Much of the indigenous population died off as they lacked immunity to such diseases. It was the worst case of indigenous depopulation in the entire Americas.

The island was plagued by brutality and plundering by English, Dutch and French pirates, much to the outrage of the Spanish government. By the 1660s it was taken over by France, and with the introduction of the French West India Company, plantations of tobacco, cotton, cacao and sugar were put into place on the rich fertile plains. Such an agricultural development required slaves, and lots of them.

By 1785 the French had some 500,000 slaves working on the island, with only a white population of some 30,000 in control. Around 40,000 slaves were brought in each year in order to replace those that had been put to death or died of disease and maltreatment. There were numerous bloody uprisings, with 'maroon' slaves escaping to hide and build communes in the mountains.

In 1804 Haiti became the first black republic in the world. From that day to this it has been a hotbed of corruption, revolution, presidential assassinations and state failure. In the twentieth century, it was subjected to the evil regime of Papa Doc, starting in 1957, which was then followed by his son Baby Doc from 1971 to 1986. From time to time, political mayhem has required US and UN intervention. In addition to all that misery and misfortune, it has suffered several devastating earthquakes.

*

Bill felt the deceleration of the boat as it pulled into the tiny port of Jacmel on the southwest coast of Haiti. He opened the hatch to observe a crowd of black faces silently staring down at him from the quayside. An open-back truck containing armed militia was awaiting his arrival. There was no mistaking it: Bill was in serious trouble this time.

'Welcome to Haiti, Mr British Spy,' declared the captain in a very loud voice. 'Look, see, I have arranged for some nice transport to take you to your hotel! I do hope you enjoy your stay here on our beautiful tropical island. Give my regards to the big man.'

Bill climbed out. He fitted a padlock to the hatch and placed the key in his pocket, although he had serious doubts about ever returning to the *Arthurian* alive.

He was bundled into the back of the truck and seated between six blank-faced soldiers; nobody spoke. As the truck drove off, he heard the captain shout out, 'Have a nice holiday!'

They sped through shanty towns of crudely built shacks and abandoned plantations, leaving only a cloud of dust behind them. Bill was overwhelmed by the stench and poverty that greeted him at every turn. It was patently apparent that people were in fear of Bill's riding companions. The civilians would scurry out of the way and deliberately avoid eye contact with any of the soldiers.

After an hour's drive they arrived at what was to be Bill's accommodation.

In a clearing in the jungle was a large decaying building. The high wall which surrounded it was capped with broken bottles and razor wire. At some time in its history it had been painted white, but now it suffered the ravages of time and the adornment of graffiti.

As they drove into the yard, Bill could see inmates clustered together in clearly defined groups. In the stifling heat and humidity, all were bare-chested and even those with the blackest of skins were covered in tattoos. One particular gang extended their tattoos to cover their entire faces and the tops of their shaven heads. Only those who were of Latino origins wore their hair long, whilst those of African descent were completely shaven from head to toe. Bill was the only white Caucasian there. He had arrived at the gates of hell, and he had just joined the queue to get in.

Bill was frog-marched into a room and strapped into a chair. Several minutes elapsed before a black man entered, armed only with electric clippers and a razor. He seemed to be a jolly sort of fellow, and chuckled to himself as he started to run the clippers up over the top of Bill's head. It was apparent that he was amused at the sight of Bill's handlebar moustache, and decided to leave it in situ. The end result of Bill's total baldness, save for his moustache, made him look far more interesting and intimidating than his skeletal frame could otherwise command. Out there, he could be thought of as a sinister mass murderer who poisoned people rather than hacking them to death, whereas in Great Britain or the USA he would just be assumed to be incredibly gay!

The jolly barber dutifully swept up all of Bill's hair and removed it before leaving the room. Bill remained alone for at least the next hour, and then the door suddenly burst open. Filling the door frame was a very overweight Latino man. His entrance was preceded by an overpowering smell of body odour, and it was evident that he had chosen to completely ignore his prostate problem, as the front of his trousers was heavily stained. This was presumably the 'big man' of whom the captain had spoken.

The big man slammed the door behind him and opened the conversation in heavily accented English. 'So, Captain Bouvier tells me you are a genuine British spy. James Bond, no less.'

'No, sir, the captain has made a terrible mistake. I'm just an ordinary working-class man who wanted to put some adventure in his life by sailing across the Atlantic Ocean, all alone. I've never really done anything exciting before and I just thought I could do—'

The big man interrupted Bill in mid-flow. 'Are you finding it uncomfortably hot in here? Would you like a drink of something?'

'That's very kind, sir, yes, it is hot. Just a drink of water would be nice. Thank you, sir,' said Bill.

The big man walked over to a cabinet on the wall and removed a tin cup. He placed it on the table, unzipped his fly and began to urinate into it. As it spilled over onto the table he directed the jet into Bill's face. He then slowly poured the contents of the cup over his head. 'There now, that should cool you down a bit. Feeling better?' With the back of his hand he hit Bill in the face, knocking him backwards onto the floor.

Bill was still strapped to the chair and he was unable to deal with the flow of blood streaming from his nose. He had to turn his head sideways in order to prevent himself from choking on his own blood.

The guards were called with the order to take him to 'the Dark Room'. Bill was removed from the chair, and then dragged on his back by his legs across the room and over to the door of the exercise yard. Four other guards joined them with their guns at the ready.

The sight of Bill's frail, emaciated little body being so mercilessly treated incited the inmates of all gangs to a pitch of instant and absolute rage. There ensued an almighty din of screaming, shouting and violent gestures toward the guards. Those from the bald, totally tattooed gang surrounded the guards and conducted some sort of terrifying group dance routine. They were the most feared of all. They were the

Mayombe Vodou, 'Voodoo'. They claimed their ancestry back to the banks of the Congo River. The guards would always avoid any dealings or eye contact with any member of that gang. Bill was hurriedly rushed through another door in the far corner of the yard.

The practice of Vodou has been inherent in Haitian culture since it first came over with the slaves from the Gold Coast and the Congo of West Africa. When spelt as 'Voodoo' it refers to a USA version of the religion which prevails around the area of Louisiana. It is a strange mix of Satanism, Catholicism, myth and magic. It is the tying of the body and the soul in a trance, and a joining of the Catholic saints and the spirits of the dead. God (Bon Dieu) is totally inaccessible, but the spirits are not. Houngans and mambos are the high priests and priestesses of Vodou, and they receive their divine rights to the priesthood from their dead ancestors whilst under the influence of trance. They are primarily there to cast good spells on those who deserve them. But evil and death can be summoned to those who are their enemies. The Vodou sense of community and belonging is incredibly strong, and Vodouists can be separated by distance only. Their brotherhood is eternal, and Haitians of all persuasions believe firmly in their powers.

Bill was deafened by the sound of the iron door slamming shut and the turning of the key. It took a long time before he was able to adjust his eyesight to the pitch darkness. He realised there was no bed and no toilet. Just a square room with a stone floor, and blackness. There was an overbearing smell of disinfectant, a leftover from the removal of a previous resident corpse. Things were not looking good.

There was a two-inch gap at the bottom of the door, which provided the only source of light and fresh air. Bill would sleep with his nose pressed up to it in order to get relief from the sweltering heat and the stagnant air in the cell. A downside to it was that it provided a highway for the cockroaches and the occasional visit by rats.

After a week of confinement, Bill's excrement lay neatly piled in the far corner, covered over by his recently acquired Hawaiian shirt. He had been on a bread and water diet only. He didn't think his body could take much more of it, but he was determined not to leave this place horizontally like the previous occupant.

On the morning of the start of his third week of solitary confinement, the door flung open. It was the big man. 'Ah! Mr James Bond, I trust you are now suitably rested!' he shouted.

Bill was far too weak to react. He could neither open his eyes fully, nor stand up.

'Get up, Mr Bond, you look as if you could benefit from some of our lovely tropical sunshine!'

Two guards picked him up and started to lead him out.

'Stop! Mr Bond, aren't you forgetting your belongings?' The big man pointed at Bill's shirt in the corner.

'No, that's fine, I'll leave it,' said Bill in a whisper.

'No, no, I insist!' The big man walked into the cell and placed his foot on the shirt, squashed it down and stamped on it several times. He then ordered the guards to dress Bill in it. 'That's better! Now you smell just like all of our other guests. I like to call it my Perfume de Port au Prince. It's an acquired fragrance, don't you think, Mr Bond?' The big man roared with laughter at his own joke.

Bill was carried into the yard and placed in the corner next to the door. He couldn't stand up and he couldn't tolerate the glare of the sun. He lay there motionless in the foetal position.

Bill was unsure as to how long he had lain there, but his opening vision was that of a towering, hugely muscular Mayombe Vodou man wearing a necklace strung with the skulls of rats. He leant down and came very close to Bill's face. With a big leering smile, he said in Caribbean English, 'Well, what have we here? A honkyman!'

Bill was too frail to even feel any fear at this point. He simply smiled and nodded his head in agreement.

'You're a tough little guy, Honkyman,' said the Mayombe.

Bill was too weak to speak. All he could muster was a big smile and a wink! At that, the Mayombe screamed with laughter and called over to all of his fellow clansmen. Bill had cracked it! The first rule of communication is a smile.

The Latinos very wisely stood well back. The Mayombe had claimed him for their own. There was no contest.

Fierce fights and brutal killings were a daily occurrence between the gangs, and the guards were mostly powerless to intervene. As a matter of fact, they thoroughly enjoyed it, and would place bets on who would come out alive. The majority of fights ended in death and the loser would be unceremoniously dumped in a jungle graveyard beyond the prison walls.

The big man was always the bookmaker at these gladiatorial events. After all, this was his personal kingdom, and he was the absolute monarch.

Bill was picked up and carried into an open cell. Each cell in the prison contained as many as fifty men, but the Mayombe cell was like no other. It was the spiritual centre, the 'hounfour', the temple of Vodou, and Bill's most recent acquaintance was none other than the houngan himself, the high priest.

Bill slept in relative comfort, and awoke to confusion as to precisely where he was. He was surrounded by the strangest of objects. The cell walls were metal bars, from which hung ornately patterned 'drapo' mats. There were masks, dolls, pictures of Christ and Christian saints, human skulls and various animal bones. There was a bowl of tropical fruit alongside an ornate gilded Catholic altar tabernacle.

Bill thought to himself, *This is seriously weird and deeply concerning.* He had the vision of his little honky head ending up as just another adornment for the room. A kind of coffee table talking piece to impress one's friends with.

He was alone as he mulled over his predicament. All the inmates were outside in the yard. The cells were all locked each evening at sundown after a roll inspection, and opened again at 7am. The inmates were free to roam during the day under constant observation from the watch tower and the parapet walkway, which went around the entire perimeter wall. The place operated like an isolated bachelor village, with wives, families and prostitutes allowed weekly visits.

Two of the Mayombe entered the cell and escorted Bill to the big open shower room. They stood guard whilst he washed himself along with his Hawaiian shirt. So intense was the humidity that it was a pointless exercise to leave it out to dry, so he just put it on again. His protectors told him that from now on, if he was ever alone then the Latinos would most definitely kill him. He was now an accepted trophy of the Mayombe, which excluded him from fraternising with any other gang. In Bill's case, the Latinos would consider it to be an extra betrayal for a white man to prefer the company of blacks to them. Not that Bill was ever given much choice.

The Mayombe high priest had the unlikely name of Jean-Pierre Napoleon. North American slaves, after they were liberated, adopted the names of either their slave masters or known presidents, which is why so many present-day black families in America are called Lincoln and Washington, and evidently something similar had happened in the high priest's ancestry.

Jean-Pierre and Honkyman hit it off right from the start. Bill proved to be a refreshing intellectual stimulus for Jean-Pierre. Jean-Pierre had lived in Paris and London and got himself into the drug business there, but returned to Haiti when Europol and Scotland Yard started to close in on him. His ancestry, superior intellect, knowledge and physical strength made it easy for him to adopt the role of a houngan high priest and take control of the gullible locals. For Jean-Pierre it was mostly playacting and mumbo-jumbo, but as time had progressed, he had started to believe in his own hype and mystical powers.

Bill was astonished at how quickly he had adapted to a life of such squalor and deprivation. To see his fellow man brutally beaten, and in some cases butchered or hanged, was all part of a normal day's events. The big man would hang people almost for looking at him in a disrespectful way, and minutes afterwards everyone would just carry on about their business as normal.

There was no shortage of basic food within the compound and marijuana was readily available at all times. Both were freely brought in by the visitors, who were only searched for weapons. The big man believed that as long as the inmates were smoking marijuana they were less likely to be aggressive and causing him inconvenience. Although Bill had never really smoked before, he also began to enjoy partaking of the ganja. It was the perfect escape from such a miserable circumstance.

About once a week Jean-Pierre would conduct a Vodou Mass, where as many as twenty or thirty prisoners would be deeply entranced and shaking violently to the sight and sounds of drums and mass hypnosis. Jean-Pierre always gave a masterly performance as the grand high priest, whilst Bill would remain passive and voyeur to all the mayhem. During one such Mass, at the peak of the ceremony, Jean-Pierre made his way toward Bill, shaking his bone rattles and chanting his mystical prayers, his eyes bulging out of their sockets. As he got close, he gave Bill a wink, turned, and returned to the believers. It was showbiz and this was the Jean-Pierre Show!

One day, on seeing Bill's solitary little tattoo of an anchor on his arm, Jean-Pierre decided that Bill should be properly initiated as an honoured member of the Mayombe. All members were recognised by a distinctive tattoo of a human skull with a sunburst halo which was placed on the left side of their chest. The artist was called for, and although he only had a piece of wood with a needle stuck in the end of it and a pot of ink, the end result was rather stylish. Bill was well pleased.

Bill had spent about twelve weeks incarcerated in Haiti's Holiday Home Hotel, as it was known, when he received a visit from the big man and two guards. He was ordered to go with them.

Bill got a nauseous feeling welling up in his throat. He was physically going to be sick and his legs became weak at the knees. Was this where he was to meet his end? He would be dumped in a shallow grave in the jungle and nobody would ever know what had happened to him. Anybody who did know him had no idea that he was even in Haiti. He would just be presumed lost at sea.

'Mr James Bond, you have a visitor,' said the big man, much to Bill's relief. He was led into a room and there, already seated, was Captain Bouvier.

'Ah! The British spy. You are looking so well. Our Haitian hospitality obviously agrees with you!'

'When am I going to be able to speak to a lawyer, and what am I being charged with?' Bill asked aggressively. 'I want access to the British Ambassador immediately!'

The captain had to hold his stomach together as he cried

with laughter. 'You British have such a wonderful sense of humour. Even when you are about to be shot, you still act as if you are in charge of the situation and totally superior to everyone around you. You really are fantastic!' he said, wiping the tears and the sweat from his face and neck.

Bill had no choice but to play his one and only ace. 'OK, how much does it take to get the hell out of here?' He put his foot up on the table, removed his deck shoe, peeled back the inner sole and counted out the two hundred and fifty dollars. 'That's all I have. I have no more money now until my family wires me some when I get to Jamaica.'

The captain's eyes lit up and a big smile came on his face. 'But Mr British Spy, why didn't you do this before? You could have saved our poor Haitian taxpayers the cost of paying for your luxury accommodation over this past three months!'

Captain Bouvier took the cash and walked through to the big man who was in the other room. Bill could hear raised voices as they squabbled over the division of the money. Eventually, the captain appeared at the door. 'Follow me,' he said.

They walked down a corridor and out through a side door which led directly to the cemetery road.

'Go!' said the captain.

'Do you mean I'm free, and I'm not going to be charged as a spy?' asked Bill in a state of bewilderment.

'A spy? Of course not. Why would the British waste time and money sending people to spy on Haiti? It's a shithole! Now go, before the big man changes his mind,' said the captain.

Chapter Eight

Bill ran like the wind, but before long he came face to face with the full horror of the prison cemetery. Half-exposed corpses lay everywhere. They had long abandoned the idea of actually burying people, and wild pigs and stray dogs feasted on the remains. Bill had become accustomed to some pretty rancid smells within the confines of the prison walls, but the smell of putrefaction on such a large scale was something that would remain in his nostrils forever. In terror, he continued to run until eventually he joined the only jungle road that led back to civilisation.

Jacmel was more than fifty miles away and there was very little traffic on Haitian roads at the best of times, but the sheer elation of being free again meant that no future obstacle would ever be too hard to cope with.

Bill was concerned that he had not been able to say goodbye to Jean-Pierre and his Mayombe brothers. He knew that they would all assume that the big man had killed Bill, which would make Jean-Pierre's hatred of the big man all the greater. 'Jean-Pierre will no doubt be casting an evil spell of horrendous fate to befall the big man for doing such a terrible deed,' said Bill jokingly to himself.

He'd walked about eight miles, and as the evening drew closer he came across the mostly collapsed ruins of a former French plantation house. He decided that this would be as good a place as any to bed down for the night, and to his pleasant surprise it still had a tap with running water, of which Bill took full advantage. The once magnificent gardens had grown into an Eden paradise of ripe bananas, oranges, lemons and grapes.

An early rise meant that he was well underway by mid-morning. He was avoiding the full heat of the day by taking a siesta in the shade at the side of the road, when he was abruptly awakened by the sound of an oncoming motor scooter. Bill frantically waved the rider down. 'Do you speak English?' shouted Bill.

'Yep! And French and German,' said the bright, smiling, mixed-race eighteen-year-old.

'What's your name?' enquired Bill.

'Rocky! I know, my mother saw it in an American movie and liked the sound of it. How about you?'

'I'm known as Honkyman,' said Bill.

'Ha! That's original. I expect you're looking for a ride, Honkyman. It'll cost you five dollars!' said the budding entrepreneur.

'I can live with that,' said Bill, and the two of them sped off in the direction of Jacmel.

Rocky had set up his own messenger business, delivering parcels from local towns to the prison. He'd seen the potential in it, because many of the families of the inmates couldn't afford to travel that often to visit them. Rocky would deliver everything from Mama's Jerk chicken to clothes or drugs. He was such a familiar face that he almost had free access in and out of the prison. He was hoping that pretty soon he would be able to expand his business and afford a van.

Upon arrival, Bill was astonished to find the *Arthurian* sitting exactly where he had left her. The lock was missing, and much of his kit ransacked and stolen, but she was still seaworthy and in reasonable shape. In the clear blue water of the harbour, Bill spotted his sextant some fifteen feet below. Quick as a flash, Rocky dived in head first to retrieve it. The thief obviously hadn't known what it was and had just discarded it. They had also failed to find Bill's secret compartment that contained his credit card, passport and English money. Rocky promised to return the following day to show Bill round and to help him prepare for his onward journey.

Over the coming days, Bill got to know the area and many of the locals. As the only white man in town he was already something of a celebrity, and even if they'd not met him, everyone knew the Honkyman.

One evening, Rocky invited Bill over to have dinner with his parents and family. Although their circumstances could only be described as abject poverty, they were amongst the kindest and happiest people that Bill had ever met. Rocky's enterprise had provided them with the luxury of Sky TV and he was determined to eventually build his parents a proper house for their retirement.

The evening was one of good food, marijuana, music and merriment and, as their time together drew to a close in the early hours of the morning, Rocky presented Bill with a farewell gift. It was a Zippo cigarette lighter and a beautifully carved ganja pipe. Bill was deeply moved and vowed to keep them as his most treasured possessions.

In the dead of night, Bill weaved his way back through the shanty-town streets. All was silent save for the occasional barking dog or the sounds of a domestic disagreement. As he turned the corner and made his way toward a well-known bar and whorehouse, he spotted a familiar battered Citroën car.

It was the one owned by the big man. Bill hid in the darkness and waited.

He'd not been there more than a few minutes when the door to the bar opened and the big man and a tall, well-built black girl appeared. They were the last to leave.

What went on in the car would seriously offend the sensibilities of the hardiest of fellows. The thought of oral contact with an enormous, unwashed, incontinent oaf like the big man turned the stomach, but a girl had to earn a living somehow in this place.

The girl was paid and left, but the big man remained in the car. Bill was scared to make a move for fear of being spotted by him. Under the influence of drink this monster was capable of anything.

Time ticked by and Bill summoned the courage to sneak a little closer. The big man had his head back in the seat and was snoring like a hog. Bill began to think the unthinkable.

The doorway that he'd been hiding in had an old loose rag hanging over it which acted as a crude mosquito net. *This is the one and only opportunity I'll ever get to improve the quality of these people's lives,* he thought to himself.

Silently, he removed the rag and twisted it into a rope. With his forefinger he slowly pushed it down into the car's petrol tank. His new Zippo was about to be put to good use. He lit it and retreated to a safe distance.

Bill watched as the flame climbed the rag. The massive explosion that followed immediately turned the car into a fireball. Completely emotionless, Bill watched the big man's arms and head move around in the car as the flames engulfed him. Although it woke the entire neighbourhood, these highly fearful and superstitious people dared not venture out of their homes to investigate.

Bill returned to his boat and slept like a log. He was amazed at how unaffected he was by the fact that he had just calmly murdered someone in a most gruesome way.

The following morning Bill returned to find that the car was still smouldering. The bones of the big man's torso had remained in situ, but his charred head had fallen off and rolled into the footwell on the passenger side. It was still distinctive on account of a front tooth missing on the left side of his mouth. A crowd stood well back as Bill approached the vehicle. They were shocked and horrified as Bill nonchalantly removed the head, placed it in his shopping bag and walked away.

Bill parcelled up the big man's head and enclosed the following letter:

My dear Jean-Pierre,
I apologise for not saying farewell to you and our brothers, but as you may appreciate, I had the opportunity to leave in a hurry and I took it. I have a long journey ahead of me, but I couldn't go without thanking you for all of your friendship and I offer you this very special gift. It is the head of the big man. I'm sorry I overcooked him a little. May his dark smile always remind the believers of me.

Forever your friend,
Honkyman

He employed the services of Rocky to deliver his parcel personally into the hands of Jean-Pierre.

A Vodou Mass of celebration was called for immediately, and the big man's head took pride of place in the Mayombe cell. Jean-Pierre, always aware of the value of publicity, spread the word that he had ordered the death of the big man through Honkyman and the spirit world. His fame as the most powerful and feared houngan high priest spread far and wide, for which he would secretly be forever in Bill's debt.

The new governor was introduced to the head of his predecessor, and things greatly improved in the prison from then on. Wildly exaggerated tales of Honkyman, the white Vodou spirit who had sailed a tiny boat from England, spread throughout Haiti, and Bill really did become a legend in his own lifetime.

He began to acknowledge and enjoy his newly acquired celebrity status. People showered him with simple little gifts of fruit and trinkets, and he was always in a quandary as to whether he should accept them or not. Rocky said that they would be deeply hurt if he rejected their kind offerings, but these people had so little for themselves, thought Bill. In his own life, it was only people like Marcus Rawley who ever received such reverential treatment from the ordinary folk in the town, and never the Bill Smiths of this world.

Bill eventually managed to phone Janice, only to hear her ear-piercing screams at the other end of the phone. She and his mother were by this time beginning to accept that he had drowned at sea. His mother had spent every day and night praying for him to St Brendan, the patron saint of seafarers and navigators. On top of that, she had had Holy Mass said at her local church, asking God to return him safely to them. It had been at least five months since he had last spoken to them from Madeira.

He decided it would be more prudent to be economical with the truth, rather than tell them that he had spent much of that time being held in one of the most violent prisons on earth, he was now a regular smoker of marijuana and he had casually murdered someone whilst being there. In his devoutly Catholic mother's eyes, that would surely condemn him to all eternity in the fires of hell. Although it was OK to kill people if you were a soldier fighting for a supposedly noble cause; God didn't mind that, apparently! Perhaps they could find some justification in that the big man had been such an evil tyrant, an agent of Satan, perhaps? So he deserved to die anyway.

In a verbal avalanche, Janice unburdened herself of all that had happened in Bill's absence. Jack and Sophie's relationship was becoming more turbulent, and Jack was proving far less than capable of handling the situation. As Bill was well aware, Sophie would prove to be more than a handful for Jack. Bill knew the day would eventually come when Sophie would tire of him. She was too beautiful, too streetwise and too clever for him. Bill expressed his deep sadness over the situation to Janice, but secretly he was more concerned that he might never see Sophie again should she and Jack part company from each other.

The memory of Sophie's sexual taunts and the passionate kiss she had given him was still indelibly printed upon Bill's mind. The desire to revisit that moment upon his return was still a personal priority for him. And although he knew that he would be playing with fire and risking his marriage, lust has a tendency to conquer all when it invades the brains of man.

As the conversation continued, Janice accosted Bill for his lack of paternal input into Jack's life, and leaving her to cope all alone with Jack's mood swings and his depressions. Bill tried to close the conversation as amicably as possible and promised to phone her again, but understandably he was unable to leave her with any forwarding address.

Chapter Nine

The time had come when Bill was feeling ready for his onward journey. He was well fed and strong enough to move on. His provisions were all checked and loaded. The sails were fully repaired, and he had ample fresh water and fuel. Rocky had tied two hemp sacks full of coconuts to the boat, one on each side. Inside the cabin he'd left a large bag of ganja, more than enough to fill many an enjoyable pipe over the coming weeks.

Fine weather with light winds was predicted for the next week, and Bill was becoming increasingly anxious to fill the sails once more. A crowd of friends, admirers and well-wishers lined the single jetty at Jacmel harbour as Bill busied himself with last-minute preparations.

To his utter amazement he could hear the advancing sound of music coming from the direction of the town. There was Rocky, leading from the front, with a Caribbean steel band and a procession of laughing and dancing people, all coming to say a fond farewell to the Honkyman. Bill was staggered and overwhelmed with emotion at the sight of it all.

'Good God, will you look at that? My mates at Rawley's would never believe this in a million years,' said Bill to himself as he gazed at the sea of smiling black faces all around him. He climbed back up onto the jetty to receive an enormous bear hug from Rocky.

'One thing I forget to ask you, Honkyman. What the hell is your real name?'

'Bill Smith,' came the reply.

'Bill Smith!' exclaimed Rocky. 'That has got to be the most uncool name in the world, Honkyman. There ain't no steel band in Haiti ever going to play a tune to a guy called Bill Smith!' He roared with laughter.

Bill suddenly remembered the remaining two hundred and fifty dollars in his other shoe. He removed it and pressed it hard into Rocky's hand. 'I'm buying a 10% stake in Rocky's Parcel Delivery Company. This is my investment money, and when I come back, I want to see a fleet of Rocky's vans all over the place, and a great big return on that investment of mine!' he said, with a huge smile on his face.

Rocky just burst into tears; he'd never seen that much money at any one time before. 'I won't let you down, Honkyman, I promise. I'll build it into a huge business, just like FedEx. I'll be the biggest employer in the whole of the Caribbean one day, you just wait and see, Honkyman,' he said, bursting with youthful enthusiasm.

'I know you will, Rocky, I have every faith in you. But I want you to promise me this. That you will always be a good employer, and that you'll be kind and fair to your employees, and never forget how you started in life. Don't ever be greedy or selfish, and one day, you'll be the most respected man in Haiti.'

As Bill sailed away, the band continued to play and the people sang and waved. Rocky ran as fast as he could, right to the very edge of the quay. Bill could faintly hear him still shouting, 'Thank you, thank you, thank you, Honkyman.' Over and over again he repeated it.

Bill knew that it was unlikely that he would ever return to Haiti, but he had left hope where he had found despair, and that made him feel good. If he'd learnt one thing from Marcus Rawley, it was the value of having faith in someone, and being in a position to give them encouragement and a helping hand. Who knows, maybe he just might return one day to check on that investment of his.

The hills of Haiti were still visible when Bill's heart began to sink once more. There on the horizon was the unmistakable shape of a gunboat looming toward him. It was Captain Bouvier again.

'My good friend, Mr Honkyman, sir,' shouted the captain from his bridge. This was a far cry from his previous cynical address of 'Mr British Spy'. 'I didn't say goodbye to you, sir, and wish you safe journey. I wanted to apologise to you for the harsh way I treated you.' His demeanour and tone were positively subservient this time. The captain was no exception to fear of the powers of the Vodou.

'I heard what happened to the big man; he had a terrible end,' the captain went on. 'I had no idea that you and the great high priest Jean-Pierre Napoleon were so close, sir.'

The wild rumours about Bill's mystical connections were obviously spreading rapidly. This was an opportunity to capitalise on them and have some fun with the captain. A good scare might make him change his ways.

'Yes, indeed, Captain. Jean-Pierre and I have always been the closest of spiritual brothers from the far ends of the earth.' Bill leaned forward for his shirt to open, allowing the Mayombe Vodou tattoo on his chest to be seen. The captain had never seen it before, and he was now in no doubt as to Bill's credentials. 'My visit to Haiti was no accident, Captain. I was drawn here to accomplish a task and I have now completed that task. You, my dear friend, were merely the instrument used to bring me directly in contact with my mission.'

Bill could see that the captain was starting to shake, for he was naturally a coward and a bully.

'I suggest you go to church more often, Captain, and mend your ways while you still have the time,' said Bill, in a stern voice of authority. 'After all, the next time you see me in Haiti I may have another mission to accomplish, and I'd hate to see you lose your head or have to experience what hell is really like before you were due to actually go there. Your friend Big Man is not in a happy place right now; that I promise you. It took him many minutes to struggle and die. His fat kept him alive and burning for a long time, you see; the skinny ones die quickly.'

Bill could see the captain glancing down to observe his own portly measure.

The captain fumbled for excuses, panicking and blaming the big man for everything, saying that he'd always been influenced by him and was afraid of him. Now that the big man was gone, the captain promised to be a much better person.

'The spirit world will inform me of your progress, Captain. I wish you good luck,' said Bill.

With that, they bade each other farewell, and as the gunboat sped off Bill chuckled to himself, knowing that there would be a marked difference in the captain's future behaviour toward his fellow man.

The winds had completely dropped and Bill could do little more than sit back in the boat and relax for a while. As he drank the milk from one of Rocky's coconuts and lit his ganja pipe, he reflected on all of his recent adventures in Haiti with far more fondness than regret. Life felt really good again. It is interesting that when you are a survivor of such dreadful brutality and you have lived in the very cesspit of humanity, you can still pick out moments of amusement and fond memory. The gentle sleep-inducing motion of the boat and the warm sunlight on his face jarred another fleeting thought to occur. *I wonder what they are doing in the Goods Inwards department at Rawley's right now.* Bizarrely, albeit briefly, he actually felt that he missed the old place.

*

Bill awoke unaware of how long he had been asleep. The sun was rising above the horizon, and in actual fact, he had slept from mid-afternoon right through until the dawn of the following morning. He had never been this laid-back before, nor had he been so joyfully at ease with life. He had also never smoked marijuana by the pipeful before. In Haiti, he had only obligingly shared a passed-around joint, but this was a new and completely different experience. There, only Jean-Pierre was able to have a fully filled pipe to himself in order to aid his contact with the spirit world.

Bill thought to himself that he had discovered the answer to the problem of his ever violent, alcohol-fuelled friends back in England. If his father had smoked joints, instead of drinking himself to death, his poor mother may have enjoyed a more peaceful life, and a better marriage. After all, nobody ever wanted to pick a fight, or beat his wife up, after smoking a pipeful of marijuana.

The days that followed were spent in a state of blissful transcendental meditative limbo. It wasn't to last. Bill's hazy composure was about to be seriously compromised by the sight of the enormous black shroud looming ahead, and it was moving fast toward him. The winds picked up with no identifiable direction and the seas were quickly raised to anger. Bill suddenly had an overwhelming fear of being struck by lightning at sea, and that would mean instant death by incineration or, worse, being alive but seriously burnt, he thought to himself.

The scaffolding pole mast and all the boat's fittings were a hotchpotch composite of different metals, aluminium, steel, brass etc., but the fittings at the top and the bottom of the mast were of copper. 'Shit! That's the perfect bloody lightning conductor,' he screamed out loud to himself. In constructing his boat, Bill had to scavenge whatever he could from wherever he could, irrespective of its nautical suitability. When the budget was funded by the weekly remnants of a working man's wage packet, all free gifts of equipment had been graciously accepted.

His decision was that if he could keep the mast at the water level it was less likely to attract a strike from the lightning, and there was only one way he could think of to do that: to lash himself to the mast and heave the vessel over onto her side. Bill battened down the hatch tightly and, with whatever ropes he could find, he tied himself securely to the mast and hurled himself backwards into the sea.

He crashed below the surface holding onto a deep breath, but almost immediately he was catapulted back up into the upright position. His weight was insufficient to counter-balance the buoyancy of the boat. It meant only one thing. He needed to crawl higher up the mast, away from the bulkhead.

Rapidly, the storm reached its full ferocity. Lightning zigzagged horizontally across the skies above him, whilst some of it would fork down into the sea close by. Back and forth he was tossed like a pole vaulter refusing to let go of the pole, and all around him the thunder clapped as deafening volleys of cannon fire.

For two hours Bill fought his lonely battle with the elements, trying desperately to keep his boat from being conspicuous above the waves. Then, almost as quickly as it had come, the storm moved on and the seas calmed once again.

Bill untied himself and fell back into the boat. He was both mentally and physically exhausted. 'Phew! That was a close shave. I think it is now time to call for Happy Hour with a nice rum and coconut milk drink and another pipe full of ganja,' he said as he reclined back into the open hatch.

'Ah! Just what the doctor ordered!' said Bill, with a satisfied carefree smile on his face, when he eventually set his pipe to one side. As he observed the lightning storm raging and clattering afar, he knew that it was now someone else's nightmare, and he offered a little prayer for the safety of any less fortunate small-craft mariners.

In the early hours before dawn, when Bill got up to pee over the side, he sighted the coastal lights of a town, north-northeast of his position. *That has got to be the southwest coast of Jamaica,* he thought. Bill's rudimentary skills of navigation had proven to be spot-on. He had become an accomplished self-taught mariner in the truest sense of the word. He had acquired instinctive practical skills that could never be taught at any naval college.

Bill had always had the good fortune to be blessed with a great deal of common sense rather than academic ability, and in a world where survival is the imperative, common sense outsmarts academia hands-down.

Bill dragged the boat as best he could up onto a deserted palm-strewn beach and propped her upright with some timber logs that he'd found above the immediate shoreline. After attaching a tethering line to the nearest palm tree, he went off to explore.

Before long, a dirt path led him up the hill behind the line of palms, and there, perched high over the bay, Bill spotted a solitary corrugated iron shack with a poorly assembled covered front porch attached. At the approach to the property, on either side of the pathway, was a garden with an assortment of crops: bananas, sugar, maize, mango and, of course, the ubiquitous marijuana plant. Chickens foraged in the undergrowth and a brightly coloured hand-painted sign on an old wooden gate declared 'Bickley Manor', which brought an immediate smile to Bill's face. Whoever lived here obviously had a sense of humour, he thought.

Bill was suddenly startled by a voice coming from within the banana grove. 'Hey there, brother!' Before him stood a tall, thin, bare-chested Rastafarian black man with a great explosion of dreadlocked hair and a scraggy greying beard. On his shoulder was a full bunch of bananas and in his right hand, a machete.

The black man approached. 'Welcome to Bickley Manor, brother. If you didn't smell so bad, I'd say that you were a lost tourist. What's your name, brother?' he asked with a big friendly smile on his face.

'I'm known as Honkyman,' said Bill.

'That's cool,' said the Rasta. 'I'm Nathan Bickley Esquire, but the folks here all call me Banjo. That's because I just love bluegrass and people hear me play my banjo for miles around if the wind's in the right direction. Now, you wouldn't be one of those white Bickleys coming here to hope to reclaim their land, would you?'

'No, not at all. What's that all about?' asked Bill.

'The Bickley family were from England, and they owned all this land when it was a sugar plantation. My folks used to work the land for them as slaves. When the British government abolished slavery, the slave-owning families all got paid huge amounts of money as compensation for the loss of their people property and the loss of the income that they generated. This place was abandoned in the mid-eighteen hundreds and then in 1898 the Bickley mansion, which stood on this very spot, was burnt down after being hit by a lightning storm. Some of the bits of timber hanging around here from Bickley Manor were used by my great-grandfather to build this house. But as you can see, he was no builder. We've lived here ever since. My folks are all dead now so I live here alone,' said Banjo, somewhat mournfully. 'Every so often, I get white folks coming up here saying their ancestors used to own the place. I just tell them that the Jamaican government owns it all now and it can't ever be sold again. That's not exactly true, 'cause I own the whole mountainside and all the land down to the beach. My great-grandfather got the title deeds to this place in 1926.'

'That's amazing,' said Bill. 'Have you got any idea what you're sitting on? This place must be worth hundreds of millions. You're a multi-millionaire, Banjo! You could sell all the frontage to hotel chains for tens of millions alone, and that's before you even start to consider the hillside land for multi-million dollar villas. You are probably the richest man I've ever met, Banjo!' he declared with wild enthusiasm.

Banjo just stood there shaking his head. 'What is it with you white folks? Why do you always want to build on top of paradise? Why would I want to become rich so that I could end up having enough money to be able to go and buy what I already had in the first place? My mother and father left me the Garden of Eden, and you don't need much money to live in it, brother!' he said, accusingly. 'Now, why don't you get your white honky ass up to the house and I'll cook us some dinner? There's a shower and soap around the back.'

Bill was more than grateful to acknowledge and accept Banjo's generous hospitality.

The shower consisted of an oil drum on stilts which was fed from the guttering of the house with a ballcock mechanism and a chain. Banjo had set a table on the porch. 'I hope you like hot food, brother. I do the meanest, hottest jerk chicken in Jamaica and I make my secret recipe sauce to go with it. I call it "Bickley's Suicide Sauce" and it comes with a fire warning on the label: "Consuming this sauce may cause spontaneous combustion",' he called to Bill, chuckling to himself.

'Sounds great! I eat hot Indian curries all the time back home in England,' replied Bill, removing the soap suds from his eyes.

Bill emerged refreshed and clean: a feeling that he'd not had in a long while. Banjo handed him a mug full of homemade mango rum.

'Wow! That's delicious. Where do you buy this stuff from?' asked Bill.

'The good Lord provides, brother. The good Lord provides. There's the sugar and there's the mango tree,' said Banjo, pointing at both.

'How on earth do you make a brew like this without all the distilling equipment?' enquired Bill.

'Where've you been all your life, Honkyman? I thought you white folks knew everything. It's simple. Take a mango. Chop the top off like you do to a boiled egg. Scoop out the inside. Pack it tight with brown sugar. Put the lid back on. Make a hole in the bottom of the mango. Put it in a sock, although one of them lady's stockings is better. And let the juice run out into a container over the next few weeks. Hey presto! Jungle juice, brother!'

As they sat and dined together staring over the most magnificent sea vista and sunset, Banjo suddenly said, 'Hey, Honkyman, I never asked you how in hell's name you got here in the first place.'

'I sailed here from England in my boat,' replied Bill.

'What? You never said that you were one of those fancy yacht sailing guys. And here's me thinking you were just a poor honky that's been down on his luck,' exclaimed Banjo with a slight touch of indignation.

'No, no, you've got the wrong idea, Banjo. I'm just an ordinary working man. I made the boat entirely by myself. I've left it down on your beach,' said Bill defensively.

'In that case, I want to make a full inspection at first light. 'Cause not only am I king of this hill and lord of this manor, I'm also my own harbour master and coast guard in these parts. I might have to impose a great big fat honky-style mooring fee!' said Banjo, jokingly.

The two of them laughed and exchanged stories well into the night. It was a night of good food, good rum, good ganja and the best of company. As the evening progressed, Banjo took up his banjo and he played it and sang as well as any Appalachian hillbilly. It was a night that Bill would remember as long as he lived.

Banjo insisted on offering Bill the 'Presidential Suite' rather than letting him return to sleep on the boat. Bill was given a Tilley oil lamp to escort him to his bedroom, and as it lit the room, an army of cockroaches scurried into the four corners and out of sight. Bill was too high, too tired and too grateful to be remotely bothered.

At 5am Bill got the full blast of the morning call from Mandela, Banjo's only rooster and master of the harem of hens. Mandela had flown up onto Bill's open windowsill in order to call everyone to rise and shine. Banjo only tolerated him in order to keep the hens' eggs fertilised and to offer a constant supply of chicken for the pot.

Bill and Banjo strolled down to the shoreline in order for Banjo to inspect the *Arthurian*. 'Jumping Jehoshaphat!' declared Banjo when first he sighted her. 'You wouldn't catch me sailing in that tub as far as Kingston, Honkyman. You are either the bravest dumbass honky I ever met, or you're the most stupid. I guess I'll have to know you better to find out.'

It wasn't the first time Bill had heard that said about him.

'If you're planning on sticking around for a while, Honkyman, we'd better get this little tub of yours to safety. This beach gets the full force of the storms. I've got the old Bickleys' boathouse around the other side of the bay. You can store it in there, it'll be safe there.'

Banjo helped Bill refloat her and was about to wade back to shore when Bill insisted that Banjo join him on board. Banjo had never liked boats, and also he had never learnt to swim. It was only when they got into much deeper water that Bill admitted that he couldn't swim properly either.

'Holy shit, now my mind's made up. You really are the stupid dumbass honky I thought you were, and that's for sure!' declared Banjo.

As they rounded the corner, there before them was the perfect protected inlet bay, complete with jetty, boathouse and additional outbuildings. Above the keystone to the main structure was emblazoned in stone the Bickley Coat of Arms, making a firm statement as to precisely who the masters were. 'This is magnificent,' said Bill. 'And you own all this as well?'

'Sure do!' replied Banjo.

'Why wouldn't you move here and live in one of these splendid stone buildings? They're much cooler than your tin shack – er, sorry, your manor house.'

'No, siree! Too much bad karma. I never come down here much except to repaint the "No Trespassing" signs. This is where they landed the slaves before processing them to the different parts of the estate. Some of them were sold on to other estates around the island. I can tell you exactly when my folks were brought here. They came here from the Gold Coast of Africa. I can tell you the first relative of mine landed here in 1723 on October 2nd. His name was No. 285. I've checked it in the archives.'

The boat was safely locked in the boathouse and as they wandered around, Banjo retrieved a key hidden from under a stone. He handed it to Bill and pointed him in the direction of one of the buildings. 'There, go and satisfy your curiosity, Honkyman,' said Banjo, who then turned his back on him and started to walk away.

The huge iron key struggled to release the rusted lock at first, and Bill had to push hard with his shoulder several times before the door gave way. 'That door's not been opened in forty years,' shouted Banjo from afar.

As Bill entered into the dank semi-darkness, there was a cold, eerie, lifeless silence to the place. Tropical climbers had made their way through the upper broken windows, but most had grown old and perished from lack of sunlight. The sandstone floors were thick with dust and dried leaves, and as Bill's eyes adjusted to the dim light, it was only then that the full horrific revelation dawned on him. There, still attached and hanging limp from the walls, were row after row of rusting shackles and leg irons: hundreds of them. At the top end of the room was what appeared to be a whipping post: a solitary cast-iron pillar with a loose ring attached to the top of it.

As Bill scanned this vast room, his heart began to palpitate with fear at being in the presence of this silent testament to such brutality. He had witnessed such dreadful things in Haiti, but the spirits of the tormented innocent souls present in this room were far more powerful than any he'd seen alive. How was it possible that these instruments of such inhumanity could remain here totally untouched for three hundred years? It was as if the last freed slave had closed the door behind him and hidden the key under that very rock.

Bill slumped to the floor against the whipping post and thought of all the broken human frames that had lain there before him. He slowly lowered his head into his hands, and wept. Banjo pressed his ear up against a window, and was touched by the sounds of Bill's distress coming from within.

More than an hour had passed before Bill reappeared into the sunlight. He quietly closed the door behind him and replaced the key in its rightful place.

As Bill approached Banjo, he was still visibly very upset, and he just couldn't contain his thoughts. 'This place has got to become a national museum, Banjo. Nowhere is the inhumanity of my fellow countrymen's history more graphically preserved than in that room. People have got to see this for themselves and to experience what I have just experienced. It's just too terrible for words alone.'

'Sweet Jesus!' Banjo retorted impatiently. 'There you go again with your honky-style theme park ideas. This is my private chapel, brother. A sanctuary preserved in silent dignity to my ancestors, not yours! And I ain't having no tourists coming here to gawp at things that you and I had nothing to do with. Slavery happened, brother! Now get over it!

'I look at it this way. If you white folks hadn't brought slavery to these islands, right now, my sorry black ass would be sitting on some log in the dust bowl of Africa wondering why the rains hadn't come. Instead, I'm here owning a piece of paradise, smoking ganja, and drinking rum with my new good friend, Honkyman. And life don't get much better than that, brother!'

Bill's tears instantly turned to uproarious laughter at Banjo's outrageous philosophical view of life. Banjo placed a brotherly arm on Bill's shoulder and the two of them headed back up toward the manor house. There was work to do.

Back at the house, Banjo handed Bill a machete. 'We've got bananas to cut, brother. Which is a job I should have done two days ago, before the good Lord sent me an unexpected lodger. Now, can you ride a bicycle?'

'Yes, no problem,' said Bill.

'Good, 'cause we got plenty of cyclin' to do in the mornin'! In this part of the world you're rich when you're a two-bicycle household. And that makes me rich, brother!' said Banjo as he pumped up the tyres on his second bicycle.

The next couple of hours were spent tying huge bundles of bananas onto each bicycle ready for morning. You couldn't see the frame of the bikes for bananas, and even finding room to pedal was a task in itself.

Bill awoke just in time to knock Mandela off the windowsill before his 5am cockerel call was due. Mandela was thoroughly humiliated by this and he strutted around the yard pecking at any hens that got in his way.

After a hearty breakfast, Bill and Banjo set off for the market some fifteen miles away, mostly over rough unmade roads. Bill rapidly started to discover muscles in his body that he never knew existed, but they needed to get there before the real heat of the day. By nine thirty they were pedalling into the market square. Everywhere, people greeted or acknowledged Banjo but offered little more than curious and suspicious glances at Bill. After all, he was the only unfamiliar white face amidst a sea of black ones.

The whole place was a brightly coloured hive of bartering and bargaining, hustling and arguing. The two of them made their way to the largest fruit and vegetable stall on the market, run by an enormously fat black woman called Aunt Nellie.

Nellie was the jolliest of souls with a loud contagious manly laugh, and when Banjo introduced Bill as his good friend, she grabbed Bill and pressed him hard into her enormous bosoms. His head completely disappeared between them and he re-emerged with his hair sticking up all over the place.

The bananas were all unloaded and Nellie counted out twenty American dollars into Banjo's hand in one-dollar bills. That didn't seem like a good deal at all to Bill. Nellie was a star businesswoman. Not only did she sell her fruit and veg from the stall; she also supplied many of the restaurants and hotels locally.

'She's just ripped you off, Banjo. Why don't we approach the restaurants and hotels ourselves? I'll bet we'd get five times that price,' said Bill indignantly, as the two of them walked away, pushing their bikes beside them.

'Sweet Jesus in heaven! Will you just shut the fuck up? You just don't get it, do you, Honkyman? Do you think I give a rat's ass if she gets a hundred dollars for those bananas? The tree cost me nothin'! To cut them cost me nothin', to cycle here cost me nothin', and I'm goin' home with a great big twenty-dollar something! Nellie buys my bananas come rain or come shine, whether I decide to come here on a Tuesday, a Saturday or a saint's day, because she can't buy them from anyone else cheaper than me. If I turn myself into some kind of businessman travellin' salesman, I'm going to have to get me a phone. Then I'm going to have to get me one of those fancy accountants, and before long, I'm going to be cycling up and down this goddamn road every time some white dude in a restaurant wants a fuckin' banana! There are two things in this life that I don't need, brother. One is commitment, and the other is ambition. Now, today's been a good day. I've got you with me and I got twenty dollars instead of ten! Now let's go and get a beer and something to eat,' said Banjo, as he got back on his bike to lead the way.

The two of them parked their bikes at a shanty-town café down in the dockland area of the town and they ordered some food. Bill was hungry, tired and aching but still thoroughly enjoying his time with Banjo. He was also blissfully unaware that his presence was being duly noted by a thoroughly unsavoury bunch of individuals sitting across the street from them. Banjo discreetly instructed Bill not to look up or have eye contact with any of them. 'Those brothers are seriously bad news. You don't want to get mixed up with them,' he said under his breath.

No sooner had their food arrived than the most menacing-looking one got up and made his approach toward them. Banjo looked up and was quick off the mark with a cheery acknowledgement. 'Jacob! My old friend, how's things going, brother?'

'Who's your little white friend?' came Jacob's dismissive reply.

'This is my good friend Honkyman. He's a sailing man from England. He's been a bit down on his luck recently and he's been helping me cut some bananas for Aunt Nellie at the market,' said Banjo, now somewhat nervously.

'So, you can sail a boat then, can you, Honkyman? I'm in the shipping industry myself, and right now I'm in the process of acquiring another boat to expand my Caribbean cargo trading business, so to speak. Pretty soon, I'm going to be in the market for a new skipper, and you look as if you might just fit the bill perfectly. I'll be in a position to offer you some very lucrative employment at nearly twice the going rate. It's strictly a short-term contract, you understand. We don't have none of them staff pension schemes in our business. Do we, boys?' said Jacob as he turned to his companions, who instantly burst into laughter at his last remark. As Jacob left Bill and Banjo to continue with their meal, he turned and said, 'I'll be in touch, Honkyman. I know where to find you.'

'Thank you, Jacob. That's very kind of you. I look forward to seeing you again!' said Bill, being all English and innocently polite.

Banjo was seriously unnerved by Bill's remark. 'Are you out of your cotton-picking fuckin' mind? I told you they are seriously bad brothers. When he says he's about to acquire a boat, it don't mean he's goin' to pay for one. It means he'll go out on the high seas and take one from some dumbass honky like you. When he says he's expanding his "Caribbean cargo trading business" it means he's not only bringing in heavy-duty drugs from South America, but he's now going into people smuggling into Florida. And when he says he's looking for a new skipper, it means that the last one is now fish food at the bottom of the deep blue sea! And if he ever found out that I own all of my own property and that the Jamaican government doesn't own it, then both you and I are going to be seeing the Pearly Gates a whole lot quicker than we planned. I thought you were stupid when I first clapped eyes on you, but I didn't think you were this stupid, brother.'

'I'm so sorry, Banjo. I didn't mean any harm by it. In England, when we meet someone for the first time and then they say, "We must meet up again and have tea together," or something like that, we always say, "Oh, that would be so nice, I look forward to it!" even though we don't mean it. In England it's called making polite conversation,' said Bill, most apologetically.

'Well, it don't work like that here, brother! Only a crazy person says, "I look forward to seeing you again" to a murdering, drug-smuggling, throat-slitting son of a bitch like Jacob, whose only true friend is Satan himself. We are in serious trouble now, brother!' said Banjo, pacing up and down in a state of severe panic.

'It will be a lot safer for you if I leave, Banjo,' said Bill. 'After all, you have been so good to me and I'll never be able to repay your kindness. I can't stay at your place and have your life in danger all because of me.'

'Hold on there, no one said anything about leaving, brother. We've got to figure a way of getting out of this situation, that's all. Jacob is not the sort of guy you say no to easily,' said Banjo.

The two of them rode home in total silence, both deep in thought.

Chapter Ten

The next few days were taken up with Bill helping around the house and completing several little jobs that Banjo had been putting off for years. Bill's carpentry and practical skills proved invaluable in fixing parts of the roof and replacing termite-infested timbers.

All the time they were expecting a visit from Jacob's men, who would insist that Bill return to the town with them. There was a tense atmosphere, and Bill hated putting Banjo under any kind of unnecessary stress, knowing full well that he couldn't cope with it.

Eventually, Bill confronted him. 'Banjo, my dearest of friends. I got you into this unpleasant situation and I'm going to get you out of it. I don't want you to argue with me, but I'm leaving to stay in town for a while. I'm not sure when I'm coming back. It may be in a week, it may be in a month. Don't worry, I'll find somewhere to stay. All I ask is if I can borrow one of your bicycles. I promise you'll get it back. Trust me.'

'I trust you more than anyone, brother. Even though you are a dumbass. I don't want you to go, 'cause I kinda got used to havin' you around. The thing is, if those sons of bitches get hold of you, when they've finished with you, they'll cut you up into little pieces, brother. And then how in hell's name am I going to be able to get my bicycle back?' said Banjo, pretending to be all serious.

Bill returned to the boat and removed the last bit of money that he had stored away in his secret compartment. It was thirty English pounds, and a twenty-euro note.

By the time he got back to the house, Banjo had already loaded the bicycle with bananas. 'I thought you could use ten dollars, brother. If you head for Aunt Nellie's place she'll help you out, but I don't know why you want to go and put your head in a lion's mouth when it ain't necessary. They're goin' to kill you, and that's for sure.'

'I need to make Jacob understand that I'm not going to help him, and that I only know how to sail little sailing boats, not big powerboats or cruisers,' said Bill, defiantly.

'I'll say one thing: you got one hell of a lot of guts, Honkyman,' replied Banjo.

It was later in the morning when Bill cycled off to endure the full heat of the day, and after a gruelling journey he finally got there at about four o'clock, just as Nellie was preparing to pack up her stall. At first, she was reluctant to take the bananas so late in the day. After hearing his woeful tale, Nellie felt sorry for him and gave him the ten dollars, on the condition that he carry the bananas to her lock-up shed and help her pack things away.

Aunt Nellie's assistant on the stall was a shy young man called Samuel and it was arranged that Bill would be accommodated at Samuel's house for the night. She also allowed Bill to leave Banjo's bicycle securely locked in the shed.

As Bill and Samuel silently weaved their way home through the narrow streets of the shanty town, they were forced to leap back and forth over the open sewer which ran down the centre of the road. There was no sanitation in that part of town and litter of all sorts was strewn everywhere. The stench took some getting used to, but Bill had endured far worse in Haiti.

Finally, they arrived at Samuel's corrugated iron, two-room home. One of his three children was sitting outside in the dirt, and she immediately raised her arms in the air for Samuel to pick her up. Bill was introduced to Kitty, Samuel's wife, and they all sat around and shared the little food that the family had. Bill insisted that Kitty take the ten dollars for his accommodation, which she reluctantly but graciously accepted.

The sleeping arrangements caused Bill a little embarrassing concern, as he was invited to share the room with Samuel and Kitty. The three children were in the adjacent room. Should Samuel decide to become a little amorous in the night, Bill decided he would just have to pretend to be sound asleep and throw in the occasional convincing snore.

All was thankfully quiet, and the following morning, Bill made his way into the town to find a bank where he could exchange his pounds and euros for American dollars. He later returned to Nellie's stall and, without formal agreement, he started to help out. This proved to be a great novelty to the locals, and people crowded around to see the white man working for Aunt Nellie. Nellie quickly realised that this was good for business. The idea that the customers could be served by a white man, and that they could boss him around a bit with their selection of goods, created great laughter and gossip within the community. Bill was thoroughly enjoying himself, and started to adopt a cheeky cockney-style sales technique which brought even larger crowds.

He continued to stay at Samuel's house for a couple more weeks and he shared with Kitty the small salary that Aunt Nellie gave him. Having a lodger was a considerable boost to Samuel and Kitty's income, and that was really the only reason that Bill put up with the less than salubrious accommodation. He still had not reacquainted himself with Jacob yet, but he knew that it wouldn't be long and so he regularly dined at the café where they had first met.

One day, down by the dockside, Bill noticed a very smart van parking next to one of the day-trip cruise boats. On the side was written 'Westminster Plaza Hotel Luxury Tours'. The driver began to unload box upon box of beautifully packaged ready-made meals onto a table next to the gangplank, all ready to take on board. Rich, mainly white, American tourists could indulge themselves with wine and coq au vin while enjoying the high life and fishing off the Jamaican coast. Bill decided to take a closer look.

Each box had a clear plastic lid and Bill could clearly see the interior, which included neat compartments for a main meal, rice and a pudding with a miniature bottle of white wine and a wine glass. 'Westminster Plaza Hotel' was printed in gold lettering on the front of each box.

Bill wondered if Samuel and his family had ever got anywhere close to eating such luxurious food in their entire lives before, let alone ever having the possibility of tasting wine in a wine glass.

He decided to hatch a plot, but he knew he had to be quick. He speedily ran down the quayside to the point where a line of fishermen sat in a row casting their rods into the dock. He politely informed them that he'd run out of bait and asked whether any of them could oblige him with some. 'Sure, help yourself,' said one.

Bill dipped his hand deep into the tin of wriggling maggots and took out a fistful. Returning to the boat's side, he awaited his chance. As the driver jumped into his van to return to the hotel, Bill scattered the maggots all over the boxes. He stood well back, and waited.

Within minutes, a busload of unsuspecting tourists pulled up at the scene. The driver got out and instructed his passengers to each take a box on board as their packed lunch. The first two went unnoticed, until an extremely large American woman let out the most bloodcurdling scream. All hell let loose with everybody shouting at the driver. Then the boat's skipper came down the gangplank and it almost came to blows. Bill could hear the skipper on his mobile phone yelling at the hotel manager and demanding replacement lunches, immediately! Both the bus driver and the skipper carried all the boxes to a nearby industrial garbage skip and dropped them in it in full view of the extremely irate passengers.

Fifteen minutes passed, with passengers pacing up and down the quayside complaining bitterly that they had paid all of this money and their trip had now been ruined. Eventually, the van arrived, and the passengers stood in line to take their lunches reluctantly from it. There were no happy faces nor signs of frivolity as each one trundled their way up on deck.

As the boat pulled away, Bill raced to the skip, removed the first six perfectly sealed boxes and ran like the wind to Samuel's house. Kitty was thrilled to receive them, but there was no time to waste. Samuel wasn't at home and so Kitty and the three children were instructed to return and collect as many boxes as each could carry. After three trips all had been removed and were piled up neatly in Samuel's house.

When Samuel returned home there was already a buzzing party atmosphere. Bill, Samuel and Kitty had plenty to distribute to all the immediate neighbours. Nothing was wasted, and even the boxes and plastic lids found use in some of the households. One thing was for sure: everyone in that entire neighbourhood possessed at least one wine glass of their very own. Bill's thoughtfulness endeared him to the locals, who were mystified as to why a white man would be living amongst them. White men were always rich in the eyes of the folks that lived in that neighbourhood.

The following day, Bill was sitting at the café when he was joined by a middle-aged Canadian from Toronto called Patrick Doyle. Patrick's parents had emigrated to Canada in the 1960s from Liverpool, and they had since made a modest fortune in the electrical industry. He explained that he was only in Jamaica for a week or so to check on his boat, *Miss Blarney*, which was moored in the marina. She had been named as a reference to his very talkative young daughter. Patrick's wife had developed cancer and it had become more difficult for them to spend time sailing together, and it was most likely that they would have to sell the boat fairly soon.

Bill and Patrick got on famously, and even found that they had mutual friends back in England. It was decided that they would take the boat out the following day. Bill quickly took to handling it, and said it was like always owning a soft-top Morris Minor and suddenly finding yourself driving a convertible Bentley.

When they returned to port, knowing Bill's predicament, Patrick put a proposition to him. 'Look, Bill, why don't you use the boat? I probably won't be back here until next year. I've got too much on my plate at the moment. You can live on it. It's got to be better than where you're staying at the moment. You could even take tourists out on day fishing trips or sailing excursions up and down the coast and make a bit of money for yourself. How about it?'

Bill couldn't believe his luck. 'Thank you so much, Patrick. That really is too kind, I do so appreciate it. I promise I'll look after her, but what if there's a mishap and she sinks? What about insurance?'

'Don't worry, no problem, it's fully insured and there is nothing in it of any sentimental value. Recently, I've realised that life is short and my priorities have changed. I'm just happy to help you, that's all,' was Patrick's reassuring reply.

Bill spent time familiarising himself with the GPS system, the rigging, the storage, cooking and toilet facilities etc., before Patrick returned to Toronto. He couldn't wait to tell Samuel,

Kitty and Aunt Nellie of his good fortune, all of whom were a little disappointed. He assured them that he was only at the port-mooring and would still see them regularly and help out on the stall if he was really needed.

Bill prepared for his first solo trip around the coast to see Banjo, but not before collecting his bike from Aunt Nellie's lock-up shed.

It was an early start for Bill. He had favourable winds and calm seas, and by midday he was rounding the corner into Bickley Port. No sooner had he tied up at the slave quay than he heard a familiar voice calling from the top of the hill. 'You ain't allowed to park that here, brother, this is government property. They'll come and impound it and you'll get a spell in the jail. You'd better move your ass double quick, brother.'

Bill waved back at him, but Banjo started to come down the hill to confront this unwelcome trespasser. As he got closer, he suddenly shouted out, 'Sweet Jesus, is that you, Honkyman? What the fuck are you doin' in that beauty? Don't you go tellin' me you stole it and that you're now workin' for that son-of-a-bitch Jacob.'

'No, don't worry, you know me better than that,' said Bill. He started up the hill to meet Banjo, but was struggling as he'd got Banjo's bicycle over his head and shoulder.

'I've got a duchy full of suicide stew on the fire, brother,' said Banjo.

'Sounds good!' said Bill, as he huffed and puffed his way up the hill.

Over dinner, Bill told of his time in the town and that Jacob was still eluding him.

'That evil dude will be on one of his trips to South America, you can count on it, which is why you ain't seen him yet. But he'll be back. Folks get all afeared the minute they know he's around. I can tell you, that nigger was born bad,' said Banjo as he inhaled an extra deep breath on his ganja pipe.

'How many men are in his gang?' enquired Bill.

'Not much of a gang, brother. It's just him and those three ugly sons of bitches that were with him the day you first saw them.'

'Well, why don't the men in the town all get together and go and beat the shit out of them? That's what I would do,' said Bill.

Banjo could hardly contain his laughter. 'A skinny little dude like you, Honkyman? Why, they'd cut off your meat and two little veggies, fry them up and make you eat them before you die, little brother. The last dumb fool to take them on came home to find his wife and kids nailed to a wall. When I say "evil" I'm talkin' serious evil, man!'

'Can't the police do anything?' asked Bill.

'What planet are you livin' on, honky? Nobody is goin' to testify against Jacob. He knows every criminal dude in and out of prison in the whole of Jamaica. Even if he was locked away it wouldn't make no difference, brother. He'd just send someone to get you,' said Banjo, who was becoming slightly frustrated at Bill's naivety.

'Well, it seems ridiculous to me that everyone lives in fear of their lives because of just four people. I'm damned sure something can be done about it,' said Bill with a determined tone to his voice.

Bill stayed in Banjo's Presidential Suite that night, instead of returning to the *Miss Blarney*. He didn't want to hurt Banjo's feelings, although the luxury of a bed with immaculately clean sheets aboard the boat was extremely tempting.

The following few days, Bill continued to help Banjo fix the roof and complete some of the jobs that he'd started before, knowing full well that Banjo would never get round to doing them by himself. Finally, Bill gave the excuse that he had to return to the moorings. He wanted to get some yacht varnish and completely re-varnish the deck on the *Miss Blarney* in preparation for starting his tourist fishing business. *Miss Blarney* had to look her very best, and Bill had run out of money.

'Hey, brother, you could give me a lift to town. I've never been on a swanky boat like this one before,' declared Banjo.

The bicycle was loaded back on board along with four times the number of bananas that Bill and Banjo could have carried on their bikes, and the two of them set sail. Banjo sat at the tip of the bow with his legs dangling either side of the bow-rail and Bill raised the spinnaker sail above his head just to show off. It hadn't really been necessary, but Bill was just enjoying the fact that he was now the new ship's master.

'This is super cool, Honkyman. Make sure you go into port real slow. I want everyone to see me sailin' in like some Hollywood hotshot. Pity we didn't have a couple of white chicks on board to complete the picture, brother.' Banjo chuckled out loud to himself.

Upon their arrival, they unloaded the bananas on the quayside, where Banjo insisted that Aunt Nellie pay him the full forty dollars. With much reluctance, she eventually gave in. Samuel and Bill were given the task of carrying the bananas to Nellie's storage shed, and when Banjo waved goodbye and started cycling back home, Bill felt in his pocket. Banjo had slipped the forty dollars into his trousers without him noticing.

Bill began the laborious business of sanding the deck before varnishing it, and as always, he was meticulous. The preparation had to be perfect, and a job that could have been done in a week took several. Nellie was grateful that, to supplement his income and pay for food and varnish, Bill chose to work for her on the stall three days a week.

Chapter Eleven

Life couldn't be any better. Bill's concerns for things back home, and his occasional pangs of homesickness, were far less frequent these days. He sometimes wondered if he could ever return to that life of grey skies, cold damp winters and an endless continuum of bill paying, career failure and marital drudgery. Now he really was living that gospel of free living, as so indelibly preached to him by his uncle Arthur. 'Live for the day because every one of them is precious, son. You must always follow your dream,' Uncle Arthur would say. But in Bill's father's family, Arthur was always referred to as nothing more than an irresponsible dreamer, a fool. Bill's father resented the fact that Bill idolised his uncle so much. After all, Arthur was the family's Indiana Jones, and Bill's father was just an unfulfilled impoverished drunk who was incapable of gaining his son's respect.

Bill arrived late to start work at Nellie's stall on this particular morning, but he was never chastised for it. He was far too much of an asset to her. His 'cheeky chappie' sales technique, especially with the older black women, was an all-time winner. They loved being teased by him, particularly the seriously obese ones, of which there were many, and Bill had them in stitches with his jokes and his innuendos regarding certain fruits or vegetables. He was becoming immensely popular with everyone.

Whilst working his audience of customers, in the midst of the crowd Bill spotted the florescence of a beauty in her mid-twenties. She was of fairer skin than those around her. She was slender and statuesque with the type of tanned, olive, silken skin that Bill had only been close to once before in his life. Her hair was not the Afro tight curl, but more a cascade of gypsy Spanish waves which fell about her shoulders. She was wearing an immaculate white sleeveless peasant girl's dress cut off at the knees, and a pair of large dark brown designer sunglasses rested on the top of her head. She was, quite simply, magnificent.

As she weaved her way to the side of the stall, Aunt Nellie greeted her warmly and hugged her tightly. The two of them linked arms and walked off chatting and laughing together. Over his sales pitch, Bill kept looking to see if she would return, but disappointingly Nellie came back alone.

At the close of day Bill questioned Nellie as to who she was.

'That's Gloria. Ain't she the prettiest thing you ever did see?' declared Aunt Nellie.

'Yes, she certainly is. What's the story on her? Is she married?' enquired Bill, anxiously.

'Hell no! The boys round here aren't smart enough for our Gloria. And you is too old, Honkyman! So you can get rid of any of those dog-sniffin' thoughts you may have, 'cause that's one little doggie bitch that ain't goin' to be on heat for you, brother,' said Nellie with a scolding, protective tone to her voice.

'No, no, I'm just curious, that's all,' said Bill.

'Her folks were big-shots not too many years ago and there was some kind of scandal goin' on,' said Nellie. 'The family moved shortly after that, but Gloria decided she wanted to stay. She still lives in their old family house just outside of town. I know she's got some fancy job in the government building in Kingston now, but she doesn't like to talk about her family no more, so don't you go upsetting her, you hear?'

Bill's previously subdued testosterone levels had suddenly spiked back up, and he couldn't get Gloria out of his mind. The days passed and there was no sight of her. He was beginning to lose hope, when suddenly, fortune finally favoured him. He was at the café reading his newspaper when a vapour trail of sweet perfume caught his attention. As he slowly lowered his paper, there she was, like a swan from *Swan Lake,* gliding across the stage before him.

'Gloria!' he screamed out.

She stopped dead in her tracks.

'I'm so sorry to startle you,' said Bill, all of a fluster. 'It's just that I know that you are a friend of Aunt Nellie's and she's a dear friend of mine also. As a matter of fact, I'm giving her a helping hand on her stall at the moment.'

'Yes, I recognise you. Nellie spoke about you with a great deal of affection. She told me what an interesting man you are. She really likes you,' said Gloria. Her voice was soft and her accent was mostly Caribbean, but there was undoubtedly an Englishness to the pronunciation of some of her words.

'Please, join me. Can I get you a cup of coffee or something?' asked Bill.

'Well, I can stay just for a couple of minutes. I have an appointment that I can't get out of in half an hour. Where are you living here on the island?' she enquired.

Bill pointed at the *Miss Blarney* moored nearby.

'Gosh, what a beautiful boat. Did you sail all the way from England in it? Nellie told me you sailed here alone.'

'No, *Miss Blarney* belongs to a friend of mine. I'm just looking after it for him. The boat that I sailed from England in is a quarter of that size, but I keep her moored further up the coast in another friend's boathouse.'

'A quarter the size?' she repeated. 'Nellie described you as a wild adventurer, and it sounds like she wasn't exaggerating. You sound like a very interesting man, Bill, and it's always a pleasure to meet interesting people.' She rose from her seat.

'I'm sorry, but I really must rush. It was nice meeting you. Next time we meet I look forward to hearing some of those fascinating stories of yours.'

Gloria extended her hand to shake his, but instead, Bill raised it to his lips and kissed it.

'Wow! A gentleman and an adventurer! I'm impressed,' said Gloria, as she turned to walk away.

Bill had never kissed a woman's hand in his entire life before. He didn't know what had come over him; it had just seemed the right thing to do at the time. He focused fully on the gentle sway of her hips and the slight curvature of her waist until she became lost in the crowd.

Bill jumped up and struck at the sky with his fist. 'Yes!' he shouted.

He sat back, ordered another coffee and silently revelled in the idea that Gloria's perception of him was now so different from what it would have been little more than a year ago. Then, he was a Mr Ordinary, a grey man in a grey world, just another face in the crowd. Now he was a buccaneer, a romantic figure, a man people were interested in and wanted to talk about. Now he really was worthy of being the successor to Uncle Arthur. Best of all, he now knew that he was assured of a future meeting with Gloria, and who knew where that might lead to? His Catholic marital vows to Janice, which once had been so sacrosanct, were not even a fleeting consideration at this time.

Over the next few weeks, in addition to thinking endlessly about Gloria, Bill continued to busy himself with preparing the *Miss Blarney* and researching his competition. Having been totally initiated into the Banjo philosophy of life, Bill needed to know the prices of all the day-trip fishing businesses on the island so that he could drastically undercut them. After all, he only needed enough money to keep himself fed with a little extra on top. Like Banjo, his general overheads were almost nil, and so were his aspirations.

His first experimental day fishing trip was for Samuel, Kitty and the children, so that he could get used to organising the order of the day for the tourists. Patrick had left vast amounts of sea fishing tackle on board, and Bill had brought plenty from his own boat when he'd been moored at Banjo's. He had also managed to arrange a deal with the café to do packed lunches for his day-trip excursions. Samuel's family were thrilled to be going out on such a lovely boat for the day, and they returned with a wide selection of fish for everyone to enjoy. As night fell, Bill escorted them home and helped them carry the catch back to Samuel's house. Naturally, he was invited to stay for dinner, and there was more than enough to include some of the neighbours.

At about midnight, Bill slowly meandered back to the *Miss Blarney* and the luxury of that clean comfortable bed. In almost pitch darkness, he had only just closed the galley door behind him when he heard the deep, chilling Caribbean tones of Jacob's voice.

'Hello, Honkyman. Nice boat you have here!'

Bill struggled to distinguish precisely where the voice was coming from, but it appeared that Jacob was lying across his bed. He felt an arm come around his neck and a steel blade was pressed under his chin, forcing him to raise his head in the air. Someone else started to tie his hands behind his back. Jacob had brought two of his goons with him.

'You may remember me tellin' you I'm in the process of acquiring a new boat, Honkyman. Well, this is it! And you remember me sayin' I'm lookin' for a new skipper. Well, you are it! Congratulations, you've just passed our stringent employment requirements, Honkyman! And your first assignment is to take a little parcel to Florida for me.'

Bill was almost standing on his tiptoes at this point, trying to avoid the slip of the blade. 'Sorry, no can do,' he replied, in almost a whisper.

'And why might that be?' asked Jacob.

'Firstly, this isn't my boat, and secondly, I don't have an American visa!'

With that, there was an almighty earth-shattering uproar of laughter from the three of them. So much so that the two goons doubled up and Jacob started kicking his legs in the air like a dying bluebottle. The laughter continued for several minutes and every time it started to die down, another one of them would say, 'He hasn't got an American visa,' and the whole thing would start all over again. Bill remained silent with nothing more than a bewildered expression on his face. There was no possibility of an escape now. Yet again, he was up to his neck in trouble.

When eventually Jacob regained his composure, he stood up and pressed his nose close to Bill's.

'Now listen up, my little man: we're going to take you on a nice holiday for a few days while we make some minor alterations to this boat of yours.' Jacob's voice was quiet and menacing.

'My friend Patrick is not going to be too pleased at having his boat messed with,' said Bill.

The uproar of laughter started all over again, but Jacob's mood suddenly changed and he took the knife from one of his goons, pushed the pointed tip of the blade up into Bill's nostril and held it there. 'I'm not finding you funny anymore,' said Jacob.

He then put his mouth close to Bill's ear. 'Oh, you are comin' with us alright, 'cause we paid a little visit to your banjo-playing nigger friend today. I'll bet they could hear his squealin' in Kingston. Let's put it this way, Honkyman: he ain't goin' to be playin' no more banjos, 'cause we cut some of his fingers off.'

Bill screamed out loud in anguish and horror and he began to sob. The thought of them torturing his dear friend Banjo was just too much to bear, and it was all Bill's fault. His head was then wrenched back by his hair and a cloth was tied over his eyes. It was so tight that it pressed uncomfortably hard against his eyeballs. Blood started to run profusely from his nose where the blade had nicked the inside of his nostril.

He'd been careless in not observing the black Mercedes that had been parked on the quayside only yards from the boat. It should have aroused his suspicions. Who else but a gangster-cum-drug-dealer would be driving such a vehicle in this town?

His plan had always been to meet up with Jacob in full public view at the café. He hadn't thought for a second that their meeting would happen like this, in stealth and under the protection of night. *If I get out of this alive I'm damn well going to have my wits about me in future,* he thought to himself.

Bill was bundled into the boot of the car and driven for about an hour through the very early morning. It appeared from the feel of it that they were driving up inclines for much of the time and he concluded that they must be in the Blue Mountains somewhere.

The car stopped, and as the doors slammed open and shut he heard Jacob shouting out instructions to everyone. When Bill was hauled from the vehicle, he noted that it was much cooler than at the coast, which confirmed his high altitude theory. He was then led into a room and forced to sit down, and his blindfold and ropes were removed. Jacob and his two goons left and locked the door without saying a word.

Jacob's third goon was more a housekeeper than a heavy, and it was he who was left in charge of guarding Bill. He was obviously not the sharpest tool in the box and Bill could hear

Jacob screaming strict instructions at him not to get too close or to engage with the prisoner.

This was an encouraging sign and Bill hoped that he could easily outsmart this goon who was being referred to by his partners in crime as Chico. Step one: get friendly and find a common ground. Step two: work at getting your captor's trust so that he will drop his guard. Chico was a Latino/Mayan, whereas the others were of pure African slave origins, which was why he was treated with an element of contempt and resentment by them.

The room contained a bed and a hand basin with a single cold tap; nothing more. A well-worn hand towel hung from a nail on the wall next to the sink.

After hearing the car speed away, Bill paused for a while before going over to the window to open it. On the outside were thick bars, scrolled in the form of a cage, similar to those you would find on a Spanish villa. The gentle cool breeze brought with it the sweet night-time fragrance of jasmine. Bill stood at the window and filled his lungs with it several times before retiring to his bed.

He slept well, and was only awakened by Chico tapping on the door. 'I've brought you some coffee,' he said, coming into the room.

'That's nice, thank you so much,' said Bill.

'Boss says I'm not allowed to speak to you,' replied Chico.

'He'll never know, will he? My real name is Bill, but as you know, out here people call me Honkyman.' Bill extended his hand to shake Chico's, but his gesture was ignored and Chico merely looked down to the ground and then turned toward the door. 'I believe you are Chico. Well, don't worry, Chico, I promise I'll not tell Jacob you've ever spoken to me.'

Chico slowly and quietly closed the door behind him without answering.

Bill got up and started to pace up and down, thinking of his plan of action. He was quickly driven to distraction by the fact that in the next room Chico had turned the television on at high volume. It was tuned to an American football game and Bill couldn't focus on his thoughts. 'For God's sake, do you have to have that bloody thing so loud? Turn the damned thing down,' shouted Bill at the top of his voice. Almost immediately his command was obeyed with no verbal retaliation from Chico.

Within the realm of psychological warfare Bill now knew that he had the upper hand. Chico had shown him an immediate subservience.

Back at the *Miss Blarney*, Samuel and Kitty had decided they would like to surprise Bill with a dinner that Kitty had made especially for him. Upon their arrival they were concerned to find that he was not around and that the cabin door had been left open. They ventured below deck calling out his name. The galley had been disturbed and the whole space was in disarray. It was totally uncharacteristic of Bill to ever leave the place in a mess, they thought. Then Kitty spotted the trail of blood from Bill's nose leading up onto the outer deck. They hurried back to inform Aunt Nellie. If anyone would know what to do it would be Nellie. Everyone began to fear the worst.

Aunt Nellie knew everybody on the island who was worth knowing, and she, Samuel and Kitty immediately called at the house of Nellie's close friend, the chief police commissioner of the Jamaica Constabulary Force. He was most welcoming, and ordered refreshments for them while he listened to their tale of concern. A twenty-four-hour surveillance operation was immediately launched on the *Miss Blarney*. The commissioner was an honourable and thoroughly incorruptible man of principle. He was very aware of Jacob's tentacles of power on the island, and finding evidence of crime, or anyone brave enough to testify against him, had thus far proven impossible.

The following morning a van arrived on the quayside with two workmen in it and within minutes the black Mercedes pulled up behind it. The workmen unloaded timber and tools and it was very apparent that they were receiving detailed instruction from Jacob. The assumption was that they were to build secret compartments below the engine block and then flood it so there would always be a couple of inches of water on top swishing around. With some oil mixed in, it would appear to be perfectly natural under the eye of a casual inspection. Bill, as a lone white English sailor, would be less subject to a thorough investigation by the US Coast Guard.

CHAPTER TWELVE

Over the next few days, Bill slowly won Chico's confidence, and bit by bit he managed to engage him in the occasional conversation. Chico had got to the point of not locking Bill's door any more, after Bill had convinced him that escaping would be a totally futile exercise. Firstly, they were far too deep into the mountains and isolated. And secondly, with all his contacts, Jacob would easily be able to find him somewhere on the island.

If he wasn't spending his time watching television or cooking, Chico would busy himself by cleaning and oiling his handgun. It was a stylish, bone-handled special 9mm Smith and Wesson, which held eight rounds in the clip. It was obviously his pride and joy and it gave Chico the respect that he had always believed he deserved. He was also an accomplished marksman. In the scrubland below the house, Chico had hung tin cans on strings from the bushes. He would spend hours using them as targets from the upstairs window, and Bill was more than impressed with Chico's abilities. Allowing Bill to watch him in action also reinforced Chico's promise that if Bill decided to make a run for it, Chico would easily be able to bring him down with a single shot.

A week had passed and Bill was tearing his hair out with boredom. He had to get word out to the authorities somehow, but could he trust the Jamaican police? That was his big question. There was every chance that Jacob would have many of the police firmly in his pocket. But regardless, Bill had to try something. He knew full well that Jacob was going to have him killed after he had outlived his usefulness. He had to outsmart them if he was to stay alive.

An opportunity finally arose. Chico was busy in the kitchen making a meal when Bill noticed that he had left his mobile phone on charge overnight. Dare he chance it? And how could he divert Chico's attention long enough to speak to anyone? Bill began to nervously sweat with the indecision of it all. If he just grabbed it, Chico might panic and shoot him on the spot. Then it came to him in a flash!

When Chico's eye was averted, Bill casually walked over to the phone and unplugged it, deliberately leaving the wire still in the wall. He slipped the phone into his underpants and held it between the crack of his buttocks, then picked up the television remote control and walked over to the open window.

Chico glanced toward the wall socket and noticed the phone missing from its charger. 'What the fuck are you up to?' he screamed.

Bill raised the TV remote to his ear and shouted, 'Police, police, put me through to the police!' Chico lunged forward, armed with a kitchen knife. As he got within grasping distance, Bill threw the TV remote out of the window. Both of them watched it bounce down the hill and into the scrubland bushes far below.

'You fucking honky bastard. I should cut you up right now.' Chico hit Bill hard in the face, dragged him to the floor and started to beat him severely. He kicked him in the ribs and kidneys over and over again in a frenzy. He then bent down and pressed the blade of the knife into Bill's mouth, slightly cutting the corners of his mouth on either side. 'If I can't find that phone or it is broken, I promise you, you are a fucking dead man,' said Chico.

He dragged Bill across the floor and locked him in his room. The corners of Bill's mouth were bleeding profusely even though the cuts were only slight.

Bill removed the phone from his backside and crawled over to the window. He watched Chico run out of the yard below and start to frantically search in the bushes further down the hill. Bill knew he had ample time as Chico was already searching in totally the wrong place. He managed to dial the American 911 emergency service, which put him through to the US Coast Guard based in Florida. He gave them all the details and descriptions and they said that they could only help him if he was able to keep the phone open so that they could track it. They said that the Jamaican police were in total cooperation with the United States. The Jamaican tourist industry had been seriously affected by bad press, and Jamaica had become known as a haven for drug dealing cartels and lottery scammers from Montego Bay. The Coast Guard also said that the new Jamaican chief police commissioner was particularly keen to eradicate those problems completely. Bill felt some consolation in what he was hearing, but nonetheless, right now, he was still in serious trouble.

He put the phone on mute and prepared to return it to the darkest of places, where it was in danger of becoming an elephant-sized enema!

Chico was still struggling to scramble back up the hill because the dry earth and rocks kept collapsing about him. He'd found the TV remote and realised that he'd been tricked, and he continued to barrage Bill with loud obscenities as he continued his climb. Bill was afraid that he was about to get yet another beating. If it was a repeat of his most recent one then there was every chance that he might not survive it.

No sooner had Chico reached the yard than from the upstairs window Bill observed the black Mercedes speeding up the drive. A dust cloud followed its approach.

Chico approached Jacob and the two goons with a cheery greeting, but he was clearly petrified that Jacob would find out that Bill had outsmarted him and got possession of the phone. When they got to the room and saw the state that Bill was in, Jacob yelled out, 'What in holy shit's name have you done, man? I told you to fucking well look after him, not nearly kill him. We need this white son of a bitch!'

Chico cowered as Jacob began to slap him around the head and face as if he were a disobedient child. 'Well, he tried to escape! I had to stop him.'

Jacob lost patience with him. 'All you had to do was lock him in the room and give him some food! That can't be too complicated even for a dumbass Indian spic like you, man.'

Chico deeply resented Jacob's regular references to his native South American and Spanish origins. There was many a time when Chico felt that he could blow Jacob away and then he would be the boss, but he would always back down from the idea when Jacob started to treat him better.

Chico was ordered to clean Bill up as best he could. The only clothes Bill had were the ones he stood up in, and they were covered in blood from now and a week ago. Also, the cuts to each corner of Bill's mouth made it difficult for him to talk. Smiling was out of the question.

Chico hovered over Bill as he washed his hands and face whilst Jacob and the two goons were busy talking in the other room. He got close up to Bill's ear and whispered, 'Where's that fucking phone? You piece of shit. I know you've hidden it somewhere.'

Bill turned toward him, his face covered in soapsuds, and said, 'I haven't the foggiest idea what you are talking about, sunshine. I made a simple mistake. I thought the TV controller was the phone, that's all. Perhaps I've stuffed it up my arse!' Bill was pushing his luck with that little throw-away line, but he was confident that Chico was not likely to make an inspection just to make sure. 'Perhaps you dropped it somewhere. I'm positive I saw you put it into your shirt pocket last night.'

Chico was beginning to doubt himself, even though he remembered plugging the charger into the wall. Bill could see the expression of confusion on his face. It wouldn't take too much to baffle Chico.

Jacob became more impatient and bawled from the other room, 'Come on, let's go.'

This time, Bill wasn't bundled into the boot of the car as before, but he was made to sit in the back, flanked by the two goons. There was a very good reason for this. Bill winced with every bump in the road, but his fellow passengers put it down to the kicking that he'd received from Chico.

They arrived at the dockside next to the *Miss Blarney* just as the light was fading. Jacob instructed everyone to wait in the car and observe for several minutes to ensure that all was clear. They remained completely oblivious to the fact that their every move was being watched and filmed.

Jacob got out first, went to the back of the car and opened the boot. There he removed a holdall which apparently contained cash, maps, the delivery coordinates, a suitcase with a change of clothes etc. He then wrapped two AK-47s and a Bulgarian Makarov snub-nosed submachine gun in a blanket and passed it to one of the goons. Chico got the job of carrying the heavy boxes of ammunition. Bill was relieved of any chores as it was very obvious that he was in a considerable amount of pain.

On board, Jacob and Bill went into the fine detail of where they were due to rendezvous with the drugs supply boat. Maps and coordinates were fully explained. The idea was that the mother ship would sail with full protection from Colombia until she exceeded their territorial waters. She would then meet up with small mule boats along the way. These would spread the risk and lessen the loss if they got caught. There were dozens of little boats like Bill's delivering drugs all across the southern coastal states of the USA. Some made it, but most didn't. The exchange would take place just into international waters off Jamaica, where Jacob would pay the cash and drugs would be strategically placed within the *Miss Blarney*.

On this particular occasion, Jacob and his goons were due to return to Colombia on board the mother ship and Bill was to continue on to Florida alone. Failure to deliver the full consignment to Jacob's team in Florida would mean that Banjo would forfeit his life and Bill would be on the run from Jacob's associates for as long as he lived. Even if he were caught and imprisoned they would never give up on killing him for failing to fulfil his obligations. That was made perfectly clear to Bill right from the start.

Early evening, Bill started the engine and *Miss Blarney* slipped her moorings and left for the open sea. They had not got out of sight of the onshore lights at Morant Point when Jacob, followed by one of his goons, turned from black to a pale green and was violently seasick.

They were well past the twelve-mile exclusion zone and at the meeting point when Bill cut the engine and a long night's wait began. To his great relief, Bill managed to find a brief window of time to remove the phone from the crack in his backside and hide it under the mattress.

For the rest of the night they remained silently bobbing around with Jacob and his seasick underling clinging on to anything they could grasp. The only sound to be heard was that of the two of them retching all night.

At around 5am they heard the unmistakable sounds of a powerful set of inboard engines roaring toward them. Jacob and his goons leapt to attention, grabbed their AK-47s and whatever weaponry was at hand and prepared themselves for a battle. It would not be the first time that Jacob had come face to face with an interfering coast guard.

Jacob raised his binoculars and scanned the horizon. In the hazy dawn light he finally declared, 'It's OK!' and within a few minutes a beautiful dark blue 56-foot Sunseeker pulled alongside. A Sunseeker had been deliberately chosen because it was a powerful luxury vessel, much favoured by the moderately wealthy, but without being too conspicuous. There are vast numbers of them parked at luxury moorings around the world and so they don't attract a lot of attention. They can be purchased new for in the region of a million pounds.

These mid-ocean transactions are usually very quick, with a simple exchange handover, and then the parties are gone. This time, though, because Jacob and the goons were returning to Colombia in the Sunseeker, everyone was invited on board for breakfast.

The principal man was a Colombian called Monolo. He was the perfect stereotypical vision of a South American drug dealer boss. He was Latino, brash, considerably overweight and festooned in gold. The chain around his neck had links as thick as a man's thumb, and it would be impossible to tell the time from his watch without being blinded by the dazzle of its diamonds. Snow white chest hair burst forth from the opening of his open-neck black shirt like the stuffing of an exploding mattress. And even Bill, with his humble council house origins, found such a vulgar display of wealth offensive and in bad taste. Monolo hugged Jacob and each of the goons in turn, but when Bill was introduced, merely a handshake was offered.

In addition to Monolo, there were three crew members and a woman called Dolores, who Bill assumed was Monolo's wife. Dolores had become a plastic surgeon's masterpiece. It was apparent that as a young woman she had been extremely attractive, but in her quest to remain a vision of youthful beauty, she had strayed down the path of bizarre enhancement. Her nose had been replaced with an upturned button, which was flanked by two grossly inflated cheekbones. Her wrinkle-free forehead and her tightly nip-and-tucked neck gave her an expressionless face. She had obviously requested that her lips emulate those of Mick Jagger, only bigger, and her breasts were so large it would be difficult to clap her hands together in front of them. It was an image that Bill found too difficult not to stare at.

The conversation was lively and varied, but when Monolo and Jacob wished to discuss matters of business, which were to exclude Bill, they would revert to Spanish. Two of the crew members acted as waiters and served the breakfast, whilst the third was the ship's cook.

All was going swimmingly, and Dolores engaged in a broken English conversation with Bill about Manchester United, her favourite football team. But all the pleasantries were abruptly interrupted when Monolo suddenly shouted out, 'Quiet, everyone!' His keen sense of hearing had picked up the distant sound of a helicopter. Everyone jumped up and immediately scrambled to action stations. Chico leapt on board the *Miss Blarney* and frantically passed the weaponry and ammunition over to the other goons.

Monolo ordered Dolores to go below deck as he screamed orders at the crew to find the key to their munitions cabinet. Everyone except Bill was running back and forth in a complete state of panic. Bill casually walked outside to the foredeck with his arms outstretched in a cruciform position.

The speed at which the US Coast Guard assault helicopter approached was remarkable. Bill was quickly deafened by the sound of its engines and blasted by the downdraught as it hovered above. Without orders or instruction, Bill sank to his knees and lay prostrate on the deck.

The helicopter tannoy system blared out the order for everybody to come out on deck with their hands raised.

Chico was having none of it; he foolishly withdrew his Smith & Wesson from its holster and fired a single shot at the helicopter's rear propeller.

An instant rapid-fire volley of three shots was returned. One went through his upper chest, a second through his throat and a final one through his head. It took less than a second for Chico to drop like a stone. His heart was still unaware of what had just happened to his head and it continued to pump a profusion of blood from the gaping wounds for several seconds afterwards.

One of Jacob's goons fired two shots up at the pilot from the window of the wheelhouse, but again a response of machine-gun fire shattered glass everywhere, splintered highly polished timbers and exploded upholstery in all directions. Jacob's goon died instantly. Monolo was unaware that below the deck, Dolores had also been hit and was enduring her own slow and silent death.

Bill lay perfectly still. Although the noise around him was deafening, his own world was silent. Throughout the entire ordeal, he stared over at Chico's body and the gruesome remains of his head. Chico's blood had made its way across the deck and had settled under Bill's face and hands. Bill was going into a state of shock.

The pilot acknowledged the waving white napkin held by Monolo, and then Jacob sheepishly followed him out onto the open deck. The staff and the remaining goon came out with their arms stretched high in the air. A US Coast Guard frigate, which had launched the helicopter in the first place, was quick on the scene, and military personnel swarmed aboard.

Those who were standing were handcuffed, taken aboard the frigate, and locked in the onboard cells. There was so much blood around Bill's motionless body that they were unsure as to whether he was alive or not. Even Jacob's passing glance convinced him that Bill was already dead.

A sailor bent down close to Bill's face to check. 'I'm OK, I'm fine,' said Bill in little more than a whisper.

'This one's alive, Captain,' said the sailor.

'Which one of those on board is an English guy called Bill Smith?' enquired the captain.

'That's me,' replied Bill, as he was gently lifted to his feet.

'Thank God you're alive, sir. We got the full briefing from your telephone call several days ago, and since then we have managed to track your cell phone. We have been monitoring Monolo Cortez for the past three years, so today is a very gratifying day for us all. We owe you a great debt of gratitude, sir,' said the captain.

The US personnel had begun removing the hoard of drugs and photographing the scene when one of the sailors shouted, 'There's a dead woman down here, Captain. And also there is a serious leak; bullets have pierced the bulkhead below the waterline.'

'Collecting evidence of drugs is our priority, sailor; leave the woman,' was the captain's reply.

Two crew members were ordered to escort Bill to the captain's cabin, where he was allowed to clean himself up. A meal and coffee were brought in, and an hour later the captain and a fellow officer sat down with Bill to get a full signed statement from him, starting with his first meeting with Jacob and leading up to his kidnap.

They were still in conversation when there was a knock on the door. A sailor entered. 'The Sunseeker is listing quite heavily, Captain. We think she'll go down in a few minutes.'

'For God's sake, unhitch the *Miss Blarney*, quickly! She'll take her down with her,' shouted Bill, in a panic. All four men ran up on deck, with the sailor screaming instructions to anyone close at hand. A crew member managed to release the guy line just as the Sunseeker lifted her stern in the air. She remained motionless in that position for several minutes. There was ample time for the entire crew to come to the side of the ship and watch.

The Sunseeker's journey to the deep was a slow, dignified affair. As water covered the deck, Chico's body washed into the cabin to join Dolores' and the goon's and all three went to their watery grave. Bill, compassionate as ever, advised the captain that he should tell Monolo of the situation and that his wife had perished in the attack.

The captain told Bill that he had telephoned the Jamaican chief police commissioner and informed him of the arrests, and that the Jamaican prisoners were being taken to the United States for trial. The commissioner had been more than happy to receive the news. There was no question of him preventing a US extradition order. The United States was more than welcome to have them where Jacob couldn't wield any power or influence on the islanders from his prison cell.

Much later, it was revealed that the composite of offences gave Monolo a total of one hundred and sixty years of incarceration and Jacob was to remain locked up for one hundred and forty years. The goon got a thirty-year sentence and Monolo's staff were returned to Colombia without charge. Jacob's operations were finally finished.

The captain was satisfied that Bill could return to Jamaica immediately via the *Miss Blarney*, and that he was not required to appear in a US court as a witness. His sworn affidavit was sufficient. The crew were more than courteous, and made sure that Bill had sufficient fuel for his short journey back to the mainland.

Chapter Thirteen

Bill's largest priority was to get back to his dear friend Banjo, and to beg his forgiveness for making him endure such dreadful torture and the loss of his fingers. *None of it would have happened if I had kept my bloody mouth shut. How can I face him, and what will I say to him?* thought Bill to himself. He opened the throttle all the way and sped toward Bickley Bay as fast as *Miss Blarney* could take him. He was in no mood for hoisting sails today. He was just going to have to face the music and there was no use in delaying it any further.

As he rounded the corner and took sight of Bickley Bay, he could see smoke rising out of Banjo's kitchen chimney. He moored up and ascended the hill as fast as his legs would take him. Banjo was sitting on the porch, rocking back and forth and smoking his ganja pipe. Mandela the rooster was perched on the back of his chair, fluttering and struggling to keep his balance.

'Well, will you lookie here and see what the cat dragged in? It's the goddamn Honkyman. I was just sayin' to my friend Mandela here that my fairweather friend Honkyman hasn't been to see me in weeks! And the last I remember is when I put forty dollars in his pocket,' said a very disgruntled Banjo.

Bill dropped to his knees at Banjo's feet, still wheezing and out of breath from his climb. 'Banjo, I am so, so, so sorry. How can you ever forgive me? With all that you've gone through, and I was never there for you. I've caused you such pain and misery.' He took hold of Banjo's hands in his and looked down at them. 'What the fuck? You've still got all of your fingers!' he exclaimed.

'You need to give the ganja a rest, brother. You is beginnin' to talk crazy,' said Banjo.

'But Jacob told me that he'd tortured you and chopped your fingers off so that you couldn't play the banjo any more,' yelled Bill.

'I ain't seen that ugly nigger in months, brother. He'd be just spinnin' you a yarn,' said Banjo.

'Oh, I am so happy!' exclaimed Bill, and he threw his arms around Banjo, kissing him several times on the forehead.

'Will you cut that out?' said Banjo, as he pushed him away.

'I've got so much to tell you,' said Bill.

'Well, you'd better place your white honky ass at the table and tell me all,' said Banjo, bursting with enthusiasm. 'Wait, wait, I've got your favourite on the stove.'

Minutes later, Banjo reappeared from the kitchen. 'One jug of Bickley's homemade mango rum, and one chicken stew with extra suicide sauce, comin' up, Mr Honkyman, sir!'

The two of them dined and chatted until dawn, as Bill unfolded his amazing story.

Over the next few days Bill remained with Banjo, where he tried his best to relax and recuperate from his ordeal. It was Chico's death that was Bill's most vivid nightmare, and the vision of how instantly destructive those three heavy machine-gun bullets had been to Chico's face and head would haunt Bill's sleeping hours for some time to come.

A week passed, and Bill decided he needed to get back to his moorings in the port. Banjo had some bananas to deliver to Aunt Nellie, and so the bananas and Banjo's bicycle were loaded on board and the two of them set sail for town.

As Bill slowly manoeuvred *Miss Blarney* into port, Banjo noticed some people pointing at them from the shore and he mentioned it to Bill.

'That's very odd,' said Bill. 'I wonder what the hell that's all about.'

No sooner had they slotted *Miss Blarney* into her berth than Aunt Nellie came running down the quay, shouting and waving. 'You is the talk of the town, Honkyman!' she cried. Nellie was dancing a rumba, a samba and salsa all at the same time. She was simply bounding with excitement. As Bill stepped onto dry land she gave him another one of those huge Nellie hugs, where Bill's head would disappear between her giant bosoms.

Days before, the chief police commissioner had telephoned Nellie and told her the full story of Bill's involvement in getting rid of Jacob and his men. Naturally, from her market stall Nellie had revelled in the gossip of it all, and in no time the word was well and truly out.

Nellie insisted that Bill and Banjo escort her home, and as they passed each shop, the shopkeepers would come running out to say 'thank you' to Bill. What Bill had failed to know was that Jacob had a stranglehold on the town through his protection rackets. Thanks to Bill, that no longer existed, and people could get on with their lives without fear or debt.

The following morning Bill decided that the boat needed a thorough spring clean. His bed hadn't had clean sheets in weeks, and he didn't want to start living like a seafaring hobo. He had been forced to live like that for far too long on the *Arthurian*. Banjo had returned home and Bill was enjoying some personal time alone. What was about to happen would once again change his life.

As he opened the airing cupboard to get the clean sheets, there in front of him was Jacob's holdall. In all the chaos of the shootout with the US Coast Guard, nobody had thought about the money. The drugs had never left the Sunseeker, and the Americans were delighted in the knowledge that they had confiscated the entire illegal hoard. It had slipped their minds to search the *Miss Blarney*.

Bill closed the curtains and locked the cabin door. He was almost too scared to open the bag, and for several minutes he just stared at it as it sat on the galley table. His Catholic upbringing left him with a serious moral dilemma. If it did contain money, it wasn't his to keep. The right thing to do would be to hand it over to the authorities. Then the question would be 'which authorities?' The American government, the Jamaican government or the Colombian government?

His human frailty made him start thinking of a hundred good reasons to keep it. He had to weigh that against the odds of getting caught if he did. After careful consideration he concluded that the odds were mostly in his favour.

He slowly unzipped the bag. Wow! He counted out one hundred and fifty bundles, each containing a thousand US dollars in what were obviously used, untraceable notes. The individual bundles were wrapped in waterproof cling-film bags.

Jacob had gone to a lot of trouble in creating a secret compartment below the engine block in preparation to accommodate the parcels of drugs. Now there was the perfect place to hide Bill's newly acquired bundles of cash. With his new moral compass in play he could put it down to booty, pirate's treasure, the spoils of war. What would his hero Uncle Arthur do in such a circumstance? 'Why, he'd keep the bloody loot and tell no one, of course!'

Once his decision was made, he hid it all away. Jacob's holdall was then cut into pieces and placed in different rubbish skips. The misery that the illegal heroin trade brought to the world still weighed heavily on Bill's mind. But there was nothing more that he could do about that. After all, he'd done his duty in getting Monolo and Jacob off the streets and locked up permanently. The Jamaican government was going to be more than happy to confiscate all of Jacob's assets, including his mountain villa. So perhaps some additional good could come from that.

Bill's only thoughts now were that he mustn't leave any incriminating evidence and he must be wise enough not to be tempted to show any sudden signs of pecuniary fortune. He would continue to arrange his daytime fishing trips and to work part-time for Nellie, as normal. As far as anyone was concerned, should the question arise, the money must have been removed from the *Miss Blarney* along with all the weaponry and then put on board the Sunseeker. It had all gone down to the deep, and there was no credible person alive to disagree with that version of the story. Even the US Coast Guard weren't in a position to say quite categorically that they had thoroughly searched every hidden nook and cranny of the Sunseeker before she went down.

Bill went to bed that night with a warm glow in his heart. He had only ever experienced the struggles of life, and his working-class parents and grandparents before him were the same. He was of northern workhouse stock. He had never known a time when he could sit back in the knowledge that next week's bills could be paid without a single care or consideration, but now he could. As he lay in his bed, he thought of Janice, and how long they had been together, and how deeply he had always loved her. If only he had been more successful, he could have given her a better marriage, a better life. If he had gone to university, perhaps things might have been different, but it all seemed so far away now.

Aunt Nellie was thrilled to see Bill turn up for work on the following Wednesday. Her action hero employee was even more of an attraction now. People came not only to buy fruit from him, but to shake his hand and to say a big 'thank you' for releasing them from the torment and fear of Jacob's gang.

Bill was back in full swing on Nellie's stall and life was good.

That is, until Bill noticed a police car making its way through the thronging crowds. It stopped a few yards from the stall. Two policemen got out and made their way toward him. 'Are you Mr William Smith?' asked one of them.

'Yes,' was Bill's nervous reply.

'Will you come with us, please, sir?' said the other one.

Bill's heart was in his mouth. Had the only remaining goon done a deal for a lighter sentence in exchange for the recovery of all the money, and given a statement in prison? Had he revealed the fact that the holdall had been left in the closet of the *Miss Blarney*, and it should still be there now?

As one of the policemen assisted Bill into the back of the car by preventing him from hitting his head on the door frame, several members of the public started to push and shove and shout abuse at them. Nellie had not quite seen what was happening at first, but as soon as she realised, she came bounding up and demanded they release him immediately. A policeman held her back at arm's length and said, 'I'm sorry, madam, we have our orders. Now will you please stand back?'

As Bill was slowly driven away, crowds of his new fans began banging on the car roof and screaming at the 'filthy pigs'.

The entire journey to police headquarters was made in silence. Bill's nerves began to get the better of him and, as always when he got nervous, his right leg began to bounce up and down.

As he arrived at the police station, he was asked to accompany the officers, but he was still without restraint at this point. Bill found himself sitting alone in a room. A large tropical fan hung from the ceiling. It wobbled back and forth as it spun. Bill tried to count the revolutions as it rotated in order to occupy his time and to help subdue his extreme nervousness.

Suddenly, the door burst open. A large black man wearing a high-ranking police officer's uniform bounded toward him with a broad friendly smile and an outstretched hand. 'Mr Smith!' he boomed. 'What a pleasure it is to meet you. I'm Commissioner Thomas Healey, the chief police commissioner for the island. I'm delighted to see that you are safe and in one piece, Mr Smith. Aunt Nellie from the market and her friends were very worried about you.'

Bill's relief must have shown on his face. 'They are very good people.'

'We've been keeping an eye on Jacob and his merry men for a very long time,' said the commissioner. 'And I have now received the film taken by our American Coast Guard friends on board their helicopter. Everything is filmed nowadays due to the need to have an accurate account of events. The world is full of professional litigants, Mr Smith. Let me show you some footage of our surveillance operation.'

Bill felt his sense of relief may have been premature and his leg started to bounce again, ever so slightly.

The computer was linked to a large screen in the office. 'Now, this is the arrival at the dockside of Jacob's Mercedes motorcar,' said the commissioner. 'There's you getting out and standing nearby. I see Jacob is removing assault rifles from the rear of the car and handing them to one of his men. I'm assuming the heavy boxes are ammunition, but what was in the holdall bag that Jacob is carrying on board?'

Without the slightest hesitation, Bill replied, 'I'm really not quite sure. I think it might have been food, because we stayed out all night and they did provide food for everyone. They didn't really tell me anything; I was only there to provide the boat and steer it to wherever I was ordered to.'

The commissioner never lowered his eye contact with Bill. 'How did they pay for the consignment, I wonder?'

Again Bill came up with a credible answer. 'I assume that in these days of advanced technology, they will have sophisticated methods of digital transfer through dodgy offshore banks. Carrying large amounts of cash is too risky, I would have thought. These are extremely clever people.'

He could feel the commissioner's eyes boring a hole of disbelief right through him.

'Ah, well, that explains it, then,' said the commissioner, as he leant back in his chair.

The commissioner was well aware of Bill's newfound popularity, and it would be foolish to interrogate him further after he had just rid the streets of such tyranny. He ordered tea for the two of them and then, much to Bill's astonishment, said, 'We are very grateful indeed to you, Mr Smith. You put your own life in considerable danger. I have mentioned your case to our new prime minister during my recent progress briefing on our battle against the drugs trade here on the island. Knowing that you don't have a permanent address here, he has asked me to personally invite you and your good lady to a reception and dinner in two weeks' time at King's House here in Kingston. In case you don't know it, it's the official residence of the Governor-General of Jamaica. I can arrange for the invitation to be delivered to your boat, if you wish.'

Bill was shocked and, for a few seconds, stumped for words. 'I'd be very honoured, sir, but I'm afraid my good lady is still in England at the moment.'

'In that case, please feel free to bring a friend, provided we have their details for security reasons, naturally,' replied the commissioner.

Shortly afterwards, the two men rose to their feet and shook hands. A police car returned Bill to town and dropped him off at the market square.

Nellie and Samuel were the first to come running up to him. 'Whatever they've charged you with, I've got the best lawyers in the country. You leave it to me,' screamed Aunt Nellie.

'No, no, I've just been invited to a dinner with the new prime minister,' replied Bill.

Nellie gave out one of her deafening manly laughs and declared, 'Well, lordy, lordy, bless my soul, you really are going up in the world now, Honkyman.' She was courteous enough not to reveal that she also was going to attend the same function. Each new prime minister invited all the known social grandees and business people as a friend-making introduction to his new premiership. Nonetheless, it was still a great honour, and certainly the grandest thing Bill had ever been invited to attend. After all, he'd never even met a prime minister before, let alone hobnobbed with one.

On the Saturday, Bill was back at the market, engaging everyone with his chirpy sales technique, when from the corner of his eye he spotted the focus of his multiple fantasies: Gloria! From afar, he watched her slowly meander down the high street in his direction, occasionally stopping off to chat with people or to examine the goods that were on sale along the way. Only a narrative from the tomes of Lord Byron could describe her with any true accuracy. She was just astonishingly beautiful. This time, her cascading raven hair was tied in a neat French roll at the back, but the same designer sunglasses remained a feature on the top of her head. She obviously had a preference for peasant girl dresses; today's was a floral turquoise, which complemented her tanned olive skin perfectly.

As their mutual glances met, Gloria was first to beam a big

smile. 'Well, what's all this I'm hearing? My wild adventurer friend has turned himself into a national hero!'

'A gross distortion of the truth. Don't believe a word of it,' replied Bill.

As she came close, she noticed the cuts to the two corners of his mouth. 'You poor thing, what happened there?'

'Oh, it's nothing. One of Jacob's men thought I didn't look happy enough, so he decided to increase the size of my smile with a kitchen knife. That's all,' said Bill, with a casual shrug of his shoulders.

'I think you have a lovely smile. And you have beautiful honest blue eyes as well; they're the colour of our Caribbean sea,' said Gloria.

Hello, things are looking up, thought Bill to himself. 'Come on, come and join me for lunch at the café,' he said, not wanting to lose the moment.

Aunt Nellie was busy serving customers when Bill shouted over to her, 'I'm just going for some lunch with Gloria. I'll be back in an hour or so.'

Nellie looked over at him disapprovingly. 'Don't you go leading that girl astray, do you hear?'

Gloria caught hold of Bill's hand in a deliberate playful defiance of Nellie's scolding, and shouted back, 'Don't worry, he won't!' The two of them went off laughing out loud, knowing full well the extent of Nellie's displeasure.

Over luncheon, Gloria was most interested in getting to know the truth of what had happened to Jacob and his gang, as opposed to the distorted Chinese whispers presently circulating through the area. An hour turned into two, and Bill suddenly realised his absence from work was letting Nellie down. When he went to pay the bill, the café owner refused to take the money. The café had also been a victim of Jacob's protection racket.

The two were about to part company when Bill said, 'Look, it's Sunday tomorrow. Why don't we take the boat out and do some sea fishing?'

'What a lovely idea, I'd like that,' she replied. 'What time do you want me there, and should I bring anything with me?'

'No, just yourself. How about at the boat for eight thirty in the morning? We'll have an early start.'

'I'll see you there,' she said. She leant forward to say goodbye and kiss him on the cheek. As Bill looked into those beautiful dark mahogany eyes her silken hair brushed gently against his face, and for a fleeting second he felt an overwhelming and exhilarating sense of déjà vu.

Back at the market stall, Bill was greeted by the sullen, dour face of Nellie.

'You is lookin' just a bit too smug for my liking, Honkyman,' said Nellie sternly. 'When that girl's parents left here and Gloria decided to stay, I made a solemn promise that I'd take care of her and make sure no harm came her way. I intend to keep that promise.'

'Don't worry, she'll be fine. She's a big girl,' said Bill as he placed a reassuring hand on Nellie's shoulder.

'You're damned right she's a big girl, and that is precisely what worries me when I see old wolves like you with saliva dribbling down your chops,' said Nellie, as she wagged her forefinger in his face.

Bill laughed and gave her a big affectionate hug. 'She's coming out on the boat with me tomorrow, and we are doing a bit of fishing, that's all. Why don't you come with us? Gloria would like that!' He said this knowing full well that Nellie hated being on the sea, because in a previous conversation she had casually told him that she always got dreadfully seasick.

'No, you go and enjoy yourselves. But you make sure your intentions are honourable, and that's all I'm saying on the subject,' said Nellie, as she turned her back on him to serve another customer.

That evening, Bill dipped into his secret hoard of cash and removed two hundred and fifty dollars. He now felt confident enough that the police chief was happy to accept his explanation of events relating to Jacob's holdall and the missing money.

He raced to the supermarket and stocked the galley kitchen with all the ingredients that he believed a man would need in order to impress a sophisticated young woman. He now knew that the champagne needed to be served chilled, and that posh people insisted on foie gras with their toast over a common pâté. He bought spices and salad and planned to make a tarragon chicken dish: the only dish he'd ever practised and mastered, so far. Very recently, he'd also discovered that Heinz salad cream, which had been a requirement in every English working-class household since Heinz introduced it in the 1920s, should be replaced by a more cosmopolitan salad dressing. A fine-quality balsamic vinegar and olive oil should do just fine.

His plan was to drop anchor out at sea, cook a lovely meal and spend a leisurely day in the arms of his Venus in paradise, with a bit of fishing thrown in.

At eight thirty in the morning to the very second, Bill saw her strolling down the quay. She was wearing a pair of white short-shorts and a stripy blue and white T-shirt with white sneakers. On her head was a matching peaked baseball cap and, of course, the inevitable trademark sunglasses.

'Permission to come aboard, Captain?' she shouted.

'Looking like that, I can say without fear of contradiction that you are the most suitably dressed able seaman to ever step aboard this vessel under my captaincy. Permission well and truly granted, sailor!' was Bill's reply.

She sat next to him at the wheel as he manoeuvred *Miss Blarney* carefully out of the harbour. Even the tiniest awkward manoeuvre would have blown his credibility as this perceived swashbuckling buccaneer. The boats were packed in tight at the moorings and weaving through them did require extra skill.

Out in the open sea Bill got Gloria to assist in baiting the lazy man's fishing lines before helping to hoist the sails. She was a keen student, and quickly learnt how to trim the sails and to watch the flow of the ribbon tell-tales. Before long she had full control and Bill thoroughly enjoyed watching her fight the wheel and guide the boat, slicing it through the waters at around twelve knots. Bill was particularly happy at the fact that she had chosen to remove her T-shirt and shorts, only to reveal a striking red bikini underneath. *This view from the stern is absolutely unsurpassable and I must savour this moment for my old age,* thought Bill to himself.

Lunchtime beckoned, and they managed to find the most romantic inlet bay with a beautiful palm-lined beach: the perfect idyllic place to drop anchor and to rest. The lazy man's fishing lines produced six modestly sized fish, but Gloria showed no interest in taking them home and she recommended that Bill give them to Nellie or Samuel.

As Gloria lay on the deck sunning herself, Bill got busy in the galley, but not before delivering her a bubbling flute of Taittinger Nocturne. He handed it to her quite nonchalantly without saying anything, as if champagne in the afternoon were all in a normal day's routine for a man such as himself. The meal was also a magnificent success and received with a flurry of gushing compliments.

Throughout the rest of the afternoon, Bill thought very carefully about his next tactical move. This first date together was not the time to leap on her at the first opportunity, he thought. Out alone on a boat, she might feel threatened. After all, this was a beautiful and highly sophisticated young woman, and she would have had numerous baying young stallions attempting to seduce her the minute they met her. *A mature man should know how to take his time, to be cool, be a little mysterious,* he thought. *If I can show self-control, but at the same time signal interest, and I return her safely home without spooking her, the prize will surely follow.*

Gloria was happy to hand over control of the wheel as they re-entered the port.

No sooner had Bill gently manoeuvred *Miss Blarney* back into her berth than Gloria alerted him to the sight of a police car with full lights flashing coming down onto the quayside. Bill's recent acquaintances, the same two policemen, stepped out of the car.

'Good evening, Mr Smith, sir. I have a letter from the Prime Minister's office for you, sir,' said one of them.

Bill politely accepted it and casually dropped it onto the galley table. 'Thank you, gentlemen,' he said, as they prepared to drive off.

Bill said nothing further. He knew that the curiosity would be killing Gloria, and after about three minutes she said, 'Well, aren't you going to open it?'

'Yes, I'll open it sometime,' said Bill, as he continued with his chores.

Another five minutes passed.

'When are you going to open it, then?' she asked.

'Sometime soon.' He was teasing her mercilessly.

'If I got a letter from the Prime Minister, and he sent a police car to deliver it, I would not be dilly-dallying in opening it,' she said, getting herself into a fluster.

'Oh, I'm sure it's nothing of any importance,' said Bill, as he started to wash the dishes from their luncheon.

'I've never in all of my life met a man quite like you, Bill

Honkyman Smith,' she declared. It was music to his ears; he knew then for certain that his bait had been taken and he intrigued her.

'OK, OK, I'll open it now, just to please you,' said Bill, with a pretend weariness in his voice. He silently read it to himself and then said, 'The Prime Minister is inviting me to a reception and dinner at King's House in Kingston, that's all. See, I told you it wasn't anything important.' He glanced back down at the letter. 'Oh, I see it says that I can bring a guest! You wouldn't happen to know anyone that might be a suitable companion for me to take along to it, would you?'

Gloria leapt into the air, wrapping her legs around his midriff and her arms around his neck. 'Yes, me, you silly man!' she shouted.

It was at that moment that Bill got his first taste of the sweet nectar of those beautiful full lips. Their kiss segued into several briefer kisses. 'I can't think of anyone in the entire world that I would want to have by my side more than you,' he said, as he engaged with those deep mahogany eyes.

'Thank you, thank you so much for today. It has been the most wonderful day that I can remember,' she said, as she tenderly kissed him again.

He knew that she had to go to work in the morning, and so the two of them walked hand in hand up into the square. Bill joined her in the taxi, returned her safely to her home, and ordered the cab driver to take him back to the *Miss Blarney*.

Her house was quite grand, and built in the colonial style. Bill had always known that Gloria's people had been comfortably off, but the size and style of the house were considerably more than he had expected. Nellie had already informed him that Gloria lived there alone, save for a resident housekeeper who had previously worked for her parents. Bill suspected that Gloria must still get some sort of allowance in order to be able to run such a large household. He was under strict instructions from Nellie not to pry into Gloria's family history, but now that their relationship was getting closer, he felt assured that she would reveal her story in good time.

Chapter Fourteen

On the Wednesday, Bill arrived as usual at Nellie's stall. Her face was one enormous beaming smile. Gloria had told her in microscopic detail of the events of her day aboard the *Miss Blarney*, and Nellie was delighted that Bill had behaved as the perfect gentleman. He had very wisely won the approval of the one person who could have scuttled his future chances of seduction.

Nellie advised Bill as to where he could hire a white tuxedo for the big reception in Kingston, and also of the only place in town where he could acquire appropriate black patent evening shoes. Bill had to get this right. In addition to the Prime Minister and the Governor-General, the British High Commissioner and the American Ambassador would be in attendance, according to Nellie, who was the fount of all knowledge on such matters.

Bill began to get butterflies; he had never been to a black tie event in his entire life before. Gloria thought otherwise of him, of course, and he was determined not to commit any social gaffes or make a fool of himself in any way.

The day arrived, and Bill had arranged to pick Gloria up from her home in a taxi. As she opened her front door to him, he gasped out loud.

Only in the cinema had Bill ever seen such radiant beauty and sartorial elegance. A full-length black satin dress hugged every contour of her perfect female form, right down to the ground she stood on. Her naked shoulders and the tops of her breasts were there for all to admire, and such a glorious sight was punctuated only by three strings of white akoya pearls. Her hair was neatly tied back in that familiar French roll that

Bill loved so much, and a diamond and pearl bracelet on her wrist complemented a pair of single pearl earrings.

'Wow, you look absolutely amazing,' said Bill, as he stepped back a pace in order to absorb the *tout ensemble* before him.

'You look pretty amazing yourself,' came Gloria's response.

Inwardly, Bill had to agree with her. He'd never been this dressed up, and he liked the idea that his white jacket accentuated the depth of his tan. His well-groomed moustache and his recent visit to the barber's gave him a distinctive British RAF fighter pilot look.

As they arrived at the grand entrance, two Jamaican soldiers stepped forward in their red and black tunics and peaked caps. One of them opened the car door and the other gave a brisk military salute. Gloria seemed to take it all in her stride, as if it were all quite normal.

As they were shown into the ballroom, they were approached by a very distinguished-looking black gentleman who was festooned with an assortment of medals and wore a red sash under his dinner jacket. He said in a loud voice, 'Gloria! Don't you look lovely?'

Gloria embraced him with a kiss and then turned and said, 'Your Excellency, may I introduce you to my friend, Mr William Smith? Mr Smith, His Excellency, the Most Honourable Sir David Allen, Governor-General of Jamaica.'

Bill gave a little nod of the head and said, 'Your Excellency.'

'You're quite the celebrity, Mr Smith,' said His Excellency. 'I've been learning a great deal about your exploits in ridding our island of some of its most undesirable sons. Well done; we owe you our gratitude. Let me introduce you to our new prime minister.'

Gloria and Bill were led through a parting of the people to a place where the Prime Minister was busily engaged in conversation. His Excellency interrupted. 'Prime Minister, this is Mr Smith, the gentleman the chief police commissioner briefed you about recently.'

'Indeed I do know of Mr Smith, and a very warm welcome to you, sir!' The Prime Minister shook Bill's hand vigorously. He then turned to Gloria and said, 'Gloria, you grow more beautiful with each passing day. How are your parents doing?'

'Missing Jamaica, I believe, Prime Minister,' was Gloria's reply.

'You must persuade them to come back,' said the Prime Minister.

Just at that moment Bill heard an unmistakable manly laugh coming from the centre of the room. Sure enough, there was Aunt Nellie in all her brightly coloured African floral finery, complete with the traditional knotted scarf upon her head. She and the American Ambassador were killing themselves laughing at what was obviously a strictly private joke. She saw Bill and Gloria and gave them an enthusiastic wave.

The toastmaster called everyone to dinner, and Bill and Gloria found themselves seated next to the British High Commissioner Dr Angus Farquhar and his lady wife. Dr Farquhar was a ruddy-faced, no-nonsense Highland Scot, with a frail, mousey, red-haired little wife. He introduced himself and opened the conversation. 'I'm Gus Farquhar, and this is my wife, Morag. Been hearing all about you, Billy! A job well done. I believe that Jacob and his boys gave you a bit of a bad time of it!'

Bill was taken aback by such overfamiliarity, and, to add insult to injury, he couldn't stand people calling him Billy. 'It wasn't too bad. They roughed me up a bit and kicked me in the nuts a few times. There was one good thing that came out of it, though. I have a much bigger smile now, since one of them cut my mouth open with a kitchen knife.'

Morag started to gag and retch at the very thought of it, and

Gloria, forever a diplomat, instantly changed the subject of conversation. Bill began to relax; he was not intimidated by Farquhar's overbearing nature, and he made sure to give back precisely what he got.

Eventually, Farquhar thanked Bill for a thoroughly enjoyable evening. 'You're my kind of man, Billy. I get sick to bloody death of attending these dinners with a load of kiss-arse sycophants. You and your wee lassie here will have to come to us for a proper dinner. Morag's a fine cook!' he said, laughingly.

I don't think so, thought Bill to himself.

As the evening drew to its conclusion and everyone started to leave, the American Ambassador approached Bill and thanked him for his contribution in capturing the Colombians and Jacob's gang. He explained to him just how important that contribution had been. Not only were the two gangs responsible for hundreds of millions of dollars' worth of drugs being brought into the United States each year, but their people-smuggling business was now proving to be even more lucrative. They had only recently become part of the global network of people traffickers. What had started off as sneaking a few Mexicans into San Diego via Tijuana had developed into an international cartel. It included everything from doing deals with the Saudis, smuggling migrants into Europe from North Africa and the Middle East in order to spread the influence of Islam, to taking control of the sex slave industry by importing underaged Russian girls as prostitutes. The Ambassador said that Bill would be a marked man should it ever be realised that he hadn't died on the deck of the Sunseeker, as was presumed by Jacob and Monolo. However, the Ambassador assured him that in conjunction with the British MI6 the US would be keeping a watchful eye on Bill's safety, without appearing to intrude into his life.

Whilst the Ambassador was speaking to him so frankly and confidentially, Bill had to pinch himself. *Little more than a year ago I was unloading trucks in the Goods Inwards department at Rawley's, and now I'm discussing my involvement in solving international crime with an American ambassador. That beats Uncle Arthur's adventures, hands down. I bet he'd be really proud of me if he could see me now.*

Gloria and Bill stepped into their taxi and Bill gave the instruction to take them to Gloria's address first. Gloria had a change of mind and exclaimed, 'No, change that address if you will, please, driver. Take us to the quayside instead.'

Bill couldn't believe his luck and remained silent.

'Well, we've still got another one and a half bottles of champagne in your galley fridge, haven't we?' said Gloria, with a smile and a twinkle in her eye.

When they got on board, Bill hardly had time to close the cabin door behind them before Gloria started to undo his bowtie. She slipped his jacket from his shoulders and threw it to one side. He stood there as an obedient child being undressed and made ready for bed. His inexperience made him think to himself, *Crikey! She's not losing any time here. Making the first move and taking control of things must definitely be a Caribbean woman thing. These women know what they want and they just go for it.*

In a split-second flashback, he distinctly remembered Sophie behaving in exactly the same way in their brief encounter.

As Gloria was unbuttoning his shirt, she gave a sudden gasp of surprise when his bare chest revealed the Mayombe tattoo of a haloed scull. She tried to step back to inspect it further, but he tightened his grip around her waist.

'Oh my God, where did you get that? I've seen it somewhere before, but I can't think where!' she said, as she gazed up at him.

'I am the only white man to be initiated into the Mayombe Vodou brotherhood. It's a long story and I'll tell you some other time,' said Bill.

The very thought that Bill might be involved in something so thoroughly mystical, sinister and primeval excited Gloria even further. 'Have you ever killed anyone?' she enquired.

'Yes!' he answered abruptly.

The role of the seducer instantly reversed, and their lips were almost touching at this point. 'I only kill people I don't like,' he whispered. He could feel her breathing become heavier and the palpitation of her heart increasing. He was in charge now.

As he kissed her tenderly, her surrender was instant and before long they were devouring each other with an animal savagery, the like of which he had never experienced before. There had always been a set formula to lovemaking with Janice, but this was raw and unbridled, it was almost brutal. It was the most exciting physical experience of his life. His harnessed testosterone had waited patiently for this moment, for this was a sexual banquet that just had to be gorged upon.

There was no rest for the two of them. Bill had become a man possessed by a demon of passion so powerful that as the first beam of sunlight streamed through the cabin window, Gloria declared that she could take no more of it. The two of them lay back exhausted and just laughed out loud with giddiness.

'Well, Mr Bill Honkyman Smith, you've surely shattered the black man's myth tonight. I've only ever had three boyfriends in my life, but I've never had the gates of heaven open up quite like that before. That was just amazing,' she announced.

Bill was more than pleased with his performance. He'd had misgivings as to whether he could make the grade with such a beautiful young woman as Gloria.

Needless to say, she didn't go to work that day. Instead, they pottered about on the boat, hardly ever allowing a kiss-free moment to pass them by, as all new lovers do.

As the evening drew ever closer, Gloria had to return home and Bill escorted her to the taxi rank in the square. Their parting was a torturous experience for both of them as they wouldn't be able to see each other until the following weekend.

Bill returned to the boat and sat on the forward deck. He lit his ganja pipe, poured a glass of the remaining champagne, and contemplated all of his blessings. Now he had everything life could offer, including that large stash of money hidden directly below his feet. It couldn't get any better. Was he now in love, or was he merely gripped by the most powerful clutches of lust? Right now, he didn't care. He'd betrayed his marital vows to Janice. He had broken that eternal promise. But at this moment in his life the prick of his conscience seemed far too small to matter.

The following morning Bill turned up for work at the market stall. Nellie knew immediately from the smile on his face, and the spring in his step, that Gloria had succumbed to his charms. She had to accept that she had lost control of her, and so throughout the day Nellie delighted in gossiping to Bill about all the guests at the Prime Minister's dinner.

In the weeks that followed, Bill and Gloria shared every possible moment, surviving more on their rampant sex drive than on food itself. They were inseparable, and close friends like Samuel and Kitty delighted in seeing them so happy together.

In reality, they were from different worlds. Outside the most basic primeval desires, the truth of it was that there was little in common. She was young, and beautiful; he was older, and not so. She was educated and sophisticated; he was practical and working-class. He had recently learnt that she was also a student of art history and philosophy, as well as being well versed in classical music. All three subjects were totally outside his collegial experience.

Chapter Fifteen

One day, when Bill was cleaning the boat in expectation of Gloria's weekend visit, he spotted Banjo cycling down the quayside at full speed waving his arms in the air.

'You gotta get *Miss Blarney* the hell outta here, brother!' exclaimed Banjo in a panic.

'What on earth are you going on about?' asked Bill, who was both startled and bewildered.

'There's a storm brewing, brother, and this ain't no normal storm. We see hurricanes here all the time, but this is goin' to be the king of them. It's due here in about three days' time and we gotta get *Miss Blarney* to Bickley Bay as quick as we can. I'm telling you, brother, not one of these boats here will survive it. They'll all be smashed to bits against each other. You take heed of me, Honkyman, I've seen this too many times before. She'll have a better chance of surviving there 'cause we have the mountain above the bay to shelter her, and she'll be on her own there.'

Bill stayed calm and put his common sense hat on. He may not have known too much about art history or philosophy, but he did know about practical physics and how things worked. 'OK, OK,' he said. He observed that lashed to the quay wall was a row of old heavy-duty truck tyres, which acted as buffers. 'I need four of those tyres.'

'What the hell do you want those for?' enquired Banjo.

'Yours is not to reason why! Just do as I say,' said Bill.

Banjo had to cut the thick attached ropes with a hacksaw and, with much heaving and panting, they managed to pile all four tyres onto the deck of the *Miss Blarney*.

Gloria arrived a little later with a small suitcase in hand. As any woman, she liked to be fully prepared for the weekend with every toiletry and smelly beauty product known to man.

'There has been a slight change of plan; we have to sail round to Bickley Bay because of the incoming hurricane. Banjo says we can stay at his place for a few days,' said Bill.

'No problem, sounds like fun. What on earth are the tyres for?' she replied.

'You'll find out when we get there.'

Banjo loaded his bicycle on board whilst Bill and Gloria prepared to leave the port and set the sails. The sailing was light and breezy and it was difficult to believe that a storm of such magnitude was on its way.

When they got to Banjo's dock, Bill ordered Gloria and Banjo to step ashore whilst he started the engine and steered the *Miss Blarney* to the centre of the little bay. There he dropped the anchor. They watched as he tied a rope to one of the tyres, lowered it in at the stern and secured it, leaving it free to swing several feet below the waterline. He did the same at the bow and again at the port and starboard midsection. He figured that in a heavy swell, if the boat had weights hanging beneath her, she would rise and fall with the waves and the swell, rather than be battered about by the surface torrent as she would be in her normal lightweight state. It was a practical theory that he was sure would work.

Bill dived into the water and, doing his recently learnt and rather unimpressive 'swim like a frog' breaststroke, he made it back to the quayside, where he scaled the steps hopelessly out of breath.

'I thought you'd be an Olympic-style swimmer,' commented Gloria.

'Believe it or not, that is the furthest I've ever swum in my entire life!' said Bill as he lay on the stone dock, still gasping for air.

Banjo had plenty of food in for a barbecue and an ample supply of Bickley's mango rum and ganja to make the evening a thoroughly enjoyable one for everyone. Before retiring, Bill ensured that the Presidential Suite was well pre-lit in order for Gloria not to witness the hundreds of resident cockroaches that would be lying in wait for her in the dark.

As expected, Bill and Gloria spent most of the night making love as silently as they possibly could in order not to disturb Banjo, although it had to be said that Banjo could sleep the sleep of the dead after two pipefuls of ganja. At 5am, as usual, Bill knocked Mandela off his window ledge perch only minutes before he was due to sound his morning rise-and-shine cockerel call.

The storm was not due to hit the island until around the following midday, and so there was plenty of time to make all the appropriate preparations. Banjo had lived through a great many hurricanes and throughout them all, his house had never blown down. This was mainly due to the fact that his great-grandfather had been a much smarter builder than he had been given credit for. Although it was built on the site of the original Bickley Manor, he had nestled his Heath Robinson construction into the only slight dip on top of the hill. He had also sloped the roof at such an angle to the wind that it acted as a natural aerofoil which pushed the airflow down as opposed to lifting it up. Banjo had all of his shutters in place and even Mandela and his harem of hens had their own storm shelter under the house.

The day remained gloriously sunny and Bill and Gloria went hand in hand down to Banjo's magnificent palm-lined beach. There they spent the afternoon frolicking in the sea and luxuriating in each other's company. Standing chest-deep in the clear turquoise waters they made love yet again.

Gloria was determined to teach Bill to swim the crawl in

addition to the breaststroke, and after several attempts and much spluttering, coughing and drinking mouthfuls of saltwater, he finally started to get the hang of it.

Bill was living the dream of every heterosexual man alive on the entire planet. *Heaven itself could be no better place than this,* he thought to himself as he lay on the sand with the most perfect woman he'd ever met.

The following morning there was still no sign of the hurricane. Gloria was not concerned about failing to attend work, as she knew that her office would probably be closed in readiness for what could become a national disaster. Hurricanes were an annual event, but this one was expected to be far worse than normal.

Bill decided to walk down to the harbour to ensure that *Miss Blarney* was sitting comfortably at her moorings in the centre of the bay, and Gloria said that she would like to accompany him. All was well with the boat, but before returning, Bill thought that Gloria should experience seeing the slave house. As she stepped inside she was instantly deeply distressed at what she saw. 'I've known about this place since I was a child; Aunt Nellie told me of its existence. My mother's people were brought into this room from Africa and chained to the wall by those very chains. I don't want to be in here anymore,' she said.

Outside, Bill put his comforting arms around her and apologised for exposing her to such sorrow. 'I've never asked you about your family before. I didn't like to pry.'

'It's not a secret. As a matter of fact everyone on the island knows about it. My father is a white man and he worked in the government at the time of our national independence from Britain. That's why I knew so many of the people at the Prime Minister's dinner; many of those people worked under my dad in those days. When my father fell in love with my mother, who was a local black woman, some people didn't approve of it. They were jealous of him anyway. They considered him to be part of the old British imperial regime. So they created a jumped-up charge against him of fraud and misappropriation of government funds. They gave him the option of leaving the country without charge, or staying and being imprisoned and ruined for life. The new prime minister knows the full truth, he is a good man, and that is why he said to me that he would like my parents to return to Jamaica.' Gloria continued to wipe the tears from her eyes as she spoke. After a moment, she looked up and gave him a weak smile. 'I know: why don't you show me that little boat that you sailed in from England?'

Bill led her to the boathouse and unbolted the door.

'Oh my God,' she shouted out, as she got her first sight of it. 'Nobody could possibly sail across an ocean in a boat like that. It's so small. It's ridiculous. You are quite an insane man, Bill Smith.' She chuckled to herself.

'Well, men like Tom McNally, Hugo Vihlen and many others have sailed across the Atlantic Ocean in much smaller boats than that,' said Bill.

'But that's completely bonkers!' she exclaimed, as she continued to walk round it and inspect it from every angle. 'It's not got a proper mast on it. It looks like a folding garden washing line!'

'How clever you are, because that is exactly what I had in mind when I first designed it,' said Bill, rather proudly.

She couldn't stop laughing at the fact that the hatch was made from a spin dryer door. 'This is quite simply the craziest boat I have ever seen in my life.'

Bill was delighted that Gloria was so interested, and it was obvious that her admiration of him had been elevated to an even higher level within the last few minutes.

'Can I get inside it?' she enquired.

'Of course you can. It might be very smelly in there. Don't

forget I lived in that confined little space for months,' said Bill.

The *Arthurian* was freestanding and propped upright with wooded supports. Gloria had to be given a leg-up to climb up onto the deck area. She opened the hatch and manoeuvred herself in very carefully. 'You're right, it really does stink in here,' she shouted.

There was complete silence for a couple of minutes. Then Gloria's head appeared from the hatch.

'You fucking dirty, slimy, deceitful, lying, perverted bastard,' she said.

At this stage, Bill was still smiling.

'Oh those!' he exclaimed, realising that she had seen the semi-naked pictures of Sophie on his cabin wall. 'I got those on the Internet.'

'No you didn't, you lying fucking piece of shit.' There was real venom in the delivery of those words.

Bill was shocked, mystified and upset at Gloria's overreaction to a few photographs of a near-naked girl. He spluttered and panicked. 'No, honestly, I really did get them on the Internet. They are just some pictures of my son's girlfriend, that's all.'

'That's even worse! What kind of screwed-up father has naked pictures of his own son's girlfriend on his wall? You are even more of a perverted scumbag than I took you for a minute ago!' she screamed. 'I can't believe Sophie would stoop so low as to put pictures of herself on the Internet like that, so that every dirty old pervert can ogle her tits.'

'Sophie? How do you know her name is Sophie?' asked Bill.

'Because she's my fucking little sister! That's why!' screamed Gloria.

'Oh my God, this can't be happening to me. No, please tell me I'm just having a nightmare,' pleaded Bill.

'Oh, you're having a fucking nightmare alright. Don't you

dare touch me.' Gloria hurriedly climbed out of the cabin and tried to jump down. Bill begged her to hear him out, and he moved forward to catch hold of her as she descended from the boat. 'Don't you dare come anywhere near me again, you lying low-life fucking monster,' she yelled. She stormed out of the boathouse and headed up to Banjo's place with Bill in hot pursuit.

Bill was almost crying at this point. How could life go from such heavenly bliss to such abject misery at the blink of an eye?

Banjo, as usual, was sitting on his porch rocking back and forth smoking his ganja pipe when Gloria reached him. 'Banjo, I'm taking your bicycle. I'll leave it with Nellie,' she screamed. She turned to Bill and said, 'Don't you dare try and follow me. We're finished!' With that she pedalled off at breakneck speed. Bill just stood there, still pleading with her to listen to him long after she had disappeared from view.

Banjo removed the pipe from his mouth and said, 'See, brother, now you know why I ain't gettin' mixed up with none of them womenfolk no more. They is nothing but trouble, brother!'

It wasn't exactly what Bill wanted to hear at that moment.

'Leave her be, brother. She'll cool down in a day or so,' said Banjo. Bill agreed and noted that she had gone off without her weekend suitcase, and so returning it to her would give him the perfect excuse to visit.

Within the hour they felt the first build-up of winds, and Banjo commented on how quickly the sea had become restless from being almost a millpond only minutes before. Bill's prime concern was whether Gloria had made it home with sufficient time to barricade herself in properly.

By nightfall, Hurricane Katherine was showing the full ferocity of her anger, with winds of one hundred and seventy-eight miles per hour. Bill prayed that Samuel, Kitty and the children would be safe. Their shanty-town home would never be able to withstand such an onslaught.

At Banjo's, by midnight the banana plantation had all but disappeared with all the plants snapped and flattened. The mango tree was uprooted and lying on its side, and Mandela's hen house had gone altogether. But lo and behold, Bickley Manor was still holding fast.

At dawn the storm showed no sign of relenting and Bill thought that he would attempt to make it to the edge of the hill and look down upon the *Miss Blarney*. He managed to crawl on his stomach the whole of the way there. To attempt to stand up would be foolhardy, if not impossible, as there were huge parts of trees and all kinds of objects, both alive and dead, flying through the air ready to impale or decapitate you. As Bill peered down, there she was, still being battered and tossed from side to side but rising and descending with the swell exactly as he had predicted. Bill's simple but ingenious strategy of applying weights was working perfectly. It looked as if *Miss Blarney* would survive the worst of it almost unscathed.

As quickly as the storm had started all was becalmed again and the sun shone once more. Birds and bees alike hovered in confusion at their new and unfamiliar surroundings.

But the eye of a storm such as this only gives sufficient time to assess the damage and little more.

As evening turned to night, the full force of Katherine's wrath returned. Bill and Banjo could do little except to strengthen and re-nail the storm shutters wherever they showed a weakness. They consoled each other throughout the night with both song and alcohol whilst hell and devastation hailed outside.

The following morning, the two of them stood on the front

porch in silence and surveyed the destruction. Where once there had been trees was now a clear vista. Banjo had the view that he had not witnessed since he was a boy. His outside shower and tank had rolled down the hill and needed rebuilding. But other than that the house remained reasonably intact.

Straight away, Banjo took his saw and started to cut the banana trees near to their bases and to clear the site. Banana trunks are soft and filled with water and they would start to re-shoot almost immediately. The *Miss Blarney* was again bathed in sunlight, and she remained motionless in the middle of the bay, looking serenely unperturbed by her recent ordeal.

Banjo was more than understanding when Bill asked him if he minded that he didn't intend to stay and help with the clean-up. Bill had to get back to town and then on to Gloria's house as quickly as possible. It would be pointless trying to sail there. Bill knew full well that the harbour would be too difficult to navigate as it would likely be filled with debris.

He strapped Gloria's suitcase on to Banjo's remaining bicycle and set off. Along the way he passed forlorn and weeping people. Some were just holding on to each other, whilst others were frantically trying to dig into the rubble of their former homes. The closer he got to town, the more anxious he became, as some houses that had appeared to be in sheltered spots were also completely flattened. As he reached the brow of the hill, there before him lay devastation of Biblical proportions. The definition of the individual roads had all but disappeared as the remains of entire houses and their contents along with boats, palm trees and everything imaginable formed a kaleidoscopic jumble of destruction.

Bill could only be guided by large still-standing landmarks such as the harbour master's house and the post office. So far, no rescue services had arrived on the scene to take charge, and everywhere people just milled around in a state of shock and confusion. The main rescue units were forced to concentrate all of their efforts on Kingston and the government areas in an attempt to coordinate the services nationwide. The entire Caribbean had been hit, and so there was no possibility of inter-country assistance except from the USA.

Bill was slowly pushing his bicycle through this sea of sorrow when all of a sudden he heard his name being called. It was Kitty and the children. They ran up to him, hugging and kissing him in sheer relief. Samuel was fine also. He was back in the area they used to call home, looking for whatever belongings he could find. They had all managed to get to the safety of St Matthew's Church and had been taken in by Father Aiden O'Malley, the Catholic priest there. If ever there was a man similar in humility and devotion to St Mother Teresa of Calcutta, it was Father O'Malley. He lived the most frugal of lives in and amongst the shanty-town poor. He had dedicated his life to caring for their wellbeing as well as their spiritual needs. The good Father's most recent project was to build a school for them, but this storm would have dashed all hopes of achieving that now. There was literally no money for such an ambitious project.

Bill had been introduced to Father O'Malley by Aunt Nellie, and shortly afterwards Bill had commented that if ever there was a man capable of restoring his faith in the Catholic Church, it would be O'Malley. Bill's affection and loyalty for the church itself had faded a long time ago, although he had retained much of his own personal religious fervour.

Bill, Kitty and the children went on together, climbing over the rubble in the direction of where Samuel was. All around them were tears of joy at souls found alive and the deepest sorrow and wailing at those found dead. As expected, in the midst of it all was Father O'Malley, kneeling in the dirt next to an old man to deliver his last rites and comforting those around.

They caught up with Samuel. He had moved on from attempting to find any more of his own belongings and was busy digging and removing corpses from the wreckage of some wooden structured apartments.

Knowing Bill's priority of concern, Samuel, Kitty and the children volunteered to accompany him to Gloria's house on the edge of town. When they got close, Bill's heart sank. He had difficulty in remembering precisely where the house had been as he'd only ever seen it in the dark. Surely, although made of timber, a large colonial house like that should be capable of standing firm against any storm.

Kitty knew exactly where the house was and her facial expression of despair said it all. She led the way to the spot, running faster than Bill could cycle.

Samuel and Bill began lifting huge sections of planks and roof tiles and throwing them to one side, whilst all the time calling out her name. Bill sobbed aloud as he continued to strain every sinew. Then one of the children unearthed the twisted frame of Banjo's bicycle. Bill now knew for sure that she had made it home. All along he had prayed that if she had not managed to outrun the storm, she would have been forced to shelter in a government building or some such place of sturdy substance. All was not lost; there was still a faint chance that she might still be alive beneath the rubble. They continued, hardly stopping to draw breath.

And then Kitty noticed a foot protruding from beneath a large timber. Frantically, they dug deeper only to reveal the limp body of Gloria's housekeeper. She was still alive, but barely. As Bill started to give her mouth-to-mouth resuscitation, he immediately felt that her ribs were mostly broken. She had suffered massive internal bleeding and she passed her last breath with Bill comforting her and holding her hand.

They removed the housekeeper's body, carefully laid it by the side of the road and returned to dig in the same area. The most likely chance was that Gloria and the housekeeper would be somewhere close together.

They were not wrong. As Bill spotted a long swathe of that beautiful black flowing hair amidst the dirt and the rubble, he gave out the most bloodcurdling scream of despair. This was all his fault. She would be alive and well if he had acted differently. Fate had dealt the cruellest of blows and he deserved to be punished mercilessly. Ever so gently Bill removed her body from the debris and cradled her head to his chest. Rocking back and forth he wept uncontrollably, his only solace being in the shared tears of Samuel, Kitty and the children.

Chapter Sixteen

Before long Father O'Malley arrived. The authorities were taking control of the situation and moving all the bodies to a central schoolhouse building. Father O'Malley was asked to identify as many of them as possible. Being the parish priest meant that he would know most of those who had perished.

With gentle persuasion the good Father got Bill to release Gloria from his embrace. He blessed her and prayed for the repose of her soul and they all joined together in tearful prayer. She was laid next to her housekeeper and in thick black marker pen, Father O'Malley wrote on her blouse in large print, 'GLORIA PALMER'. It seemed so matter-of-fact, so cold and clinical.

Samuel untied Gloria's suitcase from Bill's bicycle and placed it by her side, and Kitty noticed Gloria's sunglasses in the dust; she cleaned them and handed them to Bill. They would be amongst his most treasured possessions for the rest of his life. With his arm around Bill's shoulder, Father O'Malley led them away from the scene. 'Go home, Bill; there is nothing more you can do here,' he said.

Eventually, Bill cycled the fifteen miles back to Banjo's place, arriving late into the night. As he approached the final hill, the clear full moon hung brightly over Bickley Manor. 'What right have you to shine so bright on a night such as this?' said Bill to himself.

Banjo had feared the worst and was still up when Bill arrived home. He said nothing to him and made no gesture of greeting. He just handed him a mug of mango rum, lit his pipe of ganja, and the two of them went outside and sat on the porch in silence. Several minutes passed before Bill burst into tears.

'Let it out, brother. Just let it out,' said Banjo as he puffed on his pipe.

Over the next few days Bill just slept and walked on the beach. Deep in thought and melancholy, he contemplated all that had happened to him since leaving Rawley's. He had carried out Uncle Arthur's instructions to the letter and followed his dream of adventure. But perhaps now it was time to return home to where he really belonged, with Janice and Jack. After all, his first priority must always be his family, and he had abandoned them for the sake of his own selfish pursuits. They were still his responsibility, and the more he thought, the more his desire to do the right thing overwhelmed him. He had to get back to town to phone Janice immediately.

'Thank God you're still alive, we have been watching it all on the television, it's just dreadful. We didn't know whether you were still at sea or on the land. Where are you now, and when are you coming home? Please, Bill, please come home,' cried Janice.

'I'm OK, I'm still in Jamaica. The town nearest to us has been almost completely destroyed and we believe that the dead are in the hundreds in this town alone. I've been staying with a Rasta friend of mine called Banjo over at his place and we managed to escape the worst of it. How's Jack?' enquired Bill.

'He's not good at all. Sophie finally dumped him, and he has had deep depressions ever since. I'm really worried that he might do some serious harm to himself. To make things worse, he bumped into her this afternoon. Apparently, she has an older sister still living in Jamaica at their old family house. Mr and Mrs Palmer are deeply worried because they can't get hold of her. There's no reply from the house phone or her mobile phone. Sophie said that if they still don't hear anything within the next two days, the entire family are going to fly out there.

Hey! I've just thought of an idea. If I can get her address, perhaps you could go round and check to see that she is still OK!'

Bill remained silent and fought hard to hold back his tears. There was absolutely nothing he could do or say to make things any better at this moment.

'Bill?'

'I promise I'll be home soon, Janice. I can't leave now when these people are in such a desperate situation. They have lost absolutely everything and I've got to do what I can to help. The local priest here is called Father O'Malley and he is carrying the burden of relief for these people almost entirely alone. I'm going to stay and do what I can to help him, at least until things are a little better.'

Bill finished the conversation by saying, 'I love you, Janice, more than you can possibly imagine.' No doubt at that moment of high emotion he meant every word of it, but in saying it he removed some of the weight from the mantle of guilt which hung so heavily upon his shoulders.

There was a silent pause and Janice replied, 'You're an honest and faithful good man, Bill, and I love you for it and I miss you very much.'

Bill continued to listen to the buzz of the phone long after Janice had put it down.

At the quayside, the mechanical cranes had almost finished lifting the remnants of boats out of the dock and piling them up on the side. As Banjo had predicted, not one boat remained fully intact.

Bill decided that if he was to be of any value to Father O'Malley he would need his own base to sleep in. Samuel, Kitty and the children were still fortunate enough to be able to stay in the relative comfort of St Matthew's, but the church was almost at bursting point with homeless families. There was only one solution, and that was to get back to Banjo's and sail *Miss Blarney* round to her old moorings.

From the entire crop of flattened banana trees, Banjo had gathered a large number of bunches that would now have only gone to waste. 'Take them with you and give them to whoever needs them,' he said. The pair of them loaded the *Miss Blarney* with as much as they could, including two dozen eggs and some boxes of mangos.

As Bill docked in the port he was greatly relieved to see Aunt Nellie still alive and standing around giving out orders to everyone. She had only just emerged from her own house, which was far more substantially built than most. Nellie was doing her best to restore the market and organise the distribution of free food. When she spotted Bill, there was a very emotional reunion between the two of them.

'Where's Gloria? I thought she was staying with you at Banjo's house,' she said anxiously.

Bill couldn't contain his grief and neither could Nellie, the second she realised something was horribly wrong. When finally she regained her composure she asked, 'What in the good Lord's name happened, Honkyman? You promised me that you would look after her and always keep her safe.'

Bill could hardly force the words out. 'We had an argument and she cycled home. It's all my fault, Nellie. She was back at her house when the full force of the storm hit. Samuel and Kitty helped me find the bodies of Gloria and her housekeeper in the rubble. There is nothing left of the house.'

'Sweet Jesus, how am I goin' to break the news to her dear parents?' said Nellie, who was still sobbing profusely.

'Samuel, Kitty and the children are all well and staying with Father O'Malley at St Matthew's,' said Bill, as he tried to offer a little good news into the conversation.

'Thank the good Lord for that small mercy,' said Nellie.

'There's fruit and eggs on the *Miss Blarney* to give out to the needy. Banjo sent them. Where do you want me to put them?' asked Bill.

Shortly afterwards, Bill met up with Father O'Malley, who was assisting a dig where they had managed to release two survivors and one dead. O'Malley asked Bill if he would help another man carry the body over to the schoolhouse for identification and storage. The rescue services were trying to control the situation, but the school was in chaos and packed with people milling around. Some rooms were being used for medical assistance to the wounded and two classrooms were used for storing the dead. Heavy-duty black zip-up bags had been supplied by this time and Bill helped to place the body in one of them.

Bill couldn't help himself. He just had to make sure Gloria had been brought to the centre. Row after row of bags lay on the ground before him. Many of the tickets were unnamed. But eventually, there it was.

Female. Gloria Palmer. Found at Bristol Street.

A young woman was cutting up makeshift bandages in the next room and Bill asked her if he could borrow a pair of scissors. He carefully unzipped the body bag just enough to remove a handful of Gloria's raven locks, but he couldn't bring himself to look into her face for that final time, such was his feeling of remorse.

That evening, on board the *Miss Blarney*, Bill spent his time refreshing his considerable skill in knot-tying and he lovingly wove Gloria's hair into a magnificent Celtic knot, similar to the one Tommy Duckinfield had made for him. He laid it on his pillow and kissed it several times before tearfully fading into slumber.

*

The first delivery of coffins arrived and the identified dead were placed in them. There was no refrigeration and it was a matter of urgency to get the burials underway. Bulldozers had cleared the main roads and Father O'Malley and his team, including Bill, were still busy systematically searching the rubble of house after house. Over the next couple of days, it became easier to recognise which houses contained the dead merely by the smell of putrefaction coming from their direction.

Bill was returning home to the *Miss Blarney* after a very hard day. He was bare-chested and covered in dust from head to foot. A small, previously white smog mask hung around his neck. Ahead of him he could see Aunt Nellie standing with a little group of people. As he drew ever closer, it became apparent that it was Mr and Mrs Palmer and Sophie. They appeared distraught but composed in dignity, as one would expect from such people.

Nellie introduced Bill as 'Honkyman'. It took two or three minutes before Sophie began to recognise him.

'Bill? Bill Smith, Jack Smith's dad?' asked an astonished and bewildered Sophie.

'Hello, Sophie! I'm so deeply sorry that we find ourselves meeting again under these dreadful circumstances. I am the person who found your sister's body in the ruins of your old house,' said Bill, disguising his inner feelings.

Aunt Nellie remained diplomatically silent, realising it would be inappropriate to reveal Bill's true relationship with Gloria.

'Do you believe that my daughter died instantly, Mr Smith?' Gloria's mother was searching for even the smallest reassurance.

'I'm absolutely positive of it, Mrs Palmer. She couldn't possibly have felt any pain, I assure you of that,' came Bill's reply. At this stage of things the Palmers were under the impression that Bill was nothing more than a volunteer rescuer doing what he could to help.

As they bade each other farewell, Mr and Mrs Palmer shook his hand firmly and said, 'Thank you so much, Mr Smith, for the compassionate way that you have attended to the recovery of our daughter. We appreciate it so much.'

Sophie stepped forward; she kissed him on the cheek and said, 'Thank you, Bill. Thank you for everything. I'm sure that you are aware that Jack and I are no longer together. He is a lovely boy, but he isn't quite mature enough for me. I wouldn't want him to give up on learning to play the cello, though, just because we are not together. He has a real talent for it and you must encourage him.'

'I will, I promise,' said Bill, and Sophie once more kissed him goodbye.

As Bill turned and walked away, the torment of guilt was almost too much. He felt like Judas Iscariot. These charming people believed him to be their friend and hero, when all along he was the core reason for their misery.

The following week was Gloria's funeral. She was to be buried in a plot next to the relatives of her mother in the beautiful cemetery high on the hill, overlooking the ocean. Bill attended the service with Nellie, Samuel, Kitty and the children. To the surprise of everyone, a cavalcade of black four-wheel drive government vehicles arrived also. It was the Prime Minister and some of his officials.

After the burial service, people mingled in conversation and Mrs Palmer approached Bill to thank him for coming and paying his last respects. As she was about to move on, Bill removed from his pocket the Celtic knot of Gloria's hair.

'Mrs Palmer, please forgive me. I took the liberty of

removing some of your daughter's hair. She had such beautiful hair. I made this with it, and I'd like very much for you to have it,' said Bill with tears now streaming down his face.

'Mr Smith, that is so beautiful and thoughtful of you. How very clever of you to be able to make such a lovely object. I can't thank you enough,' she exclaimed. Then, as she was about to leave, she turned and said, 'Mr Smith, a woman's intuition tells me that there was more to your relationship with my daughter than we are presently led to believe.' She looked him firmly in the eye.

'We were the very best of friends, Mrs Palmer. The very best of friends. I would even go as far as to say "soul mates",' he replied.

She raised the lock of Gloria's hair to her mouth, kissed it, and pressed it to her breast to show Bill how much it meant to her. With a warm, appreciative smile, she turned and moved on to speak to the other remaining mourners.

Just then, Sophie came bounding up. 'Well, it looks as if we will be on our way back to living here fairly soon. The new prime minister has been talking to my dad and he has just offered him a position in his Cabinet. Apparently, some of my father's old adversaries in government are now in prison or in exile, according to the PM,' she said with a light-hearted glee in her voice. 'How long are you staying in Jamaica for?'

'I'm not quite sure, but I will be returning to England sometime in the not-too-distant future,' said Bill.

'Well, if you are still here when we move back, you and I should meet up. I was speaking to Nellie, you know, that fat woman from the market, and she tells me that you are living on a beautiful yacht which is moored down at the quay. I absolutely love sailing. Perhaps you could take me out on it sometime!' said Sophie with great enthusiasm.

Her frivolous disregard for the solemnity of her own sister's funeral turned Bill completely cold. Suddenly, she wasn't as pretty anymore. *As a matter of fact, I really don't think I could ever fancy you again,* thought Bill to himself.

After the funeral, Bill decided that he needed a break from working in the hurricane's aftermath and set off to stay at Banjo's for a few days.

Back at Bickley Manor, Banjo was keen to find out how much of the town was still standing, and whether Nellie was still alive and well. He'd not seen Bill since the day of the storm some two weeks prior, and, much as he would have been willing to help, he had no bicycle to travel there with. Bill's distressed and sombre expression told him that things were far worse than expected. Being the friend that he was, Banjo listened attentively and with compassionate understanding as Bill unburdened himself of the whole sorry tale.

'You need a break from all that stuff, man. You're gonna make yourself seriously sick. Shit happens, brother. You didn't set out to get that girl killed. How in hell's name could you have possibly known that the horny little missy on your wall was gonna turn out to be her baby sister? This life is made up of "if only"s, man. If only the chicken hadn't crossed the road. If only I hadn't poked a stick in my eye. Sweet Jesus, brother, you gotta stop blamin' yourself all the time. You is a good man with a great big heart,' said Banjo.

Bill listened in silence as Banjo tried to make things better by ranting and raving in Bill's favour.

'There is something I have to do, Banjo. I'll need you to help me,' said Bill, calmly and quietly.

'I don't like the sound of that. What crazy notion is runnin' through that honky head of yours? I'm tellin' you, brother, it's always better to sleep on decisions first before you go actin' on them. I'm talkin' sense right now, Honkyman, and you'd better listen good, d'ya hear?' Banjo was almost scolding him.

'I know you are, Banjo, and I appreciate your concern for my state of mind, but this is something I've been thinking about since Gloria's death. We'll do it tomorrow evening. Just go along with me on this one, my friend,' said Bill.

Banjo left the room, still tutting and shaking his head with concern.

The following morning, Bill sauntered down to the boathouse. He wanted to take a final look at his trusty floating home, the *Arthurian*, and spend a little time alone with her.

'Well, old friend,' he said aloud, 'you and I have now come to the end of our journey together, and the time has come for us to part company. You have sheltered me and protected me against everything the ocean and the elements could throw at us, and I am eternally in your debt for that, but our adventure is now done. I feel I just can't sail in you any more after Gloria.' He slowly walked around her, tenderly touching all of her oceanic battle scars and scrapes. He took in deep breaths of that unforgettable smell of the sea and the salt that came out from her flaking paint and her barnacle-covered hull. Bill climbed aboard and sat on the deck next to the open spin dryer door hatch. With great care, he reached down into the cabin to remove that precious photograph of him and Janice taken at St Bernadette's youth club, and placed it inside his shirt. 'It is only fitting that I take nothing more than that from you.'

By the evening, Bill invited Banjo to join him down at the boathouse.

'I want you to help me to launch the *Arthurian*,' said Bill.

'Is that it? Is that what all this mystery stuff is about? Why didn't you just say that in the first place, brother? I didn't sleep last night wonderin' what crazy notion was in your head.'

'I'm going to give her a Viking burial,' said Bill.

'Viking burial! What in God's name is one of them? Ain't those the white dudes with cow horns on their hats?'

'Yes, you've got the right idea, but historically there is little evidence to prove that Vikings actually did put horns on their helmets,' said Bill.

'I ain't lookin' for a history lesson, brother. I'm just wonderin' what is goin' on with this Viking burial thing.'

'At the receding tide we set her alight and push her out to sea. There is going to be just one difference between this Viking burial and the traditional ones. I'm not going to be on board when she goes down,' said Bill, much to Banjo's relief.

'Why would you do that, man?' asked Banjo. 'You spent years makin' that boat, it don't make any sense to do such a thing, Honkyman. You love that little boat! You and her are real partners.'

'Yes, I do love her dearly, and that is precisely why I have to destroy her. I look at it this way, my friend. It is the penance that I have to pay to God for the atonement of my sin. Gloria was the last person to sit in the *Arthurian* and that is how it will now remain for evermore,' said Bill with a melancholic tone to his voice.

'There you go again, brother. Blamin' yourself for everything. I hope you ain't thinking of letting that outboard motor go down with her as well, are you? I can't think the good Lord would have much use for one of them. I got a little rowin' boat in the back room that would fit that just fine.'

'Of course you can have the outboard, Banjo. After all, Viking burials didn't include outboards,' said Bill with a smile on his face.

Bill helped Banjo get the rowing boat out and attach the outboard motor to the back of it. They decided to give it a test run and, lo and behold, the engine fired up with the first pull of the cord. Banjo let out a loud cheer. He was thrilled to bits with his new gift and the two of them lowered it into the water. 'I don't like boats at the best of times, brother, but I have a mind now to potter around in the Bay and do me a little fishin',' said Banjo.

They released the support beams and manoeuvred the *Arthurian* down the slipway and into the water.

'Are you absolutely sure you want to go ahead with this, Honkyman?' asked Banjo, anxiously.

'Yes, I've made my mind up, there's no turning back now,' replied Bill.

Banjo handed Bill the cigarette lighter that he used for lighting his ganja pipe. They attached a tow rope from the *Arthurian* to the little motored rowing boat. As the *Arthurian* bobbed around in the water, Bill was revisited by the vision of her in the dock at Liverpool, and the excitement that Tommy and Les had when Bill chugged her around for their first inspection of her seaworthiness. A lump came into his throat. He felt like the master of an old and much-loved pet dog on the day he had to take it to the vet to have it put down.

Bill decided that he wanted to be able to remember exactly where her final resting place was, and so, rather than allow her to drift out to sea, he would drop the anchor before setting the torch to her. The little rowboat fought hard to tow her at first. It was as if the *Arthurian* knew of her fate and was struggling, aware that the end was nigh.

When they got just past the centre, at the perimeter of the bay, Bill dropped the *Arthurian*'s anchor for the very last time. Climbing on board, he lit a rolled-up rag and dropped it into the hatch just where his pillow was. For a couple of minutes he peered in, just to ensure that the fire had caught. First to feel the lick of the flames were the Internet photographs of Sophie, but then Bill spotted Tommy's Red Ensign and before the flames caught hold he managed to rescue it. 'That is definitely coming home with me,' said Bill to himself.

Banjo sat on the wall at the quayside with his legs dangling over the edge as he watched the entire proceedings. Bill joined him, and the two of them observed in silence as the smoke billowed out of the *Arthurian*'s hatch.

'You and them Vikings sure is the craziest bunch of dumbass dudes ever to walk this earth, brother,' said Banjo, breaking the silence.

At that point, a small gas canister used for Bill's cooking stove exploded, sending a plume of flame shooting up in the air which ignited the sails.

'Whoa!' shouted Banjo.

Quickly, it became a floating inferno, and acrid, toxic smoke from the ignition of the high-density foam and resin caught alight. Bill was deeply affected as he watched the painted Union flag and the words 'Cohen's Emporium' blister and distort before being engulfed by the furnace. The mast began to list to one side as the fire raged on. And then, in the most dramatic way possible, a half-tin of petrol which had been kept below the cabin floor exploded, sending flaming bits of structural resin in all directions. The remaining part of the hull sank, leaving only small fragments of burning debris afloat. *Arthurian* was no more. In a little prayer to Uncle Arthur, Bill felt sure he would have agreed that Bill had done the only right and honourable thing possible.

The two of them continued to sit in silence, staring out to sea, for several more minutes until Bill said, 'Sorry about your bicycle.'

'Does that mean I ain't a two-bicycle household no more?' replied Banjo.

'Yep, I'm afraid so. We recovered it from under the rubble of Gloria's house,' said Bill.

'As you know, brother, I don't worry my head about material things. Forget about it.'

'I'll buy you another one,' said Bill. And the two of them continued to sit in silence until the last flaming embers disappeared.

Chapter Seventeen

Over the next week, Bill finished restoring the outside shower and toilet facility whilst Banjo worked to get his crop of fruit trees back in order, ready to yield afresh.

Bill had done what he could and he returned to the town in order to help with Father O'Malley's project of rehousing the homeless, including Samuel and Kitty.

The tin shacks began to rise again, and Samuel was busy re-erecting his old place on roughly the spot it had originally stood. For the moment Bill allowed him to continue, but he had other plans in mind for Samuel and his family.

On the outskirts of the shanty town, closer to the market square, was an area of bungalows. They were of solid construction, mostly breezeblock with corrugated iron roofs. Apart from roof damage, most of them had survived the storm reasonably intact, including Aunt Nellie's house. They had proper facilities of electricity and running water, with gardens big enough for some fruit trees and a chicken run. They also had clearly defined property boundaries with title deeds as proof of legal tenure.

Bill knocked on the door of one of them. A 'For Sale' sign, which had been crudely painted on the wall with a paintbrush, had obviously been there a very long time. The paint had faded and was partly covered by more recent graffiti. The yard was an unkempt mess of mud and discarded items.

A large black man wearing shorts and a torn white T-shirt answered the door. Bill stated his enquiry and the man invited him in. Five or six children and the mother were sitting around the living room. Just then, two large dogs entered and began barking at Bill. They were scolded by the father and led into another room.

Apart from the overbearing stench and general squalor of the place, the building appeared to be sound. Bill was shown around with the entire clan following him from room to room. It was a substantial property with three good-sized bedrooms, a bathroom that had never seen a toilet brush or bottle of bleach and a kitchen that was in similar condition. The plumbing and the electrics appeared to be in reasonably good shape as the house had only been built about thirty years before. Much of what was required was little more than elbow grease and cosmetics.

'How much is it on the market for?' asked Bill.

'Forty-five thousand American dollars,' came the reply.

'And how long have you had it for sale?'

'It's a good area here but things don't always move very quickly. It's our Caribbean way. We don't like to rush into things. We painted the "for sale" sign four years ago,' said the father of the household.

'I'll give you thirty thousand US dollars and not a penny more. I don't do things the Caribbean way and I am in a rush. It will be thirty thousand in cash. I'm not in the business of negotiating, so take it or leave it,' said Bill as he made his move to leave the room.

The husband looked at the wife, and the wife looked at the husband. In unison they both said, 'We'll take it.'

'I will instruct a lawyer to draw up a contract, and once it is established that you do actually have a legal title to the freehold of this property we will exchange contracts fairly quickly and you will get your money,' said Bill with his businessman's hat on.

As Bill walked away from the property, he could hear the yelps of excitement coming from the family who had just had their lives turned upside down. Bill walked back to the *Miss Blarney* and thought to himself, *Wow! That was easy. I like being rich.*

The following morning, Nellie recommended her own lawyer in Kingston, but Bill didn't give her any information as to why he required the services of the law. Eventually, curiosity got the better of Nellie and she pressed Bill on the matter.

'I'm doing a bit of real estate business and I need you to help me find some decent tradesmen, if you would, please, Nellie,' said Bill.

'Sure, no problem. Am I guessin' this means that you is thinking of settling here in Jamaica full-time?' enquired Nellie.

'My plans are a little vague at the moment, but who knows what lies ahead? Anything is possible,' said Bill, not wanting to give too much away.

Over the coming weeks the property conveyance went through without a hitch. Bill had to pay the lawyer some under-the-table money in order to overcome the question of why Bill had walked into his office with just over thirty thousand US dollars in cash. Once work began, Bill asked Samuel and Kitty over to assist in the planning of the garden, and he also sought their advice as to what colour the house should be, both inside and out. They were thrilled and excited at the prospect of Bill living in a permanent home nearby. Kitty joked with Bill that he might need the service of a cleaner and housekeeper when he eventually moved in. She had been a domestic servant for white people before, and so she had experience of working in nice houses such as this one, she said.

Nellie's workmen had cleared the property of all the rubbish. They installed a new fully tiled bathroom and kitchen. The garden was now mostly laid to lawn with a selection of palms and fruit trees. There was a new enclosed hen house and chicken run at the bottom of the land. It was unrecognisable from when the previous occupants were in residence.

Nellie paid an impromptu visit as the workmen were tidying up and putting the finishing touches to it. She was anxious to know that they had done a good job and that Bill was satisfied with their work. She was amazed at the transformation and how clean and comfortable it now was. 'You'll be as happy as a hog in a mud bath in here,' she remarked.

Elsewhere, poverty and devastation were still prevalent. It was heartbreaking to witness, and Bill was deeply affected by it. There was a clearly defined line between the haves and the have-nots. The rich people were merely inconvenienced by the hurricane whilst the poor suffered pitifully.

Bill stocked the house with the essentials, such as kitchen utensils, beds, bedding and some basic furniture, all ready to move in.

Samuel and Kitty were invited over to see the completion of the work. Kitty was particularly keen to accept Bill's invitation as she had not seen it since the decorating had been completed and the furniture brought in. She entered the house, surveying all around in wonderment like a child entering Santa's grotto. 'Oh, Bill, it's just beautiful,' she said.

'I'm so glad you like it. See, Kitty, I took your advice and painted it in all the colours that you suggested,' said Bill, seeking confirmation of approval.

'Yes, you certainly have, and I'm very flattered, Bill, it looks wonderful,' said Kitty, as she continued to explore the rooms. 'You must be really excited! When are you moving in?'

'I'm not!' said Bill.

'Oh, have you just done it up to sell it again and make a quick profit?' enquired Samuel.

'No, I've done it because I want you and Kitty and the

children to move into it,' said Bill. 'I want you to have a decent roof over your head, Samuel. I want your children to have the best start in life and the best education we can give them, and I want that more than anything for you.'

Samuel dropped to his knees, covered his face with his hands, and wept into them. Kitty flung her arms around Bill and hugged him tightly. She couldn't speak. There was an element of absolute joy and of disbelief at the same time. This didn't happen in the real world.

'We could never afford to pay the rent on a property like this,' said Samuel, as he gazed up at Bill.

'Who said anything about rent?' asked Bill. 'Men of property don't pay rent; only tenants pay rent.'

'I don't understand,' Samuel replied.

'I have arranged it with the lawyer that on Tuesday, the three of us are going to his office in Kingston. There, the ownership of this property is being transferred into both of your names. You will own it and the land it stands on, and nobody can take it from you from that day forward. It's yours!'

Samuel's whole body was shaking as Bill helped him to his feet.

'When I first came here you took me into your home. You shared your food with me and offered me every possible kindness. This is just my way of paying you back,' said Bill, as he placed his arm over Samuel's shoulder. 'I think it wise that you let people think that you are renting it at a greatly reduced rent, even Aunt Nellie. You know she can't keep a secret. There is always the possibility you may suffer resentment from people if they think that you suddenly own the property outright.' He smiled. 'Now, come out and see the garden. We need to go to the market and buy some good laying hens for that hen house of yours.'

They were overwhelmed with excitement and they couldn't

wait to get back to the children and make preparations to move in. Bill learned that day just how enjoyable an experience it is to give rather than to take.

He knew in his heart of hearts that he couldn't keep Jacob's money for himself. Even though one hundred and fifty thousand dollars was more than he had ever dreamed of possessing in his life, and it would change his and Janice's lives forever, his conscience just wouldn't allow him. Every penny of that money had been extorted by protection racketeering and the misery of drug addiction. It was from these very people, the poorest in society, that Jacob had built his fortune, and somehow Bill had to get it back to them where it rightfully belonged.

The solution came to him the following day. At first light, Bill found Father O'Malley busy helping some volunteers lay a single pallet of breeze blocks in the building of his new school. The good Father had abandoned the idea of employing a contractor to do the building. After all, where would he get the hundred thousand dollars required to erect the basic structure with toilets, wash basins and a roof? With the help of a little unpaid labour, Father O'Malley was building it brick by brick himself.

'How's it going, Father?' asked Bill, chirpily.

'Well, Bill, at the present rate of progress, I reckon I should have it completed in about ten years,' said the Father, wearily.

Bill smiled. 'Have you thought of praying for divine intervention?'

'There is never a night that goes by when I don't ask the good Lord for a little help with this project, Bill. I fear that God has a lot more pressing problems to deal with around the world than my little school,' said the Father.

'Perhaps your solitary voice is too small a sound for him to hear! What you need is to get your entire congregation in on the act. Get them all to pray out loud together at Mass. Aren't you the one that keeps preaching to everyone that if you have enough faith, you can command a mountain to move, and it will? Isn't that what it says in the Bible?' enquired Bill, pretending to be a bit naive.

'Well, yes, it does say that, but there are things in the Bible that aren't meant to be taken too literally. Let's say they are to be given a little bit of licence for flexibility in the interpretation,' said the Father.

'Tut, tut, Father! Oh ye of little faith,' replied Bill, as he left the conversation.

The following Sunday, Bill attended Mass at St Matthew's Church and midway through the Mass, Father O'Malley spotted him in the congregation. Their recent conversation must have registered with the good Father because when he rose to the pulpit to give his sermon he started off by saying, 'I want to start by thanking all of our volunteers who are so good in helping me build our new school. I fully appreciate that the work is very hard and the progress is slow due to our lack of funds. The one thing that I as your priest am guilty of is never seeking your help in asking our blessed Lord for help and guidance in completing our task. So I think it is time for all of us to say a very loud prayer to him, and we'll keep on asking him every Sunday until he hears our prayers.'

Bill felt quite smug at the fact that he'd had some influence on the priest and he went into the sacristy after Mass to meet him. 'I'm very impressed, Father.'

'Well, Bill, what you said was quite right,' said the Father. 'I'd forgotten the fundamental principle of faith in the Lord to provide the answers and the solutions. I realised that I needed help, and if all of my flock have total faith then we have a better chance of our prayers being answered.'

As the priest was busy removing his vestments, Bill

discreetly undid the latch to the sacristy window just enough so that it wouldn't be noticed. He had a plot in mind.

Bill knew that Father O'Malley had a routine whereby he would lock the church each night and return to his home in the shanty town. He would then get back in the morning to reopen the church at 7am. You could set your clock by him.

Bill said his goodbyes and hurriedly made his way back to the *Miss Blarney*. There he counted out one hundred bundles of a thousand dollars each and removed the cellophane wrappers. He loaded the loose cash into two pillowcases, making sure to remove, as far as he could manage, any trace of cocaine powder. He waited until the dead of night.

When all the town was asleep, Bill successfully made haste unnoticed through the streets and got to the church at around 2am.

It was a considerable relief to find that Father O'Malley hadn't observed the unlatched window, and Bill threw the two bags in before climbing somewhat clumsily through it himself. His heart began to palpitate with an uneasiness at doing such a daring deed.

With no street lights to help lead the way, the place was in almost complete darkness, save for the flicker of the solitary lamp of perpetual light which burns to the side of every Catholic altar. There is an unpleasant eeriness about wandering a darkened church by night, and Bill had no inclination to linger any longer than was necessary. He ascended the altar steps and sprinkled the cash over the altar, taking great handfuls and throwing them up in the air. Some of the notes landed on top of the large altar candlesticks and the tabernacle, as if they had fluttered down from heaven itself. The rest he scattered around the floor. With the job complete, he couldn't wait to make a hasty retreat from the place. Making sure he left no trace of entry, he balanced the latch so that when he closed the window with a bang, the latch would drop into place and lock the window again.

Back at the *Miss Blarney* his nerves were still shaking him and before retiring to his bed, he lit a pipe of ganja and sat back to contemplate his good deed.

By the afternoon of the following day, Bill was sitting quietly on the deck of the *Miss Blarney* when some excited locals ran up to ask him if he had heard the latest amazing news. Father O'Malley had received a heavenly gift of all of the money for the new school. 'It's a real miracle!' they cried. Rumours were spreading like wildfire that he had had a vision from the Virgin Mary, who had given him the money personally. It all added credibility to the Father's already saintly status within the community.

It was several days before Bill bumped into the holy man himself.

'I'm sure that by now you must have heard of our great good fortune, Bill,' said the priest.

'Indeed I have, Father. You see, one must never underestimate the power of prayer! I'm told that the Virgin Mary had something to do with it,' said Bill, with a big smile on his face.

'Yes, apparently she did, and it would appear that the Blessed Virgin has an interesting pastime. As I counted the notes I noticed a build-up of white powder on my fingers. It would appear that the Holy Mother is not averse to snorting the odd bit of cocaine! Now, what do you think about that, Bill?' asked the priest, looking hard into Bill's face with a knowing expression.

'Well, that is a turn-up for the books, Father. Mind you, who could blame her after what those rotten bastards did to her son?' answered Bill, chirpily. 'God has a habit of surprising us all; he works in some very mysterious ways, Father!'

'We'll pray and be thankful, and say nothing more about it.

Except only that it's going to change the lives of the youngsters of this community forever. With an education they will have a chance in life that would be impossible otherwise. Whether it was the Holy Mother herself, or just some kindly soul with a conscience, I am eternally grateful, and I say that the gates of heaven should open wide to the one who is responsible for this remarkable gift,' said the good Father, resting his hand on Bill's shoulder.

Bill felt good about himself. He had secretly left a legacy that would benefit the future of so many of these people. He had never really felt comfortable benefiting from Jacob's drug money. It was on a par with wearing blood diamonds and knowing where they came from.

Samuel and Kitty moved into their wonderful new home, and a couple of days later Bill arrived back at the *Miss Blarney* to find a small basket full of eggs neatly bedded in straw. They were the first results of their new laying hens. Bill was touched by their thoughtfulness; he'd not eaten such delicious freshly laid eggs in years.

Aunt Nellie had got the market back up and running, and Bill returned to work for her, three days a week. In the aftermath of Hurricane Katherine's terrible destruction, understandably, the tourist trade had completely collapsed, and there was little chance of Bill embarking upon his day fishing business now. He was running out of money; there were only a couple of thousand dollars of Jacob's money left, and he still had one more debt to pay.

He got the bus into Kingston. Things were returning to normal there and Bill made his way to a bicycle repair shop that he'd noticed on a previous visit. Sure enough, there it was, back in business. The roof had disappeared but it was business as usual. Bill did a deal on a beautiful traditional-styled bike with four gears and a basket on the front. He then got the shop's owner to weld a wide two-wheel basket trailer together and bolt it onto the back. He knew from personal experience how difficult it was to ride a bike loaded with bananas that were only tied on at random. This would make Banjo's transport problem immeasurably easier, and Bill spent the entire day assisting the owner with its construction. His next stop was at the paint shop, where he purchased three tins of paint: black, green and gold, the colours of the Jamaican flag, which represented the black community that lived there, the lush green tropical vegetation on the island and the sun that shone upon it.

Bill cycled back to the *Miss Blarney* and set about the job of designing the bike's colour scheme. His meticulous eye for detail ensured that it was a professionally finished job and after three days' work he was delighted with the end result.

Life returned to its normal leisurely pace and Bill sailed over to Bickley Bay to deliver Banjo's present. He found him out in the garden planting mango trees. The place now looked remarkably well ordered by Banjo's standards.

'Hey, brother, your timin' is perfect, man! I've got four more mango trees to plant,' said Banjo.

'Yes, of course, but first I've got a present for you, and I need a helping hand to carry it up the hill,' replied Bill.

'A present for me? You already gave me an outboard motor, man. Since you's been gone I've already been out fishin' twice and caught dinner both times, brother. I don't need no more presents from you; you're too good to me as it is.'

'Well, let's say this is payment of a debt more than a present,' said Bill.

The two of them strolled down to the quayside and there, standing proudly on the deck of the *Miss Blarney*, was Banjo's new quad-wheeled trailer bike, resplendent in its Jamaican livery.

'Wow! Well, ain't that the most beautiful thing to behold next to the first time I saw Tina Turner's shakin' ass?' screamed Banjo.

The two of them unloaded it off the boat via a makeshift gangplank. Banjo rode his new toy round and round the slave house and up and down the quayside, singing and whooping out loud as he went. Bill showed him the use of the gears; he'd never owned a bicycle with changing gears before.

'This is one awesome machine, brother,' shouted Banjo. He was like a five-year-old on Christmas morning. They managed to get it up to the house and Banjo parked it right in front of the porch, where he could just sit and stare at it with joy.

Back at the town, Bill bumped into an equally jubilant Father O'Malley. He had just secured a contract with a Canadian company to complete the building of the new school, and they were due to start almost immediately.

'What are you going to call your new school, Father?' enquired Bill.

'I was going to dedicate it to St Matthew just as our church is. But I'm open to suggestions,' said the priest.

'Why not name it after the church's most recent saint, St Mother Teresa of Calcutta?' asked Bill.

'What a wonderful idea, Bill. St Teresa's School it is!' said the priest. He repeated it over and over to himself as he walked away.

It had been several months since Bill had spoken to Patrick in Toronto, the owner of the *Miss Blarney*, and so he telephoned him.

'Bill! You're alive!' shouted Patrick from the other end of the line. 'I thought you might not have survived the hurricane when I didn't hear anything from you, and there was no way I could get a hold of you.'

'It has been devastating here and there has been considerable loss of life,' said Bill. 'I've had little call to use the phone recently. I've spent a great deal of my time helping the local priest to rescue and restore some order to the place.'

'I can only assume that the *Miss Blarney* didn't survive the hurricane? We watched the news coverage and saw the boats in the harbour all smashed to bits. It showed them being dragged out of the water and piled high on the quayside,' said Patrick.

'Well, you may be surprised to know that the *Miss Blarney* is in perfect shape. I managed to get her over to a small protected bay which is owned by a friend of mine. I stopped her from being tossed around into oblivion by tying submerged tyre-weights to allow her to rise and fall with the swell,' replied Bill.

'Oh my God, that's amazing,' said Patrick. 'The thing is, Bill, I don't quite know what to do. The insurance company has already paid me out! They didn't take any convincing that the little boat was lost, and they just paid up straight away. I think the best thing would be for you to paint the name out and re-register her under a different name. When you fill out the form, you will just have to say that the boat was never given a name. My wife eventually died and it is highly unlikely that either my daughter or myself will want to go back to sailing in the Caribbean. So congratulations, Bill! You are now the proud owner of a very nice sailing boat, and I can't think of a nicer person to own her. Happy sailing! If you give me an address, I'll send you the relevant receipts and paperwork.'

Bill couldn't believe his luck. Or was it just good karma? Perhaps the good Lord really was repaying him for his compassion toward others.

Now, Bill was able to use Samuel and Kitty's new home

address for his own correspondence and as a contact point. But the fact was that he was going to have to keep his recent promise to Janice and to end his wandering days fairly soon.

In his solitary moments aboard the *Miss Blarney,* he was beginning to spend more of his time soul-searching. Much as he loved Janice and Jack and missed them both, if truth be known, could he ever really settle back in England? He'd wholeheartedly embraced his new carefree, laissez-faire lifestyle of no responsibilities. Nowadays he awoke each morning to the sunshine, waving palm trees, and the rhythmic sounds of the clinking of ropes against hollow aluminium masts. Save for his loyalty and obligation to Aunt Nellie, he had nowhere to clock in at and no pressing engagements. In England he awoke each day to grey skies and police sirens, and having to endure copious amounts of parochial small talk from unworldly pub politicians down at his local working men's club.

Here, he was somebody, he was liked and respected by everyone. He kept asking himself, 'Could I seriously return to being just another faceless working-class bloke living in a council house?' Surely, he'd moved on from that. More than ever, he could appreciate why his uncle Arthur couldn't settle down again after living the sort of exciting lifestyle that Bill had now also lived.

Bill made contact with the Jamaica Yacht Registration Office based in Florida and made progress toward registering his ownership and naming the vessel. He had carefully painted out 'Blarney' from both sides of her bow. There was only one suitable name that Bill wanted to replace it with, and that was *Aye, Miss Gloria.* He was sure that the double entendre would not go unnoticed by those who knew him well on the island.

Chapter Eighteen

Weeks passed, and Bill appeared to be no closer to returning to England, although the intention was always there. Samuel and Kitty had settled into their new home and were becoming acclimatised to what they had always previously perceived to be a luxury lifestyle. Samuel's good fortune now spurred him on to make sure not only that his children got the best education, but that they could always hold their heads up high in life. He wanted them to grow up not only educated but sophisticated also, just as Gloria had been.

For the first time in their lives they had a dining table to sit at, and Samuel was insistent that the whole family would sit together for their evening meals. He relied heavily on Bill to teach his children good table manners. Although Bill was from humble beginnings himself, his strict mother of Irish descent was a stickler for good manners at all times. 'Manners maketh the man!' she would always say. Bill distinctly remembered being scolded by her for holding his knife like a pen or for putting his elbows on the table. Children were 'seen and not heard' in Bill's childhood household, and no child would ever get up from the dinner table without saying, 'Please may I leave the table?' It was always 'may I?' and not 'can I?' At school, Bill remembered being mocked by some of his classmates for being too la-de-da posh whenever he asked the teacher if he could be excused.

One night, Bill was returning home early to the *Aye, Miss Gloria,* having had a thoroughly enjoyable afternoon meal with Samuel and Kitty. Kitty had gone to a huge amount of effort and cooked the most delicious meal for everyone.

As he approached the quayside he noticed the cabin door was open. It was of little concern to him and he couldn't remember precisely whether he was responsible for it or not. After the big hurricane clean-up, apart from a Coast Guard vessel, Bill's was the only boat afloat in the harbour. Everybody knew she was his and so no one would touch her.

As he started to descend the steps into the galley, he realised he had a visitor. It was Sophie!

'Hello, big boy, remember me? I like the name of the boat,' she exclaimed.

'Hello, Sophie. What brings you back here so soon?' asked Bill, with an almost cold tone of disdain. He was really not pleased to see her at all, and made no effort to embrace her or to show her any signs of affection, although his inner man couldn't help but observe that, as always, she did look tantalising, alluring and nubile in her white V-neck T-shirt and hip-hugging jeans, ripped at the knees.

She sat on the built-in galley table and began swinging her legs back and forth, just as she had done in his shed back in England.

Bill scanned her from top to bottom, trying not to allow his gaze to linger too long on the contours of her breasts. She was wearing open Roman sandals and he'd never noticed before how perfect and beautiful her feet were. Everything about her body was soft and unblemished.

Bill was determined to keep her at arm's length. He knew what was really behind that innocent little girl façade. He'd seen the real Sophie, and her callous behaviour shortly after Gloria's funeral. She was the siren that could lure him to his death, a manipulative vixen, a clever, self-indulgent, spoiled young woman who took plenty and gave little. He realised that the loss of her older sister now meant that her parents' affections would be lavished solely upon her. They would be extra protective of their only remaining daughter.

She was highly dangerous and Bill knew how vulnerable he was at this point in the conversation. If he continued to show signs of hostility, who knew what she might accuse him of if she took a dislike to him? On the other hand, if he made a sexual advance, the result could be the same. He was between a rock and a hard place. He was an older man, a foreigner. Who would believe him over a beautiful, innocent eighteen-year-old Caribbean girl, whose father now worked closely with the Prime Minister? He decided to remain as pleasant and as diplomatic as possible.

'My mother thinks that you were screwing my sister,' she said.

Her comment came like a thunderbolt out of the blue, and Bill was startled but remained outwardly calm.

'Yes, your sister and I did make love. I adored her,' was Bill's quiet response.

Sophie laughed out loud. 'Did you shag her on that bed over there?' she enquired. Before he could find an answer, she jumped off the table. 'Have you got any wine in this place?' she asked.

'There's an opened bottle of white wine in the fridge. It may not be that great; I used some of it for cooking a few days ago,' said Bill.

'Do you want some?' she shouted, as she poured herself a glass, then drank it down in one and topped it up again.

'No, I'm fine,' said Bill.

Just then, from behind him he felt her two hands grasp his shoulders. She leant down and her hair fell over his chest. He could smell the clean fragrance of her perfume and feel her breath on the back of his neck as she started to kiss it gently, moving round to the lobe of his ear. She whispered, 'I want you to take me on that bed. I want you to do everything that you did with Gloria. I want you to do it with me.'

Bill could feel his battle of resistance starting to flounder, and his irrepressible arousal rising fast. 'I was in love with Gloria, Sophie, and I'm not in love with you,' he said, fighting hard to resist the waves of sensual pleasure that now flooded over him.

'I don't care,' she whispered. 'I just want you to fuck me till it hurts.'

That was it. Bill's battle was lost, and he swung her round so that she was sitting on his knee. Sophie was a woman who liked her sex hard and rough, and even violent. She dug her nails deep into Bill's flesh like a cat with its prey and the two of them writhed from one side of the room to the other, crashing against the cupboards and knocking things to the floor. The whole place looked like a demolition site by the time they got over to the bed. Eventually, after an exhausting hour and a half, they fell back and dozed in each other's arms. Bill was now eating of the forbidden fruit, and it tasted ever so sweet.

Sophie was first to wake, and she carefully stepped over the clutter and debris as she headed in the direction of the water closet. Bill observed her curvaceous naked body as she went. Gloria had been slightly taller, more slender and statuesque than Sophie, whereas Sophie was more womanly and rounded. Her breasts were larger than Gloria's; she was more breeding stock than racing stock, which, as an older man, was Bill's preference. More mature men generally prefer their women to have a bit of meat on their bones.

Suddenly, Sophie realised the time. Her parents would be worried as it was now just after midnight. They both quickly got dressed.

'I'll walk you home,' said Bill.

'OK, it's not far. My parents are renting a house until we can get something more permanent,' said Sophie.

They kissed in the dark near her parents' gate and Bill

waited until Sophie was safely inside the house. Both parents were still up and Bill could hear her father shouting, 'What time do you call this? Where the hell have you been?'

'I spent the evening with my friend Carole. I've not seen her since we lived here when I was a little girl. I was just on my way home at about nine when I bumped into Bill Smith, you know, the lovely man at the funeral. We got talking about Gloria and how we both miss her so much, Daddy. Did you know that he was madly in love with her? And you'll never guess what he has called his yacht. He's called it *Aye, Miss Gloria*. Get it? "I miss Gloria",' said Sophie, trying to lighten the mood and divert the wrath of her father.

'Oh, isn't that wonderful, darling?' said her mother. 'How sad for the poor man. They must have been very close for him to do that. It's odd that she never mentioned that she was in a relationship in any of our most recent correspondence from her.'

'I know, why don't we invite him over for dinner, Mummy?' said Sophie, bursting with enthusiasm.

As usual, Mr Palmer was outgunned; it was the price he paid for living in a house full of women.

'What do you think, Daddy?' asked Sophie.

'Well, I don't see why not. He seems to be a nice sort of chap,' said Mr Palmer.

Bill returned to the boat, lit his ganja pipe and said to himself, 'Oh my God, what have I got myself into now?'

He thought to himself that heading back home before any serious collateral damage was done to his marriage was his best option. If it ever got back to England that he'd had sex with his own teenage son's ex-girlfriend and her sister as well, heaven only knew what repercussions that would have. Janice would be devastated and would more than likely divorce him. Janice's vows of marriage had always been sacrosanct. His own mother would never forgive him either because she and Janice had always been very close. His mother would think that he'd committed the most grievous mortal sin, akin to murder. And as for poor Jack, the fact that his own father had just gone and shagged the first true love of his life didn't bear thinking about.

The following day Bill decided to telephone Janice. He was determined to be happy and upbeat and tell her how much he loved and missed her, and that he was so looking forward to seeing her again. A manly voice answered the phone.

'Hello, Jack! How are you, son? I hardly recognise your voice any more, it's been too long. Is Mum there?' asked Bill, chirpily.

'It's not Jack,' came the reply.

'Oh, who are you, then?' enquired Bill, somewhat taken aback.

'It's Don, Don Wilson.'

'Don Wilson! What the hell are you doing there? Put Janice on the phone, it's Bill here!' Bill's voice pitched slightly to anger and impatience.

'She's just popped out for a minute, Bill. I just called round to see that Jack was OK,' came Don's hesitant reply.

'Well, put Jack on the phone, then!'

'He's not here either.'

Bill was suddenly not happy. 'Tell Janice that I'm coming back home very soon!' was his angry command.

'Shall I tell her to phone you back when she comes home?' said Don, somewhat sheepishly.

'No, I don't have a bloody phone here!' Bill put the phone down abruptly. That hadn't gone to plan at all. What the hell was that bloody Wilson up to?

Bill's mind began to race and he started to scan the passage of time for clues. Wilson used to regularly call round on the pretext of encouraging Jack to join his son Mark in various sports events. On more than one occasion Bill had found him in the kitchen having a cup of tea with Janice. It had all seemed quite innocent at the time. Perhaps it was; perhaps it wasn't. No, Janice would never betray her marriage vows.

Then Bill remembered how keen Wilson had been to take her down to St Ives in his car in order to attend Bill's final farewell launch, instead of having her join Bill, Les and Tommy in the Transit van. And how she was tipsy with Wilson by the time Bill arrived at the Sloop Inn. It was all fitting into place, now. 'That bloody Wilson has been sniffing round my Janice for years! I'll bloody well kill him when I get hold of that sneaky bastard,' shouted Bill.

Bill had to seek solace from his friend Banjo, and the very next day he set sail for Bickley Bay. He hadn't slept well at all.

Back at Bickley Manor, Bill poured out the whole sorry tale to Banjo, who listened silently whilst he rocked back and forth on his chair, puffing on his pipe. Bill, on the other hand, paced up and down to unburden his angry tirade. Eventually, Banjo leaned forward to give his learned counsel.

'What the hell is it with you honkies? You get yourselves all uptight about nothing! So what if your woman has the odd bit of jiggy-jiggy with some dude? It don't mean nothing, brother! Here in the Caribbean our women do it all the time! We is all at it, man.'

'What?' screamed Bill. 'That's why nobody here ever knows who their father is! Where I come from, we have standards, we have moral codes, we have marriage vows, we have rules! It's what makes us a civilised society!'

'Well, well, well, will you listen to the high 'n' mighty moral honkyman? You weren't thinkin' those thoughts when you were dippin' your white dangly bit into those two little honey pots, brother!' was Banjo's defensive retort. 'Look, man, from what you tell me about your woman, maybe she hasn't been jiggy-jiggy with this guy. But, if she has, you gotta forgive her, brother. After all, womenfolk get lonely and need a bit o' lovin' just like us menfolk! So you think hard, brother. It ain't no big deal. And that's my advice, so let's have a smoke and some of my latest batch of Bickley's magic mango juice, and stop worryin' your head, brother!'

Bill began to feel a little bit better about the whole business and apologised to Banjo for his outburst. The more he thought about it, the more he convinced himself that there was no way that Janice would betray him. For a start, she didn't really care much for sex at the best of times. She nearly always appeared to be bored by it and considered it to be more of a Catholic wife's duty. She was far too religious and she would be scared that Bill's mother, or one of the local gossips, would find out that she had a lover.

However, back in England, Janice went into an overloaded panic when Don told her that he'd answered the phone to Bill. 'What on earth did you say to him?' she asked.

'I told him I'd just popped round to see that Jack was OK. I don't think he bought that idea, though. He was not happy that you weren't at home and neither was Jack,' said Don.

'Oh, my God. What are we to do now?' said Janice, as she stared out of the kitchen window.

Don stood behind her and put his arms around her waist and cupped her two breasts in his hands.

'Get off, I'm not in the mood,' said Janice as she shrugged him away.

Don persisted and laughingly tried to kiss her neck. 'You were certainly in the mood last night, you gorgeous horny woman.'

'Look, Don, this is serious! Bill's a good man, and my marriage could be on the rocks if he thought that you and I were at it!' said Janice, who was now beginning to feel the remorse.

'Oh, don't worry about him. He'll soon find someone else. You were going to leave him anyway. He's got to find out sooner or later, so why not tell him now?' said Don, beginning to sound slightly agitated.

'No, it's not fair. Bill has only stayed on in Jamaica to help rescue and to bring comfort to those people suffering there. I can't do that to him at a time when he is only thinking of others.' She went over to the front door and opened it for Don to leave. 'I think you should go now, Don. I need some time on my own.'

He kissed her as he left and said, 'I'll phone you later!'

She didn't answer.

Janice was now in a state of moral inner turmoil. She had never intended to have an affair with Don; it had just happened. It had started long ago when Bill had begun building that damned boat and he had progressively become obsessed with it. Don had slipped in and given her the attention that Bill had neglected to. Don made her feel desirable and sexy, whereas Bill hardly noticed her even when she made a great effort to look nice. Janice was always aware of one thing, though, and that was that Bill loved her. They had been together since they were teenagers and things had just become stale, that was all. They were both totally without sexual experience in those early days, and their repression and fear of religious damnation had prevented either one of them from ever experimenting.

Janice was about to take the biggest gamble of her life. She decided that she would confess to Bill's mother and seek her advice. She thought that it was better to attempt to make her an ally by letting her know, before Bill found out about the whole sordid affair. She hoped that her mother-in-law's almost saintly nature would be understanding and forgiving.

The following afternoon, she went round to Bill's mother's house. Bill's mother could read Janice like a book and the second she opened the door she said, 'There's something wrong. Come on. Tell me all about it; I'll put the kettle on.'

Janice was handed a cup of tea and she burst into tears as she unravelled the whole story. Bill's mother listened patiently and at the end of it said, 'Who knows about this?'

'Only you, Don and me,' came Janice's sniffly reply.

'Well, for the time being we all say nothing. Little said takes little mending; nothing said takes no mending at all.' Bill's mother was a wealth of old-fashioned, but highly profound, sayings. 'You know, Janice, we are only human, and we all have our frailties and our expectations. Let me tell you my little secret. Bill's father was a drunken fool; he was a bad provider and only ever thought about himself all the time. I stuck with him for the sake of Bill until it was too late for me. Over those years I was married to him, I had three secret lovers. It was the only thing that kept me sane. Every time he came home drunk, I would look at him and know that there was someone else out there who thought that I was attractive and of value.'

Janice's jaw nearly dropped to the floor. To hear such a frank confession from Bill's deeply religious mother was absolutely mind-blowing. Janice had always been under the impression that Bill's mother was the archetypal downtrodden wife with no life of her own, when all along she was bonking outside her loveless marriage.

His mother asked, 'Do you love Don?'

'No, I still love Bill, he's nothing like his father. It's just that Don was so different, so affectionate and flattering. It all seemed really naughty and exciting at the time.' Janice hesitated. 'I desperately don't want my marriage to end. Bill is a good man. He would be devastated if he knew that I'd had sex with another man. I don't think he could cope with it.'

'Finish with Don, if that is the case, and just put it down as one of life's little experiences, and get back to making your marriage work. We'll say nothing more about it,' Bill's mother said.

Janice walked home on a cushion of air. She felt that her problem shared really was her problem halved. Her admiration for her mother-in-law had just gone through the stratosphere.

Don didn't take the news lightly, but the truth of the matter was that the excitement of seducing another man's wife was beginning to fade a little. He was the sort of man who would be looking for his next conquest. As a matter of fact, unbeknown to Janice, he already had another woman in his sights, and so Janice would have lost everything and forfeited her marriage by staying with him.

CHAPTER NINETEEN

In Jamaica, Bill was back in port. The mooring fees were soon to be due, now that he was the new boat owner, and he had to think of a modus operandi. He only had about fifteen hundred dollars of Jacob's money left and he would need that for his airfare home.

He could always moor the boat at Banjo's for free, but, realistically, how often was he going to be able to return to the Caribbean to go sailing? He would never be that rich a man. He had been away far too long, and there were pressing engagements he needed to deal with back home, so sailing her back to England was also a non-practical solution.

The answer to his prayer came a week later. Bill was busying himself in the galley when he heard a tapping on the hull of the boat. It was Mr and Mrs Palmer and Sophie. His initial thought was of trepidation that they were going to confront him over the Sophie incident, but that was instantly dismissed by Mrs Palmer's big smile. 'Mr Smith, do please forgive us for calling upon you like this, but Sophie insisted that we come down to see your lovely boat. I hope I'm not too presumptive in saying that *Aye, Miss Gloria* has some reference to our late daughter?'

'Indeed it does, Mrs Palmer. Your daughter was the most wonderful and beautiful young woman and I don't mind telling you that I loved her very much,' said Bill.

Sophie, who was standing behind her parents, started to lick her lips in a very provocative way and make lewd gestures by rotating her two forefingers around her nipples. Bill ignored her silly little game.

'Gloria never mentioned that she was in any kind of serious relationship,' said Mrs Palmer, enquiringly. 'There was the occasional boyfriend, but nothing too serious, and she would always tell us that she had moved on from whomever.'

'I think that Gloria was a little hesitant to tell you because of the considerable age difference between us. She probably wanted to wait a little longer to make absolutely sure of her feelings before telling you,' said Bill.

'I'm sure she would be very flattered if she knew that she had a beautiful boat like this one named after her,' said Mrs Palmer. 'If you are not otherwise engaged, we would be delighted if you would join us for dinner tomorrow evening, Mr Smith. It may be a little rough and ready as we haven't finished unpacking yet. We are looking for a house at the moment and so we are only in rented accommodation for the time being.'

'I'd be delighted to; that would be lovely. Please, now that you are here, come aboard and have a look round,' said Bill.

All four of them descended into the cabin. As Mr and Mrs Palmer were inspecting the sleeping area, Sophie had her hand behind her back, trying to rub Bill's genitals. Bill pushed it away and continued to explain the workings of the Perkins diesel engine, the GPS and the galley kitchen.

The Palmers were quite taken with the boat and, shortly afterwards, said their goodbyes. 'Until tomorrow evening, then,' said Mr Palmer with his parting handshake. Sophie kissed Bill on the cheek and winked at him before leaving.

Come the next day, Bill arrived at the Palmer residence suitably dressed and armed with a bottle of French wine. Throughout the entire dining experience, Sophie tortured Bill by running her bare foot up and down his trouser leg and generally made a nuisance of herself. Naturally, Bill was petrified that one of her parents would notice, and the more tormented Bill appeared to be, the more Sophie delighted in expanding the risk of being caught. Mr and Mrs Palmer were the most gracious and charming of hosts and the food was magnificent, but by the end of the evening Bill was a nervous wreck from the antics of Sophie.

Sensing that the Palmers might possibly be interested in buying the boat, Bill employed a sales tactic before leaving. 'I was wondering, perhaps I could repay this wonderful evening by inviting you all to go sea fishing this weekend. How does that sound?'

It took a millisecond for Sophie to shout out, 'Oh, that would be super! We'd love to go. Wouldn't we, Daddy?'

Mrs Palmer responded, 'Well, it would be rather nice, but we don't want to intrude.'

'No, I'd be thrilled to take you out. The weather forecast is for perfect sailing conditions for the weekend. It will be fun,' said Bill, with great enthusiasm.

On the Friday, Bill got the bus into Kingston to buy two bottles of champagne and some quality food in preparation for the Palmer trip. He was desperate to make a good impression. At 8am sharp, he spotted the family heading down toward the mooring.

'Permission to come aboard, Captain?' shouted Sophie. That was exactly what Gloria had said the day that Bill took her out on their very first sailing date together.

'Permission granted,' was Bill's reply.

The Palmers had come loaded with bags. They had also brought champagne.

'Oh, you needn't have brought anything with you, I have ample champagne and food in the fridge, but thank you anyway,' said Bill, politely.

'I think the time has come to break with the formalities,' said Mrs Palmer. 'Don't you? I'm Audrey Palmer and my husband is Charles.'

'I'm Bill.'

Sophie interrupted. 'Everyone on the island calls him the Honkyman, Mummy.'

Charles Palmer appeared surprised and spoke up. 'You're not one and the same Honkyman that everyone in Government House is talking about? The chap who is responsible for getting rid of the drugs gang from Colombia as well as that dreadful local Jacob's gang?'

'Oh, it was nothing, Charles,' replied Bill, rather modestly.

'Forgive me, I didn't make the connection. I had no idea that we were in such esteemed and heroic company!' insisted Charles. Audrey was keen to learn the full story and pressed Bill to reveal all, but Bill continued to dismiss it as a trivial event.

'Have you sailed before, Audrey?' asked Bill, trying to change the subject.

'Yes, indeed. When Charles worked for the Jamaican government before, we were very keen sailors. We had a much smaller boat than this one, called the *Cirrus Cloud*, but when the children came along we had less time, and so reluctantly we got rid of it. We always said that we'd love to take it up again when the girls were older, but circumstances changed and we had to leave for England. I'm sure Gloria will have told you of our misfortune.'

'Yes, she did, and it's a small consolation that you have been able to return here to the place you love most of all,' said Bill.

'We are close to Gloria and that's important to us,' responded Audrey.

Sophie had gone below deck and reappeared wearing a black bikini the size of three postage stamps.

'For goodness' sake, Sophie, haven't you got something less revealing to wear? You're almost completely naked!' cried Audrey.

'Oh, don't be so old-fashioned, Mummy. I'm sure Bill's not embarrassed, are you, Bill?'

'No, no, Sophie's not got anything that I've not seen before, Audrey,' said Bill. Sophie laughed out loud. Only the two of them knew how true that throwaway remark was.

Within the hour they were heading into deep water and Bill set and baited the rods for everyone. Things couldn't have gone better. Almost immediately Charles hooked a yellowfin tuna. It took him at least an hour to land it, and when they finally pulled it on board and Bill got his weighing scales out, it landed at eighteen pounds six ounces. Shortly after luncheon, Sophie and Audrey, aided a little bit by Bill, landed a ten-pounder. Not exactly prize-winning fish, but respectable nonetheless. It was a glorious day and things couldn't have been more enjoyable. Bill managed to avoid paying close attention to Sophie by sticking closely to Charles. It created a 'boys on one side, girls on the other' scenario, which greatly lessened the burden on Bill. A sexual innuendo too far by Sophie could have scuttled the day and changed her parents' view of Bill.

'So what are your plans, Bill? Are you planning on staying here in the Caribbean?' asked Audrey.

'No, I have some pressing engagements back in England that need attending to,' said Bill.

Sophie glared over at him. He was petrified at that moment that Sophie would remind Audrey that back in England, Bill was the dad of her former boyfriend, Jack. That very same boy that Audrey had started to give cello lessons to. At their first meeting before Gloria's funeral it had been glossed over and, in a distressed state, Audrey had not quite grasped the connection. Had she really thought about it, she would have realised that Bill was already well and truly married and totally unsuitable for her daughter, Gloria. Sophie didn't let the cat out of the bag; after all, she didn't want to spoil things for herself.

Back at the port, Charles and Audrey thanked Bill profusely for such a lovely day and were delighted to take the smaller of the two fish with them.

As Sophie came to say her goodbye, she kissed Bill on the cheek, and whispered, 'You owe me one!'

Bill smiled and waved as they all left. He then headed straight for Samuel and Kitty's house, where they sliced the largest tuna into steaks and Bill returned with just sufficient for himself.

The following morning was Sunday, and Bill was washing the blood from the previous day's catch off the deck, when he spotted Sophie coming toward him. She climbed aboard, flung her arms around him, kissed him and forced her tongue into his mouth. 'Great day yesterday! Guess what? My mum and dad want to know if you would consider selling the *Aye, Miss Gloria*. They were talking about it all last night.'

'That's good. What else did they say?' asked Bill.

'You've got to fuck me first!' said Sophie as she tried to pull him in the direction of the cabin door.

'Sophie, you can't start blackmailing me!'

'Yes, I can!' was Sophie's cheeky response. 'What do you think they'd say if they knew that my teenage boyfriend's father had had his wicked way with me, and come all the way to the Caribbean and shagged their other daughter as well? You naughty man!' She laughed. 'I know, why don't you try to screw my mum as well? You never know; she might be up for it. She thinks you're wonderful and charming. Then you'd have a hat-trick!'

'Don't be disgusting!' said Bill as he followed her down into the cabin, undoing the belt of his trousers as he went.

The rest of the day was a rampant one, and as they later lay in each other's arms in conversation, Bill thought that he would plant a different kind of seed in her mind. 'You know, Sophie, if you succeed in convincing your parents to buy this boat, just think of the parties you could have on it without your parents being around. You could have the pick of the crop. Young men would be queuing up for you when you've got a boat like this.'

'You're right, I could!' replied Sophie, as she pondered the thought.

The Palmers didn't take a great deal of convincing, and before long Bill received another visit from Charles and Audrey. Sophie had diplomatically decided to stay away. The three of them relaxed on the deck in the glorious sunshine and opened a bottle of wine. Charles began the conversation. 'You know, Bill, Audrey and I were wondering if, as you are returning to England, you might consider selling the *Aye, Miss Gloria*. We had such a wonderful time here and we know that our daughter sailed on it with you. The fact that it bears her name, it would mean a lot to us, and we would always treasure it and look after it. We know approximately what the value is but we are limited to a budget, what with selling our house in England and moving back here. Our budget limits us to about twenty-five thousand pounds. I know you would probably be able to get a lot more than that, and I'll perfectly understand if you say no. But what do you think?'

Bill remained silent for an agonising couple of minutes whilst he pretended to ponder the proposal carefully.

Eventually, he broke the silence. 'Charles, I thank you for your kind offer. Gloria and I did indeed share the happiest moments together on this boat. As a matter of fact, I can honestly say that they were amongst the most treasured moments of my life.' At this point Charles and Audrey were expecting a refusal and Bill could see the sadness in their faces. He continued. 'There are no people in this world that have more right to own this boat than you two. I would be delighted to accept twenty-five thousand pounds for her and I know that wherever you sail, Gloria's spirit will always be sailing with you.'

Audrey screamed out loud with joy and flung her arms around Bill's neck. Charles jumped up and shook his hand warmly.

'How can we arrange payment?' asked Charles. 'Our money is still in our bank account in England.'

'That's perfect, I'll give you my English bank details and we can arrange a simple transfer,' said Bill.

Charles recharged all the glasses and raised them for a toast. 'You propose it, Bill,' he said.

Bill raised his glass high and said, '*Por siempre juntos*! It means "always together".' It was a toast that he'd learnt from Uncle Arthur.

They all agreed that it would take another couple of weeks to deal with the documentation and the money transfer before Bill could vacate the boat and return to England.

On the Wednesday, Banjo cycled into town with the first delivery of bananas on his new amazing 'mean machine' bike. Aunt Nellie was highly impressed with Banjo's patriotically coloured contraption, and the people all gathered round as Banjo showed off by cycling up and down the market square. Bill briefly met Banjo and they arranged to meet at the café when Banjo had completed his business with Aunt Nellie. 'Hey, Honkyman! The lunch is on me this time, brother,' shouted Banjo as Bill ambled on down in the direction of the café.

Bill ordered coffee, and as he sat alone, in his mind's eye he could see Gloria's hourglass figure disappear into the crowd just one more time. He considered all the things that he would miss about this island paradise that had become his home. The broad pearly white smiles on the faces of the black children. The hustle and bustle of the market. Aunt Nellie's raucous laughter and the vibrant colours everywhere. But most of all, he would miss the sincere and unconditional friendship of Samuel, Kitty and Banjo. They were his true friends. He was reminded of something Uncle Arthur had once told him about the many exotic friends that he'd made all around the world. He had said, 'Always make new friends, but always keep old friends. For new friends are silver, but old friends are gold.'

Just then, Banjo arrived. 'Hey, Honkyman, what's with the misty eyes, brother?'

'I've got something to tell you, Banjo,' said Bill. 'I'm going back to England.'

Banjo was obviously shocked and upset. He'd forgotten that Bill had another life on the other side of the world. 'You can't be doin' that, brother! What am I gonna do? Why, you and I are Paul McCartney and Stevie Wonder, man! Ebony and ivory, livin' in perfect harmony!'

'I know we are, Banjo, but I've got to get back to my wife and son. We'll write, and perhaps I'll bring them over to see you! How about that?' said Bill, trying to make things a little easier.

'Shit! This ain't good, man,' exclaimed Banjo. 'When are you planning on goin'?'

'I'm not going for another couple of weeks yet,' said Bill, as he tried to think of something to cheer Banjo up. 'So, I know, why don't we load your delivery bike onto the boat and we'll sail back to your place for a few days?'

'Now you're talkin'!' said Banjo.

Back at Bickley Manor, Bill had one last promise to fulfil, and that was to rebuild the hen house for Mandela and his harem. They spent the next couple of evenings listening to Banjo sing and play whilst Bill rocked back and forth on Banjo's favourite seat, smoking and drinking the night away.

With the arrival of Bill's last day at Bickley Bay, he wandered down to Banjo's beautiful palm-lined shoreline and walked waist-deep into the sea where he and Gloria had made love. He wanted to rekindle the thoughts of as many of those indelible moments as possible, before they were filed away to a distant memory.

Banjo walked down the hill to where Bill was later preparing the boat to return to the town for the last time.

It was a deeply emotional goodbye, particularly for Banjo, who said it felt like there had been a death in his family. Banjo hugged Bill and said, 'Thanks for everythin', Honkyman. You've been the best friend a man could ever ask for.'

'That will never change, Banjo. We'll always be the best of friends,' replied Bill. He started the engine and manoeuvred the *Aye, Miss Gloria* slowly out of the bay.

'Remember! Ebony and ivory, brother!' shouted Banjo as he waved frantically from the quayside.

'I will, Banjo. I will!' replied Bill.

As he got to the point where the *Arthurian* lay at rest, Bill hoisted the mainsail and gave Banjo his final wave.

Aunt Nellie was also deeply upset to learn that Bill was returning to England. Apart from anything, he was her best salesman. People came from other towns and villages just to be served by him, and everyone enjoyed his cheeky sales banter. He would be greatly missed.

Bill booked his flight, and a couple of days before his departure, he went to see Father O'Malley. St Teresa's School was making great progress toward completion. The walls were up and the roof was almost on.

'I know the money came from you, Bill. I don't know how

you got it, I can only guess, but I pray that it didn't come to you by dishonest means,' said Father O'Malley.

'Father, I can promise you one thing. I didn't steal that money; it came to me by accident. I could have kept it, but I felt that I had to return it to where it truly belonged. I wanted to make sure it created some perpetual good for these lovely people who have so little,' replied Bill.

'Well, God bless you for that, Bill. Have a safe journey, and you will always be in my prayers,' replied the good Father.

Most upset of all were Samuel, Kitty and the children. How could they ever thank him enough? He had changed their lives beyond their wildest dreams. But Bill was just happy to know that they were no longer trapped on the treadmill of poverty and that the children would now have a real chance to prosper.

Charles and Audrey had acquired a car by this time and had agreed to take Bill to the airport. On the morning of his departure, he tidied the boat as best he could and collected his few precious belongings including his ganja pipe, Gloria's sunglasses and Tommy's tattered Red Ensign. Other than that, all he had were his Hawaiian shirts and a few other meagre belongings. Bill said goodbye to *Aye, Miss Gloria,* and walked with Charles to the car.

Charles informed Bill that he'd received confirmation that the money had been successfully transferred and would be in Bill's bank account when he got home.

Sophie was seated on the back seat and on the journey to the airport, she said, 'We'll miss you, Bill. Tell Jack that I'm sorry for everything and make sure he doesn't fall behind with his cello. I hope that he has found a nice new teacher.'

Audrey chipped in. 'I didn't know that you knew someone who played the cello, Bill.'

To which Sophie replied, 'Yes, remember my friend Jack Smith who started lessons with you shortly before we left

England? Well, Bill is his father! I'll explain it all later, Mummy.'

Audrey looked perplexed and started to silently unravel the story in her own mind. Did Bill still have a wife and family in England?

Just then, they arrived at the airport and Bill thanked them, bade them farewell, and checked in alone.

CHAPTER TWENTY

It was the evening of November 10th when he arrived back at Manchester Airport. The daylight had already disappeared by about 5pm. The air was chilled and the rain fell as a cold unwelcoming drizzle. Amber street lighting glowed with an eerie hue and ashen-faced people scurried about their business. Bill had forgotten just how sallow and unhealthy an English complexion looked in this artificial light. There was no laughter in these streets, and almost everyone wore black and sombre winter clothing. He took the bus back to his home town, and as people embarked at each stop, they flapped their wet umbrellas open and closed; their dank clothing steamed next to him. To Bill, it seemed that he'd arrived in some preparatory place for hell in those first impressionable moments. It all seemed familiar, but somehow alien to him now.

Little had changed since he had last trodden this old home turf. The same dogs barked at his intrusion as he passed their guarded garden territories. He stood at the gate to the path leading up to his front door. The sitting room light was on. Janice knew that he was arriving soon, but he'd not given her an exact date. He could just see the top of her head as she sat watching the television.

He lingered there until the rain started to drip onto his eyelashes and off the end of his nose. He could still turn back, he thought. It was not too late. He had the money to stay in a hotel somewhere and fly back to his island paradise tomorrow. The entire direction of his life depended upon what he did within the next thirty seconds.

Just then, he watched Janice get up and go into the kitchen, and it was then that he made his decision. He couldn't remember whether he'd ever taken the front door key with him, and so he was obliged to knock on the door.

It took Janice two or three seconds to recognise him with his deep mahogany suntan and broad moustache. She let out an ear-piercing scream and flung her arms around him. 'Bill! Oh my God, you look so different! Come in and get out of those wet clothes, you'll catch your death of cold,' she said, as she walked him into the sitting room with her arm still firmly around him. 'You get by the fire and dry off and I'll go and make us a nice cup of tea. Have you eaten?'

'Yes, I'm fine, but I've not had a proper cup of English tea in a long time.'

'We've all been sick with worry about you, when we didn't hear anything from you for months on end,' she called out from the kitchen.

Bill looked around the room at the ageing wallpaper and the same old pictures on the mantelpiece. It all seemed a lot smaller and slightly grubbier than he recalled. The settee and chairs were the same as when he and Janice had first got married. This whole house needed a complete makeover, Bill thought to himself, and now he'd got a bit of money to do it.

Janice reappeared with a tray of tea and Jaffa Cakes and placed them on the coffee table. 'What happened to the sides of your mouth?' she enquired.

'Oh, it was just a slight misunderstanding I had with some drug dealers, that's all,' replied Bill.

'Wow! I have to say, you look really great, Bill!' said Janice as she sat opposite him, looking him up and down. In her mind's eye she was discreetly comparing him with Don Wilson, who had gone to seed and developed man-boobs and a paunch. Bill, on the other hand, was incredibly fit now and looked it.

At that point they heard the key turn in the door; it was Jack. 'Hi, Mum!' he shouted from the hallway.

'There's someone here to see you, son!' replied Janice.

Bill stood up as Jack entered the room.

'Dad!' Jack shouted, and came over to give his father a hug. 'You look really amazing, Dad.'

Jack seemed a different person from when Bill had last seen him. He'd grown up, he seemed confident, he'd become a man.

'It's so good to see you again, son. I've missed you very much.'

Jack had never before heard those words coming from his father. 'I've missed you, Dad,' he said.

'You and I have much to catch up on, son,' said Bill. 'I spent far too much of my time following my own dreams and not enough time with you when you were growing up. I want that to change, son. I believe you've become a great cellist now!'

'Well, not yet, but I'm trying. I got a new teacher recently because Mrs Palmer went back to Jamaica. Apparently, Sophie's older sister was killed in a hurricane,' said Jack.

'I know. I met the Palmers and Sophie out there whilst I was helping the local priest do some rescue work,' said Bill.

'You know, Dad, I got very depressed when Sophie dumped me. But the more I thought about it, the more I realised how much I owed her. I would have never had any interest in classical music or learning to play an instrument like the cello if it wasn't for her. And as for sex! Wow, Dad! She really made a man of me in that department, I can tell you!' declared Jack.

It was on the tip of Bill's tongue to say, 'Mmmm! You and me both, son, you and me both!'

Janice was thrilled to hear Jack and Bill chatting together like this; it warmed her heart because it had never happened before.

For the rest of the evening, Bill endured a constant barrage of questions about his voyage and his adventures until jetlag got the better of him and he had to retire to bed.

In the bedroom, Janice felt an uneasiness and slight embarrassment about stripping off in front of Bill. It was almost as if they were just starting on a new relationship. Bill also felt strange and inhibited. As he peeled off his shirt, Janice was startled to see his Mayombe skull tattoo. 'Oh my God, what made you get that? You've never really been a big fan of tattoos before,' she exclaimed.

'It's a long story, I'll tell you some other time,' replied Bill.

The two of them snuggled into each other. His body felt so very different from the one that she remembered. Bill glanced over at her milk-white skin in contrast to his, and Janice was also thinking the same thought. 'This is like being in bed with a black man!' she declared.

'And precisely how many black men have you slept with, Mrs Smith?' said Bill, in jest.

They both went into a fit of the giggles until sleep started to get the better of them. Any thoughts about Don Wilson never crossed either of their minds.

The following morning, Bill insisted that he and Jack spend the day together and the pair of them took the tram into the centre of Manchester. Bill's first visit was to the bank to discreetly confirm that his twenty-five thousand pounds were safely in there, and all was well.

'You and I have got a lot of making up to do, son. For a start, I've missed two of your birthdays and two Christmases, so let's start by dealing with that,' said Bill.

They made their way to Forsyths, one of the oldest suppliers of musical instruments in the country. Jack was abounding with excitement and headed straight for the student cellos.

'What about this one?' enquired Bill.

'Dad, that one will be thousands of pounds, it's a serious quality orchestra piece!' replied Jack.

Just then, the assistant appeared. 'A beautiful instrument, sir! And we have it very competitively priced at the moment. It's a German-made Paesold Stradivari cello.'

'How much is it?' asked Bill.

'We have it marked at only three thousand pounds, sir.'

'We'll have it!' said Bill.

Jack almost went into a state of apoplexy at his father's uncharacteristic generosity and his newfound ability to pay for it.

'If this is your dream, son, then you have to be dedicated to fulfil it,' said Bill. 'I want to pay for you to have additional lessons to the ones you are already having.'

At that, the assistant interrupted. 'A friend of mine was a cellist with the Hallé Orchestra here in Manchester for many years. He's in his retirement now, but teaches. He's an excellent teacher, the very best! I can give you his phone number if that would be of help?'

'Wow! That would be really great, thank you so much,' said Jack.

'If you want to make music your life then you will have to work at it every day, just like any professional athlete,' said Bill.

It's not easy carrying a cello on a crowded tram at rush hour in the build-up to Christmas, but that was how it got home. Janice couldn't believe her eyes when she saw them struggling up the driveway with it and the two of them killing themselves laughing. Jack was babbling on so much about it that his mother had to tell him to slow down. She could hardly make out what he was saying, he was so excited. Bill then declared, 'Come on, Mrs Smith, we're all going out for dinner tonight!' This day had shown Bill just how precious his family was to him.

Jack started with his new teacher within the week and then got himself a part-time job working in the local fish and chip shop. He wanted not only to have a little spending money for himself but also to be able to pay something to his mother toward his keep. The rest of his time was spent almost entirely practising his music.

Bill's first week back was joyous way beyond his previous expectations. Janice was a different woman now; she was attentive to Bill's every need, always trying to please him instead of constantly finding fault and putting him down. In return, Bill continued to appreciate that giving was a far greater joy than receiving. Although he told Janice he'd saved money working for Aunt Nellie in Jamaica, he did withhold the fact that the sale of the *Aye, Miss Gloria* had made him twenty-five thousand pounds richer.

In the bedroom, they'd become as young lovers, spontaneous and carefree. One afternoon they made love on the kitchen table in broad daylight, throwing caution against being seen to the wind. That was something that Janice would previously have thought outrageous and sinful. Her stifled religious upbringing had always led her to believe that sex was primarily for procreation and not for fun. It was to happen in the dark and under the duvet.

One morning, she was busying herself upstairs tidying and making the beds. Bill was in great humour and in a mischievous mood that day. He sneaked up behind her and pounced. The two of them rolled around on the bed laughing and frolicking, but in the fun-filled furore, and with Bill's enthusiasm to remove his trousers, his loose change scattered around the floor. When the time came for them to get up, Bill scrambled on all fours to retrieve his money from under the bed. Janice, still naked and enjoying the mood of the moment, jumped on his back, pretending to ride him like a horse. It was then that Bill spotted the Visa credit card lodged between the leg of the bed and the bedside cabinet.

'Hey, look what I've just found!' said Bill, as he stood up. He read out the name of the card's owner. 'Donald Steven Wilson.'

Janice jumped back in horror, and immediately grabbed her dressing gown to cover herself up. Don had reported his card missing or stolen a couple of weeks before. It was patently obvious that he had dropped it in a similar scenario to the one that Bill and Janice were engaged in now.

'I knew it! I fucking well knew it. The minute that bastard answered the phone, I just knew that you and he were at it together! And in our fucking marital bed as well, you evil cow!' Bill's bawling could be heard well beyond the confines of their home.

Janice sat on the bedroom chair in floods of tears with her head hung low. 'It was a stupid, silly, thoughtless mistake and I'm so, so, so sorry. He means nothing to me. It just happened when I was really low, that's all. You were so preoccupied with this obsession of yours to be just like your uncle Arthur, and I was having terrible problems with Jack's depression and things. I felt so alone. On my own, I struggled to pay the bills on top of everything else.'

'Oh, that's bloody marvellous! So he paid you to have a shag! My wife, on the bloody game! We won't have long to wait for that to spread around the Sports Club. We'll have all of Don Wilson's pals knocking on the bloody door before you know it! What is the going rate these days?'

'It wasn't like that!' pleaded Janice. 'He was kind when I needed it most, and he genuinely cared a lot about Jack. I never took money from him, ever! It was your mother who helped out with the bills when I was stuck.'

Bill's male ego and his armour had been severely dented and he had to retaliate in the only way that he knew how. 'Yes, well, you're not the only one who has been shagging away from home. I've been screwing around with women in the Caribbean, lots of them! And you know what? They were all black women!'

Janice raised her head. 'You're a man! I expected that to happen. I didn't think for a second that you would be celibate for all that time. I realised that women would be very attracted to a man like you, who is exciting and who had just single-handedly sailed across an ocean in a tiny boat. They would look at you as an interesting Errol Flynn sort of man. A proper man!' she said, still sobbing.

Bill's vanity had just received a full-blown massage. Her comments stopped him in his tracks. Did this mean that Janice's view of him was that he was 'a proper man', compared to other men? Bill had never dreamed that Janice thought of him in this way. He had always believed that she thought him to be somewhat weak and a bit of a failure, instead of a powerful man who warranted respect.

He stared down at her. She was shaking violently and seemed so frail and vulnerable. Banjo's 'jiggy-jiggy' speech came to ring in his ear: *'You gotta forgive her, brother! After all, womenfolk get lonely and need a bit o' lovin' just like us menfolk! So think hard, brother. It ain't no big deal.'*

Janice continued to repeat over and over again, 'I'm so sorry, I'm so sorry, I don't want us to end. This marriage means everything to me. You're the only man that I've ever loved.'

Bill could hesitate no longer and he bent down, grasped her by her shoulders and gently lifted her toward him. He began to tenderly kiss away the tears that continued to stream down her face. 'And you, Janice Smith, are the only woman in the world that I have ever truly loved, and I will continue to do so until the day I die.'

With that, the two of them squeezed each other so tightly that Janice had to whisper, 'I can't breathe!'

Bill realised that his feelings for Gloria had been little more than an infatuation masquerading as love. It had also pandered heavily to his vanity. With Sophie, it was a carnal and primeval lust. Nothing more, nothing less. Only with Janice did he share the purest reciprocal love. As life becomes mundane it can often appear dormant and faded, and only when challenged or threatened does it come out fighting.

They both vowed that from that day forward they would never let a day go by without saying to each other, 'I love you.'

It is a lesson to be learned by all of those who are fortunate enough to have love in their lives.

Chapter Twenty-One

Bill had an important person to call upon. It was the man who had always had so much faith in him and helped him make his adventure possible, Marcus Rawley.

When he had left, Janice had taken Bill's only suit to the cleaners. It was hanging in the wardrobe, and with a smart white shirt and tie Bill looked every bit the tanned and successful businessman.

His arrival at Rawley's caused quite a stir. His old workmates in the Goods Inwards department were still there. Still making tea in the same dirty old kettle, and still smoking like chimneys and flicking their cigarettes in the same old empty oil drum. Debby, the receptionist, screamed out and ran over to give him a big hug.

'Mr Rawley will be so excited to see you, Bill. He's often mentioned you over the past couple of years. I'll tell him you're here,' she said.

'Bill!' came the sound of Marcus's booming voice. 'Come in, come in.' He led Bill into the magnificent chairman's office. 'I can't tell you how worried I was. I knew when you arrived in Madeira, but then we heard nothing. It was only recently that a man called Duckinfield called and told my receptionist that you were in Jamaica.'

'I spent a few months in prison in Haiti before that. They said I was a British spy,' said Bill.

'That sounds horrendous. Is that where you got those scars to your mouth?' asked Marcus.

'No, I got those in Jamaica. I was kidnapped by a gang of drug dealers and got on the wrong side of one of them, that's all.'

'Gosh! And what about the voyage, how did that go?' enquired Marcus.

'Well, if it hadn't been for a boatload of passing Americans, I wouldn't have made it. I was starving and slipping in and out of consciousness. We were about three quarters of the way across when they spotted me drifting. I owe them my life.'

'What happened to *Arthurian*? She got you there OK!'

'She certainly did! Through shark attacks and giant storms, she took everything the elements and the monsters of the deep could throw at her,' said Bill.

'You've certainly accomplished your dream. I'm sure that old uncle you used to talk so much about would be thrilled. You should write a book,' said Marcus.

'I might just do that, Marcus,' replied Bill.

Just then there was a tap on the door and in walked Miss Knowles with a tray of tea and biscuits. 'Welcome back, Mr Smith. Nice to see you have returned home safely. You're looking very well, if I may say so, sir,' she said as she placed the tray on Marcus's desk.

Marcus walked over to it, sat down, and began to pour the tea. 'Bill, you may remember that I said to you that the door to your employment was always going to be left open for you. Well, I meant it. I know it is probably a bit too soon after returning from such a different lifestyle, but I have a proposition to make to you. Bob Oakley, our internal operations manager, is retiring shortly and I want you to step into his shoes. It's a big challenge and, more than anyone, I know that you are a man who can handle any challenge that is thrown at him. It would mean being responsible for the maintenance of the machinery, the goods inwards and everything in between. I'd want you to keep an eye on time and motion and to think of ways to increase efficiency. I'd like you to work alongside Bob for a few months and step in the day after he leaves. To start with, you would be on a few pounds more than you were on when you left, but the day you take over, your salary will be exactly double that. If all goes well, in five years you will be offered a position on the board with an optional share purchase scheme. You'd have a financially secure future, Bill.' He leant back in his chair. 'Don't make any decisions yet; go home and mull it over with Janice for a week or so and let me know. You're a remarkable man, Bill, and I have an enormous amount of respect for you. Now, why don't you start to put pen to paper on that book I was talking to you about?'

'Marcus, I don't know what to say, except thank you so much. I certainly will think very carefully about your proposal and I'll let you know soon,' said Bill, as he stood up to shake Marcus's hand.

'I've brought our boat over and moored it at Conwy,' said Marcus. 'Perhaps we could go sailing together in the spring. You might teach me a thing or two!'

Bill laughed out loud. 'I doubt very much if there is anything that I know that you don't.'

Bill walked home alone along the banks of the canal and passed the spot where his father had drowned. He paused awhile to give a fleeting thought to how miserable his father had made him and his mother's life by being so dictatorial and self-centred; never a caring thought for the feelings or aspirations of others.

Marcus's amazing offer had now put Bill at a crossroads in his life. Over the past few days he had thought seriously about suggesting to Janice that they all pack up and move to Jamaica, where they could live a more simple and carefree life together.

But the practicality of that just wasn't there. Janice had previously been homesick after a week in Benidorm. She would never cope with the heat, for a start. And although she would get on famously with Father O'Malley and easily become an active member of his church, Bill knew that it would only be a honeymoon period that wouldn't last. In Jack's case, he would be able to resume his cello lessons with Audrey Palmer, but the Sophie situation would rear its ugly head and the whole thing would end in tears. Bill was torn; he wanted Jamaica, and he wanted Janice and Jack as well. Should he resume the mantle of conformity and responsibility, mostly for the sake of his family? Or should he sacrifice his family for the sake of his own free and leisurely lifestyle?

He thought it was time he caught up with his dearest old friend, Tommy Duckinfield. Tommy had always been a fountain of sound advice.

When Bill arrived at Tommy's house, he peered in through the window only to observe him sitting eating fish and chips, still in its paper, whilst watching the football on TV. Bill tapped on the window with a coin.

Startled, Tommy leapt up from his chair and took an inquisitive look at the intruder glaring in at him from his window. Suddenly it dawned on him. 'Bill, you old sea dog!' he shouted. He hurried to let him in. 'You look bloody great! What the hell happened to your mouth?'

'It's a long story. Put the kettle on,' said Bill.

'Have you seen what's happened to Cohen's Emporium?' asked Tommy as he made the tea.

'No, why? What's Les up to these days?' asked Bill.

'Oh, I'm sorry, mate, didn't you know? Les died nine months ago. It was only a small funeral, we all went to his local synagogue. I had to wear one of those little hats. I think they call them kippahs. When I went round to his house, the rabbi and a load of his relatives were there. The rabbi said that I'd have to wear a kippah on my head. I thought, *Fuck me! The*

Catholics have some potty ideas, but who the fuck wears a kipper on his head at a funeral? I was relieved when I saw what it was, I can tell you!' He pointed down at the remnants of his fish and chips. 'Anyway, the Emporium is now a Chinese chippy. That's where these came from.'

Bill was upset. 'How can you be so casual about it? Les was our closest pal!'

'It was nine months ago, and I've had time to get over it. There was nothing we could do to get in touch with you. Janice knew about it, but she must have forgotten to tell you when you last phoned her. Once we knew that you'd landed in Jamaica, I went round to Rawley's to let them know you'd made it.'

'Yeah, thanks for that, Tommy. What did he die of?' asked Bill.

'Cancer. It was very quick from finding out. It only took weeks and he was gone.'

Bill nodded. 'I suppose you knew that Don bloody Wilson has been shagging my Janice while I've been away.'

'Yes, I did hear a rumour that he'd been sniffing round her. I wouldn't worry about him. He's tried it on with some of the factory girls at Rawley's, and he's always been a bit of a joke with them. Apparently, he's got a donger the size of a cocktail gherkin. Some of those girls have deliberately gone with him just to report back on how small it is!'

Bill felt a little more assured by that snippet of information; his dominant position in the lion pride had been restored. He phoned Janice to tell her where he was, and he and Tommy continued to talk well into the night.

The following day, he felt an overwhelming urge to go and find Uncle Arthur's resting place so that he could pay his respects and tell him of all of his amazing adventures. He knew that the cemetery was just outside Liverpool because he vividly remembered the funeral and how upsetting it had been. Where in the field they had placed Arthur was another matter, but he did remember that it was not far from a tree and near to a corner. When he got there he was astonished at how vast the place had become, and after hours of wandering up and down the aisles of stones he realised that he was going to have to do some research.

At the local cemeteries office he was led into a private wood-panelled room with a large desk and handed three enormous leather-bound ledgers.

'These are the ones for the approximate date of the deceased,' said the rather sullen and dour assistant.

There it was, Arthur Thomas Smith. Grave number 1254.

Bill raced back to the cemetery. He'd been shown a map in the office, but remembering the exact location proved more difficult. Then he spotted it. The tree was considerably bigger now and Bill approached what he thought at first was a cleared area. But then he realised that this was a place for the unmarked graves, the pauper's section of the cemetery. Deeply saddened, he looked down at a small metal plate wedged into the ground on the end of a spike, just peering out from the uncut grass. Grave 1254.

This was not right! How could a man so heroic, so brave, so interesting and strong, a man who had travelled the world, fought with sharks and escaped from headhunters, end his days and be remembered as nothing more than a number? No, Bill knew he just had to do something about this. Uncle Arthur deserved to have a proper monument.

As Bill walked through the cemetery gates with his head hung low with sadness, there across the road was a cemetery stonemason's shop. Bill marched over to it; today was the day that Arthur Thomas Smith was going to get the dignity and respect that he so rightly deserved.

The stonemason's assistant appeared courteous and helpful, albeit somewhat pompous.

'I'd like a white headstone for my uncle,' declared Bill.

'Certainly, sir. We have a range of the Italian Carrara marble headstones, but I have to say that they are more expensive than some of the others in our range. After all, your uncle would be in the very best of company. Michelangelo produced nearly all of his greatest works from the very same quarry, including his statue of David. Perhaps Welsh Ffestiniog slate may be something that you may consider, sir. Or we do a slightly less expensive Cornish granite.'

Bill was put out by the assistant's automatic assumption that they may be out of his price range. 'Do I look poor?' he asked indignantly.

'No, absolutely not, sir! It's just that sometimes people are unaware that headstones are a lot of money and they get a little shocked. I'm forever hearing, "Gosh, I had no idea that they were so expensive," and so I like to warn people in advance.'

Bill pointed at a beautiful Carrara example standing as a window display piece. 'How much is that one?'

'You have excellent taste, sir. That one is around the top of our standard range. That one would be in the region of three and a half thousand pounds. If you are looking for a bespoke hand-carved piece in Italian Carrara marble, it could start at around five thousand pounds.'

'I like that one!' declared Bill.

'Very good choice. Do you have details as to what you would like to have engraved on it, sir? The charge is by the letter over a certain number of characters,' said the snooty assistant.

'Give me a piece of paper and I'll think of something,' said Bill.

He wrote, 'Here lies the body of ARTHUR THOMAS SMITH, an Explorer, Adventurer and Merchant Seaman.'

'I'll have to give you the exact date of birth and the day of his death later,' said Bill.

'You can phone that through to us, sir.'

Bill filled out the appropriate forms, left a ten percent deposit, and returned home a very happy man.

He was informed that before the cutting began, once they had all the correct details, he would receive a picture of exactly how the stone would look. Upon receiving it, he realised that it was a very large stone for such a small amount of writing. Then something came to him that had never occurred to him in his life before: his own mortality. Why not be buried alongside his own hero, Uncle Arthur? It would be perfect. There would be ample room below the written words to include a similar accolade to his own accomplishments. For example, it could read:

Also WILLIAM SMITH Esq., Nephew to Arthur Thomas Smith.
A Lone Yachtsman and Philanthropist.

A whole range of grandiose acknowledgements came in and out of Bill's head for posterity to remember him by.

After his approval, he had a three-week waiting time for the stone to be put in place. Bill couldn't wait with the excitement of it.

The day arrived when he received the letter thanking him for his final payment and informing him that the stone had been erected on plot 1254. Janice, Jack and Bill all got in Janice's little car and drove to Liverpool. It was a very special day for Bill. They parked by the cemetery gates and Bill led the way on foot. Long before reaching the plot, Bill stopped them in their tracks. 'See if you can spot Uncle Arthur's grave from here! Go on, tell me: which one do you think is his?'

Janice and Jack scanned the sea of graves until Janice said, 'Well, it can't be that big white one on its own over there!'

'Yep! You guessed it,' said Bill.

There it was, in all its magnificence, standing entirely alone in the centre of the unmarked graves. Bill couldn't have been more proud; his much revered uncle Arthur had finally been acknowledged.

'That must have cost an absolute fortune!' declared Janice.

'Well worth every penny, my darling, well worth every penny!' replied Bill.

'I don't know where all this money has come from, but I hope you didn't do anything dishonest to get it,' said Janice.

'What, me? No, have no fear, I got a bit of money saved through nothing more than hard work and good fortune,' replied Bill.

As they stood admiring it, Bill gave Janice and Jack strict instructions that this was where he also wanted to be eventually laid to rest.

Bill then suddenly exclaimed, 'I know what! Whilst we are here in Liverpool, why don't we go to see if the old Empress pub in Toxteth is still there? That's where Uncle Arthur and his merchant seaman pals used to meet up. He was always talking about the Empress. It might be knocked down by now, because I know that they have cleared a lot of the old terraced streets around that area. It's worth a try; they may even serve food.' He was already starting to lead the way. 'I think the Beatles used to hang out there sometimes. It was Ringo Starr's local when he was growing up because he lived just across from it on Admiral Grove. I always remembered that Uncle Arthur said that Ringo's mum, Elsie, was the barmaid there. He once showed me a picture of him and Ringo sitting in the pub together.'

Janice and Jack were not overly enthused or impressed but went along with it as it was meant to be Bill's special day.

As with all Scousers, the landlord was most friendly and

welcoming. He had a Toxteth accent so thick that you could cut it with a knife. 'Sorry, mate, we don't do food,' he said.

Janice ordered her usual glass of stout ale, and Bill ordered pints of bitter for Jack and himself.

'So, what brings you to these parts? You don't look like touristy Beatles fans,' said the landlord.

'No, we are here because we've only just got round to putting a headstone on my uncle's grave and this used to be his favourite pub. So as part of our pilgrimage we thought that today we would follow in my uncle's footsteps.'

'What was his name?'

'Arthur Smith. He was a merchant seaman,' said Bill.

'Arthur Smith? Oh, yes, Arthur Smith, I know who you mean. He was a bit before my time but I still hear some of the old timers mentioning him. He was always known as a great storyteller,' said the landlord. 'Old Harry Clough used to be his best pal on the ships; the two of them sailed together for years. He still comes in here, does old Harry. He must be well in his eighties now.'

'Oh, great! That's fantastic. When does he come in? I've got to meet him,' said Bill.

'I know he's gone down to Bristol this week because his sister is going into an old people's home somewhere down there, but he should be back next week. He usually comes in each evening at around five o'clock, has a couple of pints, and leaves by about eight. He doesn't like to be out late these days because the roads are too dangerous for an old guy on his own. The yobbos and druggies are prowling around after ten looking for a fix. He got mugged one night and they forced him to take them back to his house. They got his war medals and a bit of cash for drugs money. I'll tell him you've called in and he's to expect you. You're Arthur Smith's nephew, is that right?'

'Yes, I'm Bill Smith,' said Bill. They exchanged farewells and Bill and the family returned home after a most successful day.

For Bill the week couldn't pass quickly enough. He wanted to learn so much more about Arthur. There had to be a hundred tales that only Harry would know. Bill thought that he should write them down. Perhaps he could include some of them in this book that Marcus had been so keen for him to write.

The week passed and Bill telephoned the Empress pub to arrange to meet up with Harry the following afternoon.

There was no mistaking Harry; he'd a rhino-skin face and a voice that sounded like a Liverpool gravel mixer. He'd been a forty-cigarettes-a-day man, and never missed a day. He was sitting in the same corner seat that he'd occupied for sixty years.

'Are you buying?' was his opening remark.

'Yes, the drinks are all on me today,' replied Bill.

'Great! I'll have a pint and a whisky chaser,' said Harry.

Bill returned from the bar carrying a tray of doubles and placed them on the table.

'That was your uncle Arthur's seat,' said Harry, as Bill drew a chair up close. 'I met your father a few times. He'd call to see Arthur on rare occasions. He was always trying to cadge money from him. I didn't like the feller very much.'

'I'm sure you liked him better than I did. He was a bloody awful father,' replied Bill.

'Come to think about it, you look a lot more like Arthur than you do your father,' said Harry as he took a closer look at Bill.

'You've got no idea how happy that makes me,' said Bill. He got his pen and paper at the ready. 'Shall we start with me asking you questions?' he asked. 'As a boy, I remember seeing lots of photographs of Arthur in different parts of the world doing all sorts of exciting things, which was what really inspired me to live the same kind of adventurous lifestyle that he'd lived. Were you with Arthur when he was attacked by a shark and survived fighting it off?'

Harry let out a loud burst of laughter. 'Yes, I was, and I was also attacked by the very same shark. As a matter of fact, so were much of the crew!' he said, still chuckling to himself. 'The only thing is, it was dead at the time. It was one that some of the lads managed to drag up on deck, and we each took it in turn to have our photograph taken with our heads in its mouth. We chopped it up and one of the lads boiled the jaws and teeth to take home. We were near Hong Kong and another lad got a couple of shillings for the fins to make soup with from some little coolie on the docks.'

'So it wasn't true, then?' said Bill, somewhat disappointed.

'Did it not dawn on you that if your best mate is right next to you and being attacked by a shark, the first thing that would spring to mind wouldn't be, *Oh! I must go and get my camera to get a shot of this before he gets completely eaten*?'

Bill, as a grown man, suddenly felt utterly stupid. As a boy, he had been so taken in by it he had never considered the possibility that the story might not be true. 'What about the time that he was shipwrecked off the Egyptian coast?' he asked.

'We were never actually shipwrecked. We ran aground on a sandbank near Egypt one time; that was because the captain was drunk and he didn't account for the high and low tide at the full moon. We were wedged on that sandbank for a couple of days. Some of the lads were allowed to go ashore, but Arthur and I had to stay with the ship in case the engines needed to start up.'

'Why was that, then?' enquired Bill.

'Because me and Arthur were the two stokers down in the boiler room. We were the only two members of the crew that would come home from the Equator whiter than when we'd left England on a winter's day!' laughed Harry.

This story was getting worse by the minute!

'Well, there is one story that is definitely true,' insisted Bill, defiantly, 'and that is the one about how he was in Ecuador in the late 1950s and he escaped from headhunters. I had the evidence of it, because I had the genuine shrunken head that he'd stolen from them. It was in my bedroom for years, until next door's dog chewed it up.'

'Sorry, lad! Arthur bought that from one of the natives who used to try and sell stuff to us whenever we docked. It was a monkey's head. He paid two shillings for it, and that seemed like a lot of money for it at the time. That's ten pence in modern money,' said Harry, still laughing to himself. 'What happened was, the government cracked down on local tribes killing each other and shrinking their enemies' heads. So, some of the smart ones who lived down near the ports would kill the monkeys to eat them. Knowing that Westerners were fascinated with the idea of collecting genuine shrunken human heads, what they used to do was chop the head off a monkey and shave its face except for the eyebrows. They would then fill the head with sand and sew the lips and the neck up. They looked exactly like a little human's face. You couldn't tell the difference. They were doing a roaring trade!' He shook his head at the fond memory of it all.

Bill was devastated. He was almost at the point of tears, such was his feeling of disappointment.

'Don't be too hard on him, lad. Arthur Smith was the kindest man alive; he'd do anything for anyone. He probably told you those stories because he knew the kind of shitty life your father was giving you. Arthur was a great reader. Down in the boiler room we didn't often get the officers coming down. It was too hot and dirty for their white tropical kit, and so Arthur would endlessly read books about the likes of Scott of the Antarctic and David Livingstone. He was just a harmless dreamer, a fantasist, a Walter Mitty, and I think that in the end he really thought that he was one of those heroic people. He believed his own made-up stories,' said Harry.

'So all that he ever did was shovel coal into a ship's furnace, and that's it?' asked Bill.

'I'm afraid so, lad. That's just about the top and bottom of it,' said old Harry.

Bill had heard quite enough, and he closed his notepad and put away his pen. He thanked Harry for spending the time with him, and he got up and left. Bill felt deeply hurt, disappointed, humiliated and embarrassed. He'd spent the whole of his life boasting to every man and his dog about his great hero uncle, when all the time the guy had been a complete phoney.

He called into a stationery shop just down the road and bought its largest red felt-tip pen and drove back to the cemetery. 'I've just spent three and a half thousand pounds on this bloody great lump of rock!' he said as he stood there staring at the headstone. Bill sat down at the front and up close, and in the space left for his own written memorial, after 'Explorer, Adventurer and Merchant Seaman', he wrote in neat red print: 'AND THE WORLD'S GREATEST BULLSHITTER'. It stood out well against the white marble and the beautiful gilt lettering above. He left with a modicum of satisfaction knowing that it would be the most talked-about gravestone in the cemetery.

He arrived home to be greeted by Janice. 'I know, things didn't go well with the old chap, did they? You've finally learnt the truth about Arthur, haven't you?' she said, rather sympathetically.

'Don't tell me you knew all along that Arthur was full of bullshit,' said Bill.

'Of course I did! The whole family have known for years; it's just that no one had the heart to shatter your boyhood dream. People tried to give you subtle hints sometimes, but you were so obsessed with Arthur it would have seemed cruel to hurt your feelings. It would be like telling someone that Father Christmas isn't real!'

'But I've gone to the ends of the earth all because of that bastard! I've been to hell and back. I've been nearly drowned, starved to death, shot at, tortured, stuck in one of the worst prisons on earth, pissed on by a guard, had my mouth slit open by a drug dealer. I've even murdered someone because of him!' Oops! Bill hadn't intended that bit of information to slip out.

'What?' screamed Janice. 'I'm now married to a murderer! You'd better tell me exactly what you've been up to, other than sailing over the ocean in that bloody bathtub of yours. And what the hell were you sent to prison for? Now I get it. That's why we never heard from you from one month to the next. And how exactly did you murder this poor person? Is that what you were in prison for?'

'No! I set fire to him in his car! And he wasn't a poor innocent man, he was a brutal killer who tortured people for fun. I had to kill him,' said Bill.

'Oh my God in heaven! I'm married to a monster!' shouted Janice.

'You don't understand, Janice, there's a horrible, evil, unforgiving, exciting, magnificent and beautiful world outside this fucking little council estate that we live on. I've seen things that would terrify you, and I've seen things so beautiful they would astonish and amaze you. I've seen mankind at his most evil and cruel, and I've seen and experienced love and kindness beyond your wildest dreams. I'm not Arthur fucking Thomas Smith! I'm the real thing! I've lived the life that he never did.'

Suddenly, Bill realised what he was saying. He owed Arthur

everything. Without Arthur he would never have set foot outside the boundaries of his council house world. He and Janice had only ever been to Benidorm once, and prior to that Llandudno had seemed exotic. Now he really was going to have to write that book.

Bill left the room and retreated to his garden shed. He'd not been in it since his return and he had to get WD-40 to release the padlock. The Union flag bunting from the unveiling of the *Arthurian* was lying in a pile on the floor. Everything was exactly as he had left it because Janice had never found a use for the space. He decided there and then that it would be the perfect sanctuary for his new literary adventure. He could become just like Dylan Thomas, following in his footsteps by creating literary masterpieces from a garden shed. 'I must begin immediately on converting this from a cold empty workshop to a cosy little nest with white-painted walls, a writing table and chair, and some curtains on those windows,' said Bill to himself.

Bill was first to rise in the morning and he went downstairs to start to prepare breakfast for Janice and Jack. Janice had started a new part-time job as a dinner lady at the local school, and Jack had a half-hour bus journey to his cello lesson later in the morning.

Bill listened as the morning post fell to the floor at their front door. Amongst the letters was a badly written one with an airmail sticker on it; it had come from Puerto Rico. It read:

Dear Mr William Smith Esquire, I am twelve years old I learn English good. Today I find your bottle on my beach by my house. I have send you letter back from inside the bottle. I live on the island of Puerto Rico at Luquillo.

Love from Rodriguez

The empty bottle of Jamaica rum that had been given to Bill by his Welsh friend Barnacle, the very same one that he'd thrown into the Bristol Channel on his trial run in the *Arthurian*, had taken almost an identical journey to Bill himself. It had taken two years to float safely across the Atlantic and had ended up in Puerto Rico. The note that Bill had enclosed was as clean and as fresh as the day that he'd written it.

'I must get that and the letter from Rodriguez framed for the wall of my Dylan Thomas shed. I'll get Tommy's well-worn Ensign framed at the same time. I know that Tommy would be very touched to see it hanging there,' said Bill to himself.

On the way back home from work, Janice called to see Bill's mother for their weekly chat and a cup of tea. Bill's mother was thrilled to learn that the troubled waters of Janice's indiscretion with Don Wilson had been calmed, and that all was well again at the Smith household. Janice made a solemn promise that Bill would never find out about his mother's extra-marital activities.

'Men always want to believe that their own mothers are pure, so, in Bill's case, let's keep it that way,' said Bill's mum, as she gave a broad wink and a smile to Janice.

On the Friday afternoon, Bill had an appointment with Marcus Rawley. Today was the decision day regarding his future and the future of his family.

Miss Knowles welcomed him into the chairman's office. Marcus was several minutes late and burst in slightly out of breath. 'Bill, my dear chap, a thousand apologies. I've been stuck in traffic for more than an hour, and I've been concerned and thinking about you a lot. What's your verdict, then? Tell me it's positive.'

Bill looked serious and pensive. 'Marcus, I want to thank

you for your very kind offer and I have given it careful consideration.'

There was a pregnant pause. Bill could see that Marcus was looking anxious and tense.

'I'd be delighted to accept!' said Bill, with an outburst of laughter.

'You bugger! You had me on the ropes for a minute then. I thought you were going to say no!' said Marcus. 'I'm delighted to welcome you into the management team, and I know that Bob Oakley will be pleased as well, knowing that he will have an able successor. Are you OK to start on Monday?'

'I look forward to it,' said Bill.

Bill raced home to give Janice and Jack the good news. 'Come on, it's celebration time! We're all going to have dinner out this evening,' he declared.

In their favourite restaurant, Bill told Janice exactly what his work contract entailed, and that it would double his salary upon Bob's retirement. If he stuck at it, in five years he would be offered a position on the board of directors. It was beyond their wildest dreams.

In a couple of years they would be able to get out of the council estate their marriage had stagnated in, and be in a position to buy a home of their own in a nicer area. That would mean that they would be the first generation in their families to have ever owned their own house, and they would be able to leave it as their legacy to Jack. It would have been paid for entirely by their own endeavour and hard work.

'In the meantime, let's give that house of ours a complete makeover,' said Bill. 'I'm sick to death of that bloody settee and chairs that we got when we first got married. The whole place needs decorating from top to bottom. Next weekend, my darling, we are going furniture shopping!'

Janice was more than thrilled. They had never been in a

position before to afford such luxury. 'I've got the best husband in the world,' she announced.

'And I've got the best dad,' said Jack. Coming from the son that he had always alienated, those words meant more to Bill than anything.

On the Monday morning, there were quizzical expressions on the faces of the men in the Goods Inwards department as Bill arrived for work wearing a suit and tie. Not only that, but he walked directly into the main reception and was greeted by the receptionist instead of clocking in at the workers' entrance. Throughout the day Bob Oakley escorted Bill around the factory, introducing him as his heir to the internal operations management job. Bill was liked and respected and continued to be referred to with affection as Captain Bill, or just 'the Captain'.

That evening, Bill returned home and sat at the kitchen table whilst Janice prepared dinner. An all-too-familiar plate was placed in front of him.

'Egg and chips, love, your favourite. Sorry, I forgot to get the tomato sauce when I was passing the Co-op this afternoon. I'd forget my head if it wasn't screwed on. I keep saying to myself that I'm going to start writing lists one of these days. Never mind, I think there's a bit of brown sauce still left in the bottle in the cupboard. You don't mind brown, do you? You like brown!'

Nothing had changed.

Bill arose from the empty plate. 'I'm going to the shed,' he declared.

'That's nice, dear,' said Janice. 'I'll bring you a nice cup of tea later!'

www.ingramcontent.com/pod-product-compliance
Lightning Source LLC
Chambersburg PA
CBHW030425310726
48979CB00009B/1623/J

9781789630039